Land Sakes

Land Sakes

A Novel

Margaret A. Graham

Revell

Grand Rapids, Michigan

© 2005 by Margaret A. Graham

Published by Fleming H. Revell
a division of Baker Publishing Group
P.O. Box 6287, Grand Rapids, MI 49516-6287

Printed in the United States of America

Library of Congress Cataloging-in-Publication Data
Graham, Margaret, 1924-
    Land sakes : a novel / Margaret Graham
        p.   cm.
    ISBN 0-8007-5973-7
    1. Widows—Fiction. 2. Cruise ships—Fiction. 3. Rich people—
Fiction. I. Title.
PS3557.R2157L36 2005
813.54—dc22   2004026491

For Alvera J. Mickelsen,
writer, teacher, speaker,
who spends herself unstintingly in helping
other people succeed.

In memory of Nancy Lee Bates,
who left the world better than she found it.

What is repugnant to every human being is to be reckoned always as a member of a class and not as an individual person.

Dorothy L. Sayers

1

The spring of the year is always beautiful in the mountains of North Carolina, and I hated to think this would be my last to see the blooming of the dogwood trees and the greening of the slopes. My heart was broke. I had been the housemother at Priscilla Home for many years when the board ups and decides I should retire. There was a bunch of new people on the board who did not know doodly-squat about what was best for the ministry.

Priscilla Home is a Christian place for women who abuse drugs, and although I was a couple years shy of seventy, I felt plenty fit to keep on as housemother. In fact, I had thought I was set for life. You never know, do you? I loved those women, and through the years I had kept up with a lot of the ones who had graduated from our ten-month program. Many of them told me I had made a difference in their lives.

Ursula, the director of Priscilla Home, had decided to go to seminary, so the board did offer me her job. "Esmeralda," the young whippersnapper of a vice president told me, "the work of housemother is too demanding on a woman your age, but we would like you to take over as director."

"No, that's not for me."

He upped the ante. "Of course, there would be a 25 percent increase in salary."

"I'm not interested, thank you."

That just goes to show you what greenhorns were on that board. They know I have got only a eighth grade education. I couldn't handle the bookkeeping, letter writing, or all that computer stuff. Besides, my heart was in helping them women one-on-one, day in and day out, not sitting in the office answering the phone and shuffling papers.

I didn't know what I was going to do. Financially, I was strapped. Never dreaming the board would do this to me, I had bought a car for Pastor Osborne. He's the pastor of my home church, Apostolic Bible, in Live Oaks, South Carolina, and for years he had been driving around in a two-door rattletrap of a compact. With three adopted children he needed a four door, but on the salary he made he could never afford one.

Ever since I came to Priscilla Home I had dreamed of the day when I could afford to buy a decent car for the Osbornes. For a long time it was only a dream. You see, when I was living in Live Oaks, I had lied to get Maria, a homeless woman, admitted to the hospital, and since I never get away with any lie, after she died, the hospital charged me with her medical bills. Only after I had paid off those bills did I see my way clear to buy a car for the Osbornes.

I called Elmer, my friend who runs the hardware store in Live Oaks, and asked him to shop around for a four-door, low-mileage car for the pastor. Elmer wanted to help too, so he loaned me the money at the rate of interest he was getting on his money market account.

I still had nine more payments on the Osbornes' car when my Chevy died. Too many trips up and down the Old Turnpike had tore it up. In the mountains, a body needs a four-wheel drive, so I found a secondhand Subaru in good shape and got a bank loan to pay for it. After that, it was nip and tuck, making payments to Elmer and to the bank, but by the skin of my teeth I was managing until this thing came up with the board.

I had no place to go. The Osbornes were renting my house in Live Oaks; I couldn't ask them to move. Besides, I needed the rent money they were paying me. Even with the rent money, my Social Security, and the three hundred a month I got as housemother, I was barely making ends meet. Having to leave Priscilla Home meant I would lose three hundred dollars' salary as well as free room and board. I tell you, the board could not have picked a worse time to pull the rug out from under me.

I went into town and put in my application at all the restaurants, the stores, and even the fast-food places, but nobody needed help. I checked the classifieds for an efficiency to rent in town. There was only one, and it was dirty as a dog bed.

The board told me I could take my time about leaving because the new director would need my help learning the ropes. Nancy, a nurse and a Priscilla Home grad, had been my assistant for three years, so she would replace me as housemother.

The fall before all this happened, Barbara Winchester had come to Priscilla Home, roaring down the driveway in a red sports car. She pulled to a stop in back and stepped out dressed like a movie star—high heels, dark glasses, the whole bit. No resident is allowed to have a car at Priscilla Home, so pretty soon I took her keys, which didn't set too well with her.

Barbara kept telling me, "I'm the heiress of the Winchester fortune, and the only reason I've come to Priscilla Home is to keep Father from disinheriting me."

"Oh?"

"Yes. Surely you've heard of him—Philip Winchester? He's on the Fortune Five Hundred list. They call him Florida's Citrus King. He owns big companies in the States and has mining interests overseas."

Well, when you've been in this work as long as I have, you take stuff like that with a grain of salt.

Like I said, Barbara came in the fall of the year with a dozen suitcases full of designer clothes, enough shoes to open a shoe store, lots of jewelry, and, hear this—*imported thermal underwear!* Seeing all that stuff, I figured she was making big bucks selling drugs.

She didn't fit in at first. But one day, after being at Priscilla Home a few weeks, she took a bunch of them clothes down to the laundry room to wash and then went outside to smoke. Some time later, I was in my room when I heard Nancy screaming, "Barbara, get in here!" She sounded historical, so I hurried down there.

Barbara got to the laundry room about the time all the rest of us did. Nancy was beside herself! "Barbara, look at this," she said and held up the thermal underwear that had shrunk to the size of my hand. "You've ruined your clothes!"

"Oh?"

Nancy kept pulling one designer outfit after another out of the washer—pantsuits, silk blouses, sweaters— some had shrunk to Barbie-sized clothes, and all the colors had run together.

"You musta never washed clothes before," somebody said.

Holding up a tiny cashmere sweater to her chest, Barbara admitted, "I've never washed a dish, much less clothes."

Seeing all that swanky wearing apparel reduced to doll clothes was bad, but it was also just about the funniest thing that had ever happened at Priscilla Home. It was all I could do not to bust out laughing.

"One size fits all!" somebody piped, and that did it! Barbara fell out laughing, which set us all off. I tell you, we were historical!

That broke the ice; it made Barbara one of us. Since she had no work clothes, she asked me to let her look through the secondhand stuff we have in the clothing room. Of course, she had plenty of the good stuff left to wear on occasions that called for such. As for the ruined thermal underwear, she framed them, and they're still hanging on the wall of the craft room.

Over time, Barbara learned a lot more than how to wash clothes. Nancy showed her how to load the dishwasher, run the vacuum cleaner, etc. The cooks taught her how to stir the grits, fry eggs, and roll biscuit dough. Driving the little snow plow was her specialty. All winter long, every time it snowed, Barbara zipped up and down our driveway like a house afire.

That girl beat all I ever saw. It tickled her pink, learning how to do stuff, and many's the time she said she wished her mother could come to Priscilla Home. She said her father told her that his wife didn't know how to do nothing.

It was strange the way Barbara talked about her mother. She never seemed to know much about her firsthand. If Barbara's family really was rich, maybe she hadn't lived at home a lot; maybe she'd been shipped off to boarding school and summer camp most of her life.

Although prayer and Bible study were all new to Barbara, over time she took to it. Albert Ringstaff, who was not only our neighbor but also our Bible teacher, came every morning to teach our Bible study. That man never tired of the questions the women asked, and I never heard anybody explain things as good as he did.

One snowy afternoon Barbara and I were in the kitchen, peeling potatoes, when we got talking.

"Miss E., all my life I've had this kind of funny feeling deep inside . . . I can't explain it. I loved to party, but after all the good times were over, I still had this feeling that didn't go away."

"You know, Barbara, God draws us to himself one way or another. Maybe that feeling bugging you has been him drawing you to himself—bringing you here so you could hear about him."

She laughed and got up to dump the peelings in the trash can. "In my case, he wasn't *drawing*—he had to *drag* me up here to these sticks!"

I'm not the teacher Albert is, but by the time we got all those potatoes peeled, I felt like I had done my best.

In the late spring when the board dropped that bomb-shell on me, Barbara was awful upset, as were the rest of the women. They wrote letters to the board, and when the board didn't answer, it was all I could do to keep them from walking out.

Barbara was pitcher-pumping me. "Let me call my father's lawyers. They'll file an age discrimination suit against this place."

I put the quietus on all of that, told them the Lord was in this and we'd just have to wait to see what he had in mind.

Even though I truly believed the Lord had his reasons for my being let go, my heart was aching. I didn't want the women to know how bad I felt, because it's like Splurgeon says: "One downcast believer makes twenty souls sad." What crying I did, I did alone in my room. And, working about the house and yard, I let loose, sing-ing the songs of Zion in a voice that sounded like a whooping crane in mating season. The girls got a lot of fun out of my singing, and it did as much for me as it did for them.

But Barbara kept harping about her mama. "I want her to meet you, Miss E."

Then one day her mother's secretary called and told Barbara her mama was going on this cruise and needed a companion.

"A companion?" I asked. "Why does a grown woman need a companion?"

"Mother has spells of light-headedness."

"I see." I was tired and excused myself to get ready for bed.

❧

There's nothing quite like a good hot bath to ease body aches and pains. As I sloshed around in the tub soaping up, I wondered if anybody in Live Oaks knew I was leaving Priscilla Home. I hadn't even told Beatrice. She and Carl spend their time traveling in that RV they got. It would have been nice to pick up the phone and call her, but Carl has never bought a cell phone, which is one thing I will never understand. Now and again, Beatrice will call me from a pay phone or write a letter. The last letter I got from her she told me to write in care of General Delivery in Seattle, Washington. They were staying a while at a campground there.

I turned on more hot water and lay back in the tub, feeling cut loose from everybody I loved. Beatrice—she's like a sister to me. We've known each other all our lives, and since neither of us have any near kin, we tell each other everything. I could write to her to give her this news, but it would be better to wait until I knew what I was going to do. Hearing the board retired me, Beatrice would most likely get historical.

But me? When you've lived as long as I have, it takes more than a bump in the road to make you go all to pieces. It's like Splurgeon says: "All sunshine and nothing else makes a desert." A bump in the road shakes you up so you don't rest on your laurels.

Sometimes it's better not to have nobody to talk to but the Lord. I didn't have to tell him how much I loved Priscilla Home, and he knew the good I could do there. But I told him if he had somebody who could do it better, I could handle that, if only I wouldn't get jealous.

I've been disappointed before. A few years back I had feelings for Albert Ringstaff. He is one dear man, a gentleman from the word go. Smart too. Before he retired, he tuned pianos for concert maestros, as he called them, and traveled all over the world. Now he lives up on the mountain, where he has a big place and a guesthouse.

Albert came here as a widower, and in time he became the only man I had ever been interested in since my Bud died. But I came to understand that the Lord had something better for me than marrying Albert. Anyway, Albert's highbrow music and friends would have proved to be not my cup of tea. As it is, I have had work to do for the Lord, and he has give me souls for my hire. It don't get no better than that.

But you never know what's around the bend, do you? Women my age are dropping like flies, so I'd have to be boneheaded not to know I was getting close home. As much as I looked forward to getting there, I did want to make the most of the time I had left. If Priscilla Home was the end of the line for me, coasting the rest of the way home would be the hardest thing the Lord ever had me do.

When the new director arrived, she made it clear that she could handle this work without any help from me. A body don't hang around where they are not wanted, so I started packing. As I was folding my underpants, my glasses fogged up. *Lord, we're coming down to the wire. Where do we go from here?* I decided I better put down a deposit on that dog bed of an apartment in town, but I really didn't want to.

I had wiped my eyes and started packing my winter clothes when Barbara came to my room. "Can I help?" she asked.

"No, just sit down and visit with me."

"Had a letter from Mother's secretary."

"Your mama has a secretary?"

"Oh yes. I don't suppose Mother has ever written a letter in her life. At least, she's never written one to me."

"I like to write letters, myself," I said. "I have this friend I've known all my life, and we write letters back and forth all the time."

Barbara stood up and looked out the window. "Father said he has never known my mother to have a friend."

"Oh no? How old is she?"

"She's in her sixties." She turned away from the window. "According to Dad, Mother only likes dead people."

I dropped the blouse I was holding and stared at her. "What?"

"That's right, dead people. He says she likes to know where they're buried and how they died, so she travels all over the country visiting cemeteries."

What kind of a wacko is this?

"Miss E., Mother is going on this cruise, and she needs somebody like you to go with her."

I laughed. "She does, does she?" *Barbara's feeling sorry for me; wants to help me out*, I thought. "Well, Barbara, I may be a lot of things, but one thing's for sure, I am not no nurse."

"She doesn't need a nurse."

"Didn't you tell me she has spells of light-headedness?"

"Yes, she does."

"Well, with all the money your family has got, it seems like you would hire a registered nurse, somebody like that."

She shook her head. "No, that's not what she needs."

"Well, your daddy will be traveling with her, won't he?"

"Dad never goes anywhere with her."

"I see." I was beginning to get the picture. Here's a bubbleheaded woman who has not got much of a marriage and has not been much of a mother. I have not got much patience with a woman like that.

"Where's she going on this cruise?"

"Alaska. The ship sails from Vancouver."

"That's nice." The room fell quiet; I kept folding clothes. To make conversation, I asked if her mother was going to fly to Vancouver.

"No, she doesn't like to fly."

"Going by train?"

"No, by car."

"I take it she's got a good car."

"It's ten years old, but it runs good."

"Oh." That told me more than she wanted me to know. If her mother was riding around in a ten-year-old car, all that flapdoodle Barbara had told us about her family being rich was just that—flapdoodle. Why, my Chevy was only twelve years old when it gave up the ghost. "Will your mother do the driving?"

"No. She doesn't have a driver's license."

So that's it—she's looking for some birdbrain to drive her mother across country in a rattletrap that's sure to be falling apart.

"Will you pray about it?"

"About what?"

"About going as a companion with Mother. Besides all your expenses being paid, you can name your own salary."

Yeah, right, I thought. *Or else she's planning to pay with drug money.* "Barbara, I appreciate your wanting to help me out, but I'll manage. I don't know what the Lord has in store for me, but something will turn up. Don't you worry about it. Now run along to bed so you won't be caught up after lights out."

"I wish you would consider it. Mother needs some-body like you."

I couldn't get the suitcase closed. Barbara helped me push down on the lid, and I snapped it shut.

"Why not, Miss E.?"

"Like I told you, Barbara, I am not no nurse. I never been on a boat, never got seasick, and I plan to keep it that way."

"You can name your own price, Miss E."

"Run along, Barbara." I heard the screen door slam

downstairs and then footsteps on the stairs. I gave her a wink. "I think I hear a 'putty cat.'"

"Oh, *her*, that old battle-axe of a director."

I smiled. "Now, now, be sweet!" She gave me a hug and left. I closed the door behind her, glad that was over.

Two days later, I had all my stuff packed and ready to go. I was going into town the next morning to rent that apartment if it was still available. Even so, I felt like Abraham must have felt when he "went out not knowing whither he went." My severance pay would keep me going a couple months, but after that, well . . . I'd cross that bridge when I came to it.

2

Albert came over that night, bringing us a mess of fish, and the girls took them to the canning room to clean. He and I walked up to the front porch and sat down in the rockers. "You catch them fish?" I asked.

"Not this time. I bought them at the trout farm."

Through the years, Albert and me had spent many an evening sitting on that porch talking, and it hurt to think that this might well be the last time.

Albert leaned his elbows on his knees and twirled that little German hat on his fingers. Reminded me of that day we went up on Grandfather Mountain. I still have a picture of him we took that day. He was wearing that same little hat with the feather on the side.

"Say you didn't catch those fish?"

"No, I didn't. Truth is, I've been having bouts of vertigo. I never know when it's going to hit me, so it wouldn't be smart to wade in the stream fishing. The doctor made all kinds of tests but didn't find anything. My wife is pushing me to take it easy, but there's a lot of work to keeping up our place. As much as I enjoy doing the work, I have to admit I'm not always up to it. When this comes on me, I shouldn't be driving, but since Lenora doesn't drive, I have to." He paused. "Say, Esmeralda, do you know of a man I could hire to help out?"

"No, I don't, but I'll keep it in mind." A chipmunk was scurrying around in the flowers. "Albert, have you heard anything about Dora?"

"Yes, I have. I saw in the *New York Times* that she has a concert next fall in Lincoln Center. It's amazing, isn't it?"

"Amazing? It's more like a miracle. When you gave her that big harmonica, did you ever dream she'd wind up a recording artist and playing that high-class music on stage?"

He shook his head. "Never. We knew she had talent, but we never dreamed she'd do anything more than play for her own pleasure."

"I tell you, Albert, the Lord does wonders, don't he? We saw Dora on TV one time—she was still wearing that old hunting coat she wore when she was here."

Albert got up and walked to the edge of the porch, propped his hands on the banister, and looked up the driveway.

"So, what are your plans, Esmeralda?"

"I found a little place in town, and if it's still available I'll rent it tomorrow." I tried to sound upbeat. "As soon as schools let out, tourists will be flocking up here, and it shouldn't be hard to find a job in one of the restaurants."

He turned around, leaned against the banister, and

folded his arms across his chest. "Lenora and I would like for you to come live with us. We have that guesthouse and we'd love having you." He smiled. "Maybe you can teach Lenora how to cook."

"Thank you, Albert, but I believe the Lord has work for me to do somewhere."

"Any idea where?"

"Can't I serve the Lord as a waitress?"

"Of course, but you are best suited for a ministry such as this one here at Priscilla Home."

"The board don't think so."

"I wish they had asked me. The way you run circles around these younger women amazes all of us. The board probably acted in haste."

"Well, it's all over and done with now. There are not many places like Priscilla Home to apply to." I laughed. "The only job offer I've had is from one of the residents. And she's just trying to help me out."

"Oh? What's that?"

"Barbara wants me to sign on as a companion for her mother. She says her family is rich, but I have my doubts about that."

"Oh, the Winchesters are wealthy, all right. Philip Winchester is one of the wealthiest men in America, and his wife comes from a family that has been wealthy for generations."

"Really? Well, they might be rich, Albert, but Barbara's mother sounds like she's nutty as a fruitcake."

"Mrs. Winchester? Well, you're probably right about that." His eyes crinkled at the corners; he was tickled about something.

"What's so funny?"

"Well, it is funny. Several years ago, as was his habit, Philip Winchester was off on his yacht with a bevy of young women, and Mrs. Winchester had his picture plastered on billboards all across the country, advertising him as a missing person 'last seen in the company of several swimsuit models.'"

We laughed. "How did he take it?" I asked.

"Matter-of-fact, he enjoyed it. Came on TV and said he was the envy of every CEO in the country." Albert sat back down. "According to the gossip columnists, Mrs. Winchester won't get on that yacht with him at the tiller. I guess there's more to it than that. The jet set lives in a different world than the rest of us."

"Well, tell me, Albert, if they're so rich, why does Barbara's mother drive a ten-year-old car?"

"That's probably another one of her eccentricities. She travels by herself a lot. They say she won't fly, even though Philip has private jets that would fly her anywhere she wants to go. Once in a while she makes the gossip columns or the headlines, usually because of some prank she pulls, like the one about putting his picture on billboards."

The more I heard about that woman, the more I was convinced she was wacko.

"So Barbara wants you to live with this woman and take care of her?"

"No. She wants me to drive her across the country and go on a cruise to Alaska with her."

"Now that sounds interesting. You would enjoy seeing Alaska."

"I don't need a vacation, Albert. I need to find a job. I'd have to be nuts to get behind the wheel of a ten-year-old rattletrap and drive across America with a loony tunes lady to take care of."

"Oh, I'm sure Mrs. Winchester would have a driver." Albert leaned back in the rocker, his hands behind his head. "Esmeralda, a trip like that shouldn't last more than a few weeks. You've never seen much of the country, and this would be a chance to see some of the states between here and Alaska . . . Besides, you could use the money, couldn't you?"

"How much do you think they'd pay me?"

"I don't know, but I daresay they'd pay you a lot more than you expect." He stood up to leave. "Esmeralda, if I were you, I'd take it."

"You would?"

"I would." He was halfway down the steps. "What have you got to lose?"

I watched my friend walking across the lawn to his car and wondered if I should reconsider the offer. I sat there mulling it over. *Like he says, a few weeks is not a long time . . . I could sure use the money . . . I can put up with anything if it don't last long . . . Like Albert said, what do I have to lose?*

My sanity, probably!

I stood up to go inside.

❧

That night after supper, I was reading my Bible, hoping some Scripture would show me whether or not I should sign on with Loony Tunes. It don't always happen that way, but as I was reading in John there was this verse that I had counted on before: "When he puts forth his own sheep, he goes before them, and the sheep follow him for they know his voice."

"He goes before them," I repeated. "To Alaska?"

I closed my Bible and sat there thinking. After a while, I went upstairs to Barbara's room. "Tell me, Barbara, does your mother have a driver?"

"Oh, sure, Percival Pettigrew."

I hesitated. Then I said, "Well, you can call home and see if she wants me, and if she does, make the arrangements. I've decided I'll go with her."

3

Nancy went shopping with me to find a dress that would be okay for evening wear. The Nearly New shop had only one in my color, blue, with puff sleeves and a wide sash that tied in a bow in back. "We'll go to the Thrifty Nifty," she said. "That's where rich women dump their duds so they can buy new."

Well, we found a blue silk gown with the tags still on it. "Never been worn," the clerk told us. It fit perfectly, and, if I do say so myself, I looked great in it. I had a strand of pearls that would set it off nice.

Nancy found a beaded bag that matched the dress, and I tried on a pair of pumps with a heel low enough for me to wear. That's all I needed. I had everything else—a parka, sweats, sweaters—all the like of that.

So I was all fixed, dressed in my navy blue suit, ready and waiting the morning Mrs. Winchester was to arrive. All the girls were crowded onto the porch to see me off, laughing and talking—giving me all kinds of advice about finding a fellow and the like. I checked my bottomless pit to make sure I had everything—sunglasses, wallet, rain bonnet, umbrella, three Gospels of John; digging around in those little compartments, I found my lipstick, comb, brush, compact, stamps, address book, note pad, pencil, pen, tissues, and checkbook. But I couldn't find my nail file. I had to go through several pockets again before I found it. Satisfied that I had everything, I closed my pocketbook and sat there holding it on my lap with both hands and trying not to fidget.

One of the girls hollered, "Here she comes!" A vehicle was turning in the driveway.

"Looks like a limo," somebody said.

It was long, I tell you. Longer than a hearse! "What kind of a car is that?"

"It's a Rolls," Barbara told me. "A Rolls-Royce. A touring car."

"Well, why didn't you tell me her car was a Rolls-Royce?"

She grinned. "I was afraid you wouldn't take the job."

There was a man in a uniform behind the wheel and a ugly-looking dog on the seat beside him. The driver looked straight ahead and did not so much as glance our way as he drove around back. The girls picked up my luggage and piled off the porch, leaving me to bring up the rear.

I did not like the looks of this—this blue, streamlined automobile and a dog on the front seat! It gave me second thoughts. *Can I handle this?*

The chauffeur was standing straight as a poker at the rear of the car, ready to load my two bags. Although he was skinny, his uniform fit. If it had been khaki, he could have passed for a World War I private. With a long nose, a neat little mustache tucked under it, and a chauffeur's cap and black kid gloves, he looked like something out of a Hollywood movie.

Where's Mrs. Winchester? I wondered. Then I saw her deep inside the backseat, nearly hid; on the other side of her was another one of them ugly mutts staring straight ahead.

I grabbed Barbara's arm. "Now, see here, Barbara, if you think I'm gonna ride in that car with two big dogs all the way to Alaska, you've got another thing coming!"

"They won't hurt you, Miss E. They're guard dogs—Afghan hounds."

"That figures—they're terrorists!"

She laughed. "No. Mother won't have bodyguards, so the dogs are the next best thing."

"Now see here, Barbara—"

"Percival, this is Miss Esmeralda McAbee. Take good care of her."

The chauffeur stiffened, tipped his cap, and held his nose in the air. "Good morning, madam." Plainly, he thought he was too good for the likes of me. Well, nobody can snub me and get away with it. He opened the door for me to get in, but I let him stand there waiting while I took my time hugging each of the girls and saying my good-byes. I wasn't done when here came Albert's station wagon down the drive. He parked in back of the Rolls and got out wearing that pin-striped suit he wears when he's going to fly from Greensboro to New York for a board meeting or something. "I see you're ready to go," he said to me.

"Yes, I guess."

Barbara introduced him to Percival, and that nozzle nose did not hesitate to reach out and shake hands with Albert. Seeing I wasn't ready to get in the car, he shut the backseat door and began showing off the Rolls to Albert.

"Is this the Silver Spur model?" Albert asked him.

"Sir, this is the Mulliner Park Ward Touring Limousine." Nozzle Nose was so proud he could have split his britches. "This motorcar is two feet longer than the Silver Spur II." They walked around to the front to look at the fancy grill. On the top was the figure of a shapely woman with wings in skin-tight drapery. "The flying lady," he said, "distinguishes the Rolls-Royce as the finest motorcar in the world."

Albert nodded. "I've known several maestros who own the Rolls, and I must say the ride is superb."

"This model, sir, is the product of the world's finest craftsmen. The coach builders of Mulliner Park Ward required fourteen months to sculpt the metal and wood that went into this luxurious motorcar."

He opened the door on the driver's side, and that hound, staring straight ahead, did not so much as look his way.

I whispered to Barbara, "You sure them dogs are housebroke?"

She giggled. "Maybe."

That didn't help my jitters one bit.

Percival was showing off the interior of the car, pressing his palm down on the soft leather seat. "Sir, the material that goes into this model is the kind dreams are made of. This leather, made of champagne-colored hides perfectly matched and hand-stitched, required the hides of eighteen cows."

Albert nodded and began admiring the instrument panel. Nozzle Nose fell all over himself explaining. "All the woodwork is Lombardian walnut, burled walnut with silver inlays."

"It's really a magnificent car."

I stood on one foot then the other, anxious to get this show on the road, but Percival wasn't done. "Sir, this odometer is designed to record one million miles."

"So I've heard," Albert said. "I understand the Rolls has built-in security. Is that correct?"

"That is correct, sir." And Nozzle Nose was off to the races. "The pin tumbler door locks are designed using an Egyptian model used four thousand years ago to seal the tombs of the pharaohs." He paused for that to take effect. Albert nodded again, so Percival went on. "The odds for forging a key for these doors are one in twenty-four thousand. One in twenty-four thousand," he repeated. "That is not all, sir; when I remove the key from the ignition, the transmission automatically locks."

I could tell that Albert was ready to leave, but Nozzle Nose kept right on talking. "This motorcar is equipped with a minibar, refrigerator, silver-plated cocktail flasks, crystal glasses, a vanity set, and a marvelous entertainment console."

"Thank you," Albert told him and threw up his hand

to me. "Esmeralda, enjoy yourself. Lenora sends her love. We'll be praying for you."

"Good-bye, Albert. Take care of that vertigo."

I turned to say one last good-bye to the girls. There were tears in our eyes; we were too full to say much.

Percival opened the door for me, and, sad as I was, I slid in beside Mrs. Winchester. Percival fastened my seat belt. I wiped my eyes. There was no turning back now.

The mutt didn't even notice me as I settled in my seat. *Some guard dog.*

Barbara opened my door a bit and poked her head inside. "Mother, this is Miss Esmeralda. We call her Miss E. We all love her very much, and I know you will too."

"How do you do," Mrs. Winchester said in a small voice. "I am Winifred Win*chus*ter."

"I see," I said. *So this is the way it's gonna be—Mrs. Winchuster, my eye! Here's somebody who won't be calling her Mrs. Winchuster. I am nobody's lackey.*

Barbara tried to speak with her mother, but her mother had nothing to say to her. "Mother is shy," Barbara explained. Then she pecked me on the cheek and closed the door.

I'd never heard anything so crazy. Why would any mother be shy around her own daughter? Whatever this Mrs. Winifred Winchester was, she didn't strike me as being shy. Dressed in an elegant linen suit with a chiffon scarf and a broad-brimmed hat with feathers, she had to be the queen of the world. It made me feel good to see that her outfit did not hide the fact that she was heavier than me. As for her face, I couldn't see much of it because of that hat and the dark glasses, but what I could see put me in mind of a Cabbage Patch doll. What nose she had was pressed in between blubber cheeks. But I must say her perfume was nice. *Must be Evening in Paris*, I thought.

The dog beside her was gazing off into the distance, still ignoring me. That was fine—I'd sooner it ignore me as growl, bark, bare its teeth, or bite a plug out of me.

Percival had put on white gloves and was wiping dust from the flying lady with a chamois. Well, he was wasting his time and mine, because once we hit the Old Turnpike there'd be dust enough to bury us. While he was polishing the chrome, the lights, and hubcaps, I was getting antsy.

I decided to check my pocketbook again. I didn't want to get on the road and find I had left something behind. I counted the bills in my wallet and found my Medicare and health insurance cards, driver's license, and credit card. After rummaging in that bottomless pit, I didn't miss anything, so I stuffed everything back in there, snapped it shut, and, with butterflies in my stomach, sat waiting for us to get going.

At last, Percival changed his gloves to the black ones and climbed in behind the wheel. He did something or other that rolled up the glass partition between the front and back seats. *Good,* I thought. *That takes care of number two terrorist.*

You'd think Nozzle Nose was getting ready for the Indy 500 the way he checked all the gadgets, adjusted his cap and gloves, then started the engine and got us moving. As we glided down the driveway, I couldn't look back; my heart was too heavy. Leaving Priscilla Home for a world I knew nothing about was the hardest thing I had ever done in my life.

4

As we were going down the Old Turnpike, Mrs. Winchester spoke not a word. It was just as well; I didn't feel like talking. My heart was heavy as lead. Closing the door on the people and work I held dear had me so full I could have busted out crying.

Sitting in that fancy car beside that rich woman and those funny-looking dogs, I might as well have been leaving the planet for some other world. I felt out of place and uneasy. Never before in my life had I felt old, but now I was feeling old, too old to once again take the bull by the horns and do what I had to do.

I think it was Mr. Splurgeon, but it might have been Pastor Osborne, who said, "The future is as bright as the promises of God." In a better frame of mind I could have taken that at face value and got help from it, but I was feeling so low I'd have to stand on a soapbox to reach bottom.

I knew Jesus don't go to pity parties, so I tried to get

this party over with as soon as possible. That don't mean it was easy.

I slipped a Gospel of John out of my pocketbook and looked up that verse the Lord seemed to have give me. "When he puts forth his own sheep, he goes before them." *That ought to be enough to settle my nerves.*

We were nearly at the end of the Old Turnpike. I saw a flock of turkeys down the hill. I would miss this road, these hills—so many memories. I leaned back, took off my glasses, wiped my eyes, and shut them.

Running through my head were the words of that old hymn "Anywhere with Jesus": "Anywhere with Jesus, I can safely go; anywhere he leads me in this world below. Anywhere without him dearest joys would fade; anywhere with Jesus I am not afraid."

No matter how many times in the past I had sung that song and meant it from my heart, I had never before put it to the test. This was the test; this was where the rubber met the road—either I was willing to go anywhere with Jesus or I wasn't.

As Percival was turning onto the paved highway, I took a gander at the dog on the other side of Mrs. Winchester. I had never seen a dog with as long a head as that one, and it had a topknot of long silky hair parted in the middle and falling down over its ears like a long-haired girl's. The hair on the dog's back was silky too, but short. I couldn't see the feet, but it wouldn't have surprised me to know its toenails were manicured. The way that dog held its head on that long, arched neck put me in mind of a fashion model posing for a camera.

"What's the dog's name?" I asked.

Out from under that hat came a small voice. "Lucy."

"Lucy?"

"The one up front is Desi."

"I see," I said, but for the life of me, I didn't. Why in the world would anybody name dogs after Lucy and Desi Arnaz?

We rode another mile or two, but then my curiosity got the better of me. "Did you say Lucy and Desi?"

"Yes . . . Lucy is stagestruck, and Desi has been known to chase after female show dogs."

I didn't know if I was supposed to laugh or what. "I see," I said again, and the more I looked at Lucy, the more I could see that she might be stagestruck. The stuck-up way she held her head made her look like somebody who, if they ain't a celebrity, wants to be one.

We rode all the way to Highway 321 without saying another word. Most women have got tongue enough for two sets of teeth, but not Mrs. Winchester. She might just as well been a mummy sitting beside me. I felt myself lapsing into that pity party again. I forced myself to say something. "Barbara said your car is ten years old. Is this the one?"

"It is."

Barbara had said her mother didn't have a driver's license, but just to see what she would say, I asked, "Mrs. Winchester, did you ever drive it?"

"No, I don't drive."

"You mean—"

"I've never learned to drive."

"I see." I couldn't imagine any able-bodied woman her age not knowing how to drive. Maybe she was epileptic or something. Could that be what Barbara meant by her having spells?

Anyway, I was going to keep talking whether Mrs. Winchester listened or not. "I use to drive around Live Oaks before I was old enough to get a license. Had to do it to get to work. My papa died when I was in the eighth grade, and I had to drop out of school and go to work. In the mill I worked on third shift and didn't cotton to walking to and from the mill at night. Of course, there's no danger in Live Oaks. It's a small town, and the only calls the sheriff and his deputy get is when somebody locks their keys in the car, or a cat won't come down out of a tree, or somebody reports hunters on posted land. Our officers of the law earn their keep writing traffic tickets on strangers coming through town. Live Oaks is not much more than a crossroads, and when a stranger comes barreling down the highway, he don't hardly know he's in a town before it's too late."

The road alongside the river was one curve after another. That car we were in was heavy; it hugged its side of the road without the tires squealing. It would've been better if the tires had squealed, because here came a Bubba hot-rodding toward us in the middle of the road! He swerved to miss us and near 'bout went over the embankment on the other side. *Whew-ee, if he had hit this Rolls, he'd of been creamed like roadkill!*

Even so, Percival did not slow down. I got a firm grip on a hand bar next to the door, and to keep my mind off it, I kept talking a mile a minute.

"Live Oaks is where I met my husband. Hands down, Bud was the catch of the day, and I was the envy of every girl in town except Beatrice. She only had eyes for Percy Poteat, so she wasn't jealous of me. Beatrice is my best friend. We grew up together, and she had to drop out of school the same as me. We went to work in the variety store before we got jobs in the mill. When the mill closed, there was no work in Live Oaks. Beatrice went to work in a convenience store in Mason County."

Well, this one-way conversation was getting nowhere. I shut up for a while and started to read the Gospel of John. My bottomless pit is heavy, and as I leaned over to set it on the floor, lo and behold, out from under that hat came a small voice. "And then?"

I couldn't believe my ears. I remembered where I left off, so I picked up from there and went right on telling her about Bud and me, about how he went to Vietnam and got wounded, and how me and Elijah nursed him until he died.

Thinking about Bud, I got quiet. After all these years, it was still hard for me to think about him the way he was after he was wounded, the way he suffered all those years.

"And then?" I heard her say.

I come to. "Well, Mrs. Winchester, I had the best husband a body could ask, so I never looked for another."

It was true; I never *looked* for another husband. Of course, there was Albert, but it wouldn't do to tell her about him.

I hardly knew where to go from there, so I ventured to ask her, "Tell me about yourself."

She was so long in answering I didn't think she was

going to, but then she did. "I had a wonderful child-hood."

I waited for her to say more. Seeing she wasn't going to add anything, I decided not to let her off the hook easy. "When did you get married?"

Again, it didn't look like she was going to come down off her high horse and answer my question. I was about to let it go at that when she finally said, "After my coming-out party."

Since it was like pulling eye teeth to get anything out of her and I have not got the patience to humor anybody, I leaned back and took a breather.

Looking at the back of Percival's head with his ears sticking out like taxicab doors and that hound beside him with its nose sticking in the air put me in mind of rednecks who ride around in their pickups with their red-bone coonhounds hanging their heads out the window. At least redbone coonhounds have got some personality, which was more than I could say for those fancy hounds. *I bet those Afghans cost a pretty penny.*

We had long since passed the Tennessee welcome sign, and I was feeling nature's call. To keep my mind off it, and because I knew she wanted me to keep talking, I decided to tell Mrs. Winchester that story about how the preacher praying for Elijah's sick mule caused a ruckus in church. And how, when the mule died, me and the Willing Workers stood our ground to keep the city from selling the mule's carcass to the dog food plant.

When I finally finished, I'm not sure, but I thought I heard Mrs. Winchester giggle.

Already past Johnson City, Tennessee, we turned to

pick up Highway 81 heading for Knoxville. Once on the interstate, I tell you, that nozzle-nosed Percival pressed the pedal to the metal. We zoomed past everything on the road; we must've been going ninety miles an hour. The scenery went by so fast it looked blurry. *Good,* I thought. *The quicker we get to a pit stop, the better.*

Mrs. Winchester opened a box of candy and offered it to me. I picked a piece that didn't look like it was cream filled and, sure enough, it wasn't. I tell you, that was the best chocolate candy I ever put in my mouth. "Is this Hershey chocolate?"

"No. It comes from an island off the coast of Africa." She plopped a whole piece in her mouth and with a fat thumb and finger picked another one and held it while waiting to finish the first piece. Diamonds in her rings caught the sun and bedazzled my eyes. The diamonds were as big as acorns with what might be emeralds on either side. I couldn't help but notice her fingernails—the polish was a perfect match for that peach-colored suit she was wearing. *Probably press-on nails,* I thought, but I couldn't be sure.

For a second time she was poking the box at me, but I said, "No, thank you." I know my limit. Apparently, she didn't know hers, because as soon as she would finish one piece she'd gobble down another. *No wonder she's bigger than me.*

It wasn't long before we were pulling into a rest stop, and none too soon—I was about to have an accident! Before Percival could get out and open my door, I was outta there, running for the restroom.

What a relief!

As I was washing my hands, I didn't hear anybody else in the johns. I thought sure Mrs. Winchester would be in there. When I came outside she was still sitting in the car. *I can't believe she don't have to go.*

Percival was guarding the Rolls from a bunch of teenagers who were circling around it and asking questions. One of them punk rockers asked him, "How much does this baby cost?"

Percival answered, "If you have to ask, you cannot afford it."

The boy gave him one of those signs, the meaning of which I do not know and don't want to know. *Nozzle Nose, you better watch out; you're pressing your luck with those kids.*

They started peeking inside the car. "Who's that lady? She own this?" one of them asked.

"We travel incognito," Percival said in that highfalutin way he has got.

They all laughed. "Anybody got a dictionary?"

One girl reached out her hand like she was going to handle the flying lady, and Percival screeched, "Do not *touch* the motorcar!"

The girl removed her hand, made a face at him, and said, "So long, Banana Nose!" As the teenagers were piling back in their van, I handed the girl a Gospel of John. "It's the best book you'll ever read," I told her, and she thanked me.

As the kids rode past yelling obscenities, Percival opened the passenger door, let out Desi, and started putting a harness on him.

A big trucker came over, picking his teeth with a tooth-pick. "What kinda dog you got there?"

"Sir, this is an Afghan hound," Percival said, fastening a long leash to the harness.

"Afghan, eh? Too fancy to hunt. Must be you buy 'em for their looks."

Percival didn't like that one bit. "Sir, I will have you know that these are not merely beautiful animals, they are very useful. Afghans were bred for hunting antelope, leopard, wolves, and any other swift prey."

The trucker grinned and, chewing the toothpick, remarked, "There's not many antelopes and such in these parts."

I smiled. Percival didn't. "These are sighted dogs," he said, his face flushed, his temper rising.

I asked him what that meant.

"It means, madam, that they are farsighted and can spot an animal at a great distance." He handed me the leash. "Would you be so kind as to hold Desi while I get Lucy?"

I laughed. "I don't do dogs," I said, but I took the leash and held it.

Still grinning, the trucker pointed at Desi's big feet. "All that hair makes him look like he's got feathers."

With Lucy in hand, Percival closed the back door. "This animal might as well have feathers; Afghans run faster than birds can fly over any kind of terrain—rocky, hilly, or desert dunes."

Getting under Percival's skin was giving the trucker a big kick. "The way that female's belly is tucked up between her flanks, she must be kin to the greyhound painted on the side o' one o' them buses."

"Sir, these animals are far superior to any greyhound; they are multitalented. As well as hunting, they excel at herding sheep, tracking, and racing, and are the best guard dogs money can buy."

"Some guard dogs," the trucker remarked. "They didn't so much as raise a hair when I come up."

"Sir, these hounds have a mind of their own. They are standoffish around strangers but not because of fear; they are simply not interested in anything unworthy of their attention."

The trucker spit out the toothpick. "Unworthy, huh?"

Uh-oh, I thought. *Now you've done it—you've gone too far with a Bubba twice your size!*

Unaware of what he had done, Percival went right on fueling the fire. "Style is important to these regal animals. The Afghan is not called the king of dogs without reason."

Bubba wasn't grinning any longer; I had to do something before he punched Percival in the nose. I motioned toward Lucy. "Look at the end of her tail. Curved like that, it reminds me of a spit curl from the twenties."

That did the trick—turned Bubba's attention from Percival to Lucy. "I'd say she's a flapper, all right."

I thought Nozzle Nose was going to blow a gasket! The idea of calling Lucy a flapper! Fortunately he didn't say anything. Once the harness and leash were fitted on Lucy, he reached for the leash I was holding and away the three of them went across the grass.

At first those hounds strutted, trotting at a fast pace, pulling the leashes taut with Percival leaning backward holding down their speed. It wasn't to last. Desi and Lucy speeded up, pulling Nozzle Nose head first. He couldn't keep up; he fell sprawling, and those hounds took off like streaks of lightning.

Percival must've been dazed; he wasn't getting up. "Come on, let's help him," I said to Bubba, and the two of us ran across to where he lay.

Bubba got Percival to his feet while I fetched his glasses and cap. Can you imagine—that cap had the Rolls insignia on the front and was lined with silk. With his nose skinned and bleeding, blood and grass stains on the front of his uniform, Nozzle Nose looked a mess. The trucker handed him a bandana. "Here, we gotta get you cleaned up." The two men headed for the restroom.

The dogs were out of sight.

5

⌘

After Nozzle Nose cleaned himself up, there was nothing to do but wait for the dogs to come back. Fast as they were, they could have been back home in Afghanistan or who knows where. I left him at the picnic tables and sat in the car.

In a few minutes, Percival gave up calling the dogs and came back to speak to Mrs. Winchester. "As you know, madam, Lucy and Desi have minds of their own. A romp like this will last half an hour or more. Shall I serve lunch?" She nodded that he should.

He folded down two tables for us, found silverware, napkins, and glasses in a cabinet, then, with a flourish, gave a fancy fold to the napkins and set our tables. From the refrigerator he brought out two plates of salad, unwrapped them, and set them on the tables. Whipping out a wine bottle and wrapping it in a towel, he opened it, poured a glassful for Mrs. Winchester, and, with the bottle poised above my glass, asked, "Madam?"

"Sweet tea if you got it," I told him.

He peered down at me like I was a crawling cockroach. "Madam, we have Perrier."

"That'll do," I said, although I didn't have the foggiest notion what Perrier was.

This thing of him calling me "madam" was getting under my skin. In my book, *madam* means only one thing, the likes of which I am not, never have been, never will be. Of course, he didn't mean it thataway, but somebody like that Bubba might not know the difference and think I was in that kind of business.

Holding tongs with his pinkie poking straight out, Percival lifted an ice cube and placed it in the glass and then put in another before pouring what looked like water.

After serving us, Percival served himself and, carrying the wine with him, left to sit at one of the picnic tables under a tree.

I looked at that plate set before me, and the only thing I recognized was a lettuce leaf. "What's this?"

With a forkful halfway to her mouth, Mrs. Winchester answered, "Caviar and avocado."

"*Caviar?*"

I hesitated, but I was hungry, so I prayed and took a taste of it. All I tasted was cream cheese with lemon. Then I forked a bigger bite. That didn't taste like nothing I had ever ate before. I took a sip of the Perrier. It was some kind of soda, but even though it had a fizz, the only thing I could say for it was it was wet and I was thirsty.

I finished that plate in no time flat and could have eaten more, but if that salad was as rich as I thought it was, it would hold me until supper time. *Caviar! Wait till I tell Beatrice!*

Percival wasted little time eating, but he kept turning up that bottle until he drank every drop. When he came back to the car, he cleared our tables, put the dishes and everything back in the cabinet, folded back the tables, and asked, "Is there anything else, madam?"

She said no. Taking a towel and what looked like grooming brushes and stuff, he went back to wait for the dogs.

"Do you think they'll come back?" I asked Mrs. Winchester.

"They always do."

And in a few minutes, they did. With heads held high and prancing like royalty, they emerged from the woods, trotting toward the picnic area, their leashes dragging behind them. Percival, frazzled and hot, stood up to take charge, and I decided to get out and help him.

Nozzle Nose must have appreciated my help, because he didn't put on airs so much and didn't call me "madam." "They have a mind of their own," he repeated. "They only return when they're good and ready."

I held the hounds while Percival went in the men's room. He came out with a mop bucket full of water and started washing Desi's muzzle. Lucy, standing by my side like the Duchess of Dogs, looked ready to go again should Desi bolt and take off.

"Percival," I said, "Mrs. Winchester keeps having me talk about my hometown and everything else I can think of. What's with her?"

He stood up, took off his glasses, and wiped his face

on his sleeve. "Madam has lived all her days in a cocoon. She is a voyeur. What she knows about life she knows only as a spectator. She has never *lived* life."

Land sakes, that woman was in her sixties. What did he mean that she had never lived life?

Percival finished washing Desi's feet, gave him a hit-and-miss brush; then it was Lucy's turn.

Despite all the time it was taking us to get the dogs cleaned up, Mrs. Winchester did not get her body out of that car and go to the bathroom. I thought either her bladder got better mileage than mine or she had a potty in that Rolls.

Well, she didn't have a potty. When we got back on the road and were bypassing Knoxville, she told Percival to stop at one of the motels. In a few minutes he pulled into one of the better ones, got out, and opened the door on my side. I had to get out before Mrs. Winchester could, and, after she went inside, I stood there watching as she went past the desk. *So that's how she does it—uses a motel restroom for her pit stop.*

I got back in the car and sat there, going over in my mind what Percival had told me about her. He made her sound like a hermit, but she was too well-dressed to be one of them. Well, in my opinion, if not *living* life, as he put it, a body would have to be in a coma, in jail, or hiding out from the law.

After Mrs. Winchester was back inside the car and we were on I-40, Nozzle Nose fairly flew. I reckon the wine inspired him to break the NASCAR speed record. As if I didn't have enough to worry about, now we had a wino behind the wheel! Even Lucy looked alarmed, like any minute her hair would be standing on end. I held on to the armrest so tight my knuckles were white, but Mrs. Winchester had turned on the TV and was so glued to a soap opera she didn't notice we were racing to break that record or our necks, one.

Well, at least she wasn't asking me for more stories. Every time a commercial came on, she plopped another chocolate in her mouth and offered the box to me. I wouldn't let go the armrest to take a piece, but I was tempted. That was some good candy!

By late afternoon, by the grace of God and the help of however many angels he sent, we were coming into Nashville, and Percival slowed down. Exiting the interstate for a parkway, we were soon rolling through the Opryland Complex. I can't tell you how fabulous that place was—gardens and streams all over the place. It looked like acres and acres of trees and flowers, fountains, waterfalls, shops, eating places, all the like of that.

When the Rolls came to a stop before the hotel entrance, a man in a uniform that would have done a palace guard proud opened the car door. I climbed out and Mrs. Winchester followed, leaving Lucy alone on the backseat.

Percival proceeded to supervise the unloading of our luggage, and I followed Mrs. Winchester into the lobby. I couldn't believe my eyes! That lobby was as big as all get out, a lot of red carpet with settees and chairs, a grand piano, palm trees, a crystal chandelier hanging from the ceiling, cut flowers everywhere you looked. I just stood there gawking! A staircase wound up to an open floor, and it was easy to imagine Scarlett O'Hara coming down those steps and making a grand entrance.

I tell you, that lobby was out of this world. I picked up a brochure at the desk to find out more about the place.

Mrs. Winchester did not stop at the desk—she just told a bellhop to take our luggage to the Presidential Suite. He knew her name, so I figured she was well-known in Opryland. *Did I hear her right? Presidential Suite?* She beckoned for me to follow. "Come on, it's 5:00."

I followed in the wake of that wide load making her way through the crowd, hurrying as fast as she could hurry.

We landed in the Jack Daniel's Saloon. The walls all had pictures and stuff about Jack Daniel—not the whiskey, the man who made the whiskey. Being inside that saloon was like being inside a barrel—it was pitch dark. Mrs. Winchester told the waiter, "In the corner." I followed her groping along behind him. With her wearing dark glasses, she might as well have been blind.

As soon as he got us seated, the man handed us a wine and liquor list. Mrs. Winchester didn't bother to look at hers, just told him to bring her a dry martini straight up. He turned to me. "And you, madam?"

"Sweet tea with a slice of lemon and lots of ice."

Mrs. Winchester's mouth fell open. "You don't drink?"

"Never have except for a toddy now and then when I've been sick. Mama used to make syllabub at Christmastime, and one time I tasted beer, but other than that, I've been a teetotaler all my life."

The way her mouth hung open you'd think I had escaped from the funny farm.

While we were waiting, I read that brochure and looked at the pictures. The whole complex was under glass with tropical gardens, a river, and pathways. I saw where they had a forty-four-foot waterfall and a light and laser show. *Sure hope we get to see that,* I thought. They even had showboat cruises. All my life I'd wanted to go on one of them paddle-wheel boats. And then there was the Grand Ole Opry Theater. I used never to miss the Grand Ole Opry on radio, with stars like Roy Acuff, Chet Atkins, and Minnie Pearl. Some of them had died, but a few were still around. If the price was right, I would've liked to see a Grand Ole Opry show.

I offered the brochure to Mrs. Winchester, but she didn't care to see it.

The bar was filling up with mostly men come for the happy hour, but I only saw one table where the men and women seemed happy; they were laughing. Perched on the bar stools, the others weren't talking much, just drinking. Humped over their booze, they looked like so many crows side by side on a telephone wire.

I wasn't comfortable sitting in there with people guzzling demon rum and the like, waiting for the devil's joy juice to kick in, and with my lungs breathing in their smoke.

I thought about something Splurgeon wrote: "Shun the company that shuns God, and keep the company God keeps." Well, I would do that if I could, but I had signed on to this job and I had to see it through.

To make conversation I said, "Can you believe—they've

got pictures of Jack Daniel on the back of every one of these chairs."

"Yes, I see. While we're in Nashville, we'll visit his grave."

"Jack Daniel's grave?"

She nodded.

Land sakes! With everything there is to see and do in Opryland, it looks like she could forget dead people for a while.

The waiter served us our drinks. Mine had a lemon slice, and hers was served in a V-shaped stem glass with an olive stuffed with something. "I thought you said you wanted a dry martini."

"I did."

"What you got there looks wet to me."

A smile creased her fat face. "Dry means it's all vodka . . . Absolut vodka with maybe a drop or two of vermouth added."

That didn't make a bit of sense to me.

I took a sip of what passed for tea. It tasted like dishwater; must've come out of a can.

After that, we didn't talk, and once she had swilled down the drink, she ordered another one.

While she waited, fidgeting with her napkin, I stirred my tea and watched the bartender wiping glasses.

After downing the second martini, Mrs. Winchester must have been feeling some effect. "I feel sorry for people who don't drink," she said, "because when they wake up in the morning, that is as good as they're going to feel all day."

She was nuts if she thought that was going to get a

rise out of me. Mrs. Winchester ordered a third drink, and I wondered how many it would take before I would have a fall-down drunk on my hands. It was beginning to dawn on me that a fall-down drunk might very well be what Barbara meant by telling me her mother had spells of light-headedness. Well, light-headed she may be, but the rest of her was all heavyweight, and I do mean heavy! If she fell down, I'd have a mischief of a time getting her up.

The martini was served, and Mrs. Winchester swirled it around once or twice, fished out the olive, and forked it over at me.

That olive had a cheese filling and was so delicious I could have eaten a jar full. Right after I swallowed it, I began to sense the bartender was watching me. I could just feel his eyes looking my way, and it made me uncomfortable. He was probably grinning—watching this country bumpkin sitting in a saloon for the first time. Or was it because he wanted to see what I would do when Mrs. Winchester fell out the chair? If that was it, I did not see one thing funny about it.

Out of the blue, Mrs. Winchester told me, "I'm a poet," and started fumbling around in her purse.

"Oh?"

Finding a slip of paper, she held it to the light of a little lamp on the table, trying to read it. "Here's one I wrote . . . I wrote it the other day. I had Percival . . ." Frowning and holding the paper this way and that, she kept trying to read it. "I had Percival drive me to the . . . to the . . . cemetery in Smithfield . . . That's where . . . where Ava Gardner's buried . . ."

If she'd take off them dark glasses, maybe she could read whatever it was she was trying to read.

"She's buried beside her father . . . with a granite marker . . . Ava Lavinia Gardner." She gave up trying to read what was on the paper. "Smithfield was her hometown . . . Did you know that? Did you know Ava Gardner was from . . . from North Carolina? . . . Brought up on a tobacco farm? She was brought up on a tobacco farm . . . Do you remember the men . . . she married?"

I didn't remember.

"She married Mickey Rooney . . . then she married . . . Artie Shaw . . . then she married Frank Sinatra. Don't you remember?"

"I think I remember her marrying Frank Sinatra."

"Good," she said, like I had passed a test or something. "Here, read my poem."

I took the paper and read to myself:

Here lies Ava, thrice married,
Her choices were certainly varied,
She got a Mickey, became one of Artie Shaw's eight,
Marriage with Frank was her belated fate.

I was surprised; she really was a poet! "How do you do that? How do you make all them lines rhyme like that?"

As she played with her glass, holding it in both hands and rolling the last swallow around in the bottom, she looked pleased with herself. "It's a gift . . . That's what it is . . . it's a gift . . . just comes to me . . ."

"Must be," I said, impressed. I handed the poem back

to her. "That's the only kind of poem I like—the kind that rhyme. Do you write a lot of them?"

"Oh, sure. Tomorrow . . ." She beckoned the waiter again.

Uh-oh. One more drink and I'll have to call the rescue squad. I looked around, hoping to see Nozzle Nose. He was probably in his room in the hotel. "Where's Percival?"

Something tickled her. "Probably taking Desi and Lucy to the pet hotel . . . or polishing . . . that precious motorcar. Or he's reading . . . he's a bookworm." She drank that last swallow and looked around for the waiter but didn't see him.

Turning back to me, she went on about Nozzle Nose. "Percival . . . Percival's in love with the Rolls." That got her giggling. "It's his mistress . . . Nothing is too good for her . . . The gas he fills her tank with . . . the gas . . . has to have the highest octane money can buy."

That struck her very funny. I'd heard of drunks who feel good at first, then after a while get mean or start blubbering, so I figured I better do something right away. "Mrs. Winchester, I think we better go."

"Must we?"

"Yes, we must, or I'll have to pick you up off the floor."

She giggled again, and I got up and walked around the table to help her out of the chair. "Want me to get the check?"

She waved that aside like I shouldn't bother.

Well now, I wasn't walking out of that joint without paying. I looked around but couldn't find a waiter.

Nobody was in sight but the bartender, so I glanced his way; he gave me the high sign that it was taken care of and winked. *That man must have a tic!*

I took Mrs. Winchester's arm, and with her leaning on me, we made our way out of that den of iniquity back to the lobby. Seeing the two of us, people smiled and got out of our way. A bellhop ducked out of sight. I tell you, it was embarrassing.

Fortunately, no one was in the elevator. I propped Mrs. Winchester in a corner and started to press the button. "What floor?"

"Top . . . top floor," she managed to say.

I punched the highest number. The door slid shut, and when the elevator started moving up, I grabbed on to her so she wouldn't fall. "You got the key?"

She shook her head.

Well, how in blue blazes did she expect us to get in that Presidential Suite? I didn't even know the number. "Do you know the room number?"

With a wave of her little fat hand she let me know it was no concern of hers.

This was a pretty kettle of fish! What would I do with her while I went back downstairs to the desk for a key? I sure as shooting didn't want to go through the ordeal of taking *her* back down there.

Reaching the top floor, the elevator door rolled open, and I pressed the button to hold it open until I could get her out.

I got her out, but the trick was holding her up while I reached around to release the door. I was fit to be tied.

A maid in the hallway scooping a cigarette butt from

a waste thing saw us, dropped what she was doing, and hurried to help me. "Mrs. Win*chus*ter!"

Of course, the maid had the key, opened the door for us, and helped me get Mrs. Winchester inside. "Your luggage arrived," the maid said. The phone was ringing, so I let her take care of Mrs. Winchester while I answered it.

"Hello?"

"Miss E.? It's me, Barbara."

I was surprised. "How did you know where to call us?"

"The secretary gave me your itinerary. Mother always stays at the Gaylord Opryland Hotel. How are things going?"

"Things could be better."

"I'm sorry. She's drunk, isn't she?"

"Not pie-eyed drunk, but not too far from it. Is this what you meant when you said your mother has spells of light-headedness?"

"Miss E., you'll have to forgive me for tricking you into this, but I had to do it. If anybody in the whole wide world can help her, it's you."

"Well, this is a lot more than I bargained for. You should have played fair with me, Barbara. I don't know how you think I can help her. The way it stands now, if I could I'd be outta here on the next bus!"

"You're mad at me?"

"No, Barbara, I guess I can't be mad at you, because for some reason the Lord led me to take this job. That means I'm in for the long haul . . . But you could have told me."

"I'm sorry; I hope you can forgive me. We're all praying for you, Miss E."

"You better. How are things going at Priscilla Home?"

She groaned. "Oh, Miss E., you wouldn't believe this director! Now that you're gone, she's worse. She walks around here like she's the warden."

"Come now, she's new. Give her a break . . . Remember, it's like Splurgeon says, 'No case is hopeless while Jesus lives' . . . Barbara, don't you want to talk to your mother?"

"No, not really. We never talk." She was quiet a minute. "Miss E., things aren't the same here without you. Everybody misses you."

"Well, Barbara, hang in there and keep praying. How's Nancy?"

"Has her hands full."

We talked on about ten or fifteen minutes—maybe longer. Barbara said all the Opryland staff knew her mother and looked out for her. "It's the same in all those other hotels she visits. They all look out for her."

"Well, it looks like I can use all the help I can get."

"All the girls send their love."

"You give them mine, Barbara."

I could hear their bell ringing.

"There goes the bell for dinner, Miss E., so I'll have to hang up. We love you. We'll be praying."

After we hung up, it took me a minute to get back to where I was at. I looked around at that Presidential Suite and I tell you, it would put the White House to shame! I was in the dining room, and there was a table and chairs in there that would seat twelve people, plus a fireplace and piano and couches and chairs and with so many fresh flowers a body might wonder who died. There was even a bar on one side of the room.

I went back in Mrs. Winchester's room and saw that the maid had managed by herself to get Mrs. Winchester ready for bed and had her propped up on big pillows. The maid was already unpacking and putting things away.

I started to ask Mrs. Winchester what we would do for supper but was stopped dead in my tracks. Without her hat and dark glasses, what I saw was a shocker. Mrs. Winchester had a glass eye.

6

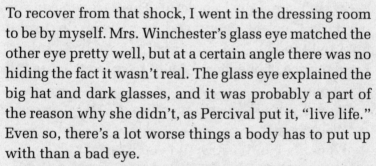

To recover from that shock, I went in the dressing room to be by myself. Mrs. Winchester's glass eye matched the other eye pretty well, but at a certain angle there was no hiding the fact it wasn't real. The glass eye explained the big hat and dark glasses, and it was probably a part of the reason why she didn't, as Percival put it, "live life." Even so, there's a lot worse things a body has to put up with than a bad eye.

I heard the maid ask Mrs. Winchester if she wanted to deposit her jewelry in the hotel safe.

"No, put it wherever you like."

The maid came in the dressing room to show me what was in that jewelry case—ropes of necklaces, gold and silver chains, pearls, broaches, bracelets, watches, and no telling what else. Rolling her eyes at me, she whispered, "She never leaves them in the safe—has me put what she's not wearing in a drawer or any old place."

That was a fine how-de-do! Maybe Mrs. Winchester didn't care if her jewelry was stolen, but I did! If ever anything was missing, I'd be the prime suspect. I tell you, this situation was getting harder and harder to deal with.

I followed the maid back to the bedroom and saw that she put the jewelry in a dresser drawer. "I'm Hazel," she told me. "There are three of us assigned to Mrs. Win-chuster. Mary will be here in the morning. Grace comes twice every day to clean."

That was a relief. With three maids to help me, I ought to be able to manage.

I was starved, but I didn't see any way I could leave Mrs. Winchester to go eat. I'd heard about room service but wasn't sure how to order it. There were menus on the desk; I picked one up and, as I always do, read it from right to left. You would not believe those prices! For the price of one meal I could have fed a house full of people.

"Would you like me to order dinner?" Hazel asked.

"Would you?"

"I'd be glad to. What would you like?"

"I'll take whatever chicken they have and decaf coffee. I'm tired and I'd like to take a bath if you—"

"Yes, I'll stay with her."

"Thanks."

My gown, robe, and slippers were laid out for me in my room, and the bed was turned down. As swell as that place was, I was too uptight to enjoy it. While I was undressing I tried to think of some way I could persuade Mrs. Winchester to stash her Fort Knox in a safe. *Land sakes, these maids, the bellhop, and who knows who else has got keys to this suite. What could make that woman so careless? Maybe whatever caused her to have a glass eye also knocked her off her rocker.*

Whatever her reason, to protect myself I had to do something about those valuables.

I was so preoccupied I didn't pay much attention to the luxury in the bathroom. It was big as a boxcar, and the marble was real—cream colored with dark veins running through it. As well as having big, thick towels with monograms, the room had any appliance you might need, plus bottles of lotions, bath oils, shampoo, and the like, enough to stock a drugstore. To top it all off, a vase of yellow rosebuds sat on a table. I touched them to make sure they were real.

I filled the tub with hot water and poured in some bubble bath. After all I'd been through with Barbara's mother, Nozzle Nose, and them dogs, I felt I was owed a good, long soak. The water was so deep my legs and arms floated like one of them astronauts in space. I wished my worries would float like that. This thing of dealing with a drunk was bad enough, but those jewels lying about gave me the heebie-jeebies.

꒰꒱

After a while I heard Hazel letting someone in the door and figured it was room service. I finished bathing and got out of the tub. Once I got dried off and was putting on my gown, I heard her tapping on the door. "Dinner is served."

"Coming." I tied on my robe and went in the dining room. The silver food warmers, crystal goblets, and heavy silverware—enough forks to furnish ten people—

were spread out as fancy as anything you might see in a magazine.

I took a look-see in Mrs. Winchester's room and saw that her supper was on a bed tray. Lifting one of them dome lids, Hazel told her, "Beef Wellington." All around the meat were ripe tomatoes topped with globs of whipped cream. Hazel was telling her, "Tomatoes with horseradish cream, asparagus salad, and charlotte russe for dessert."

Mrs. Winchester did not so much as look at the tray.

"Will that be all?"

Mrs. Winchester nodded.

I followed Hazel to the door, thanked her, and locked the door behind her.

Sitting down at that dining room table, I felt like the queen bee. I gave thanks, then lifted the lid from the main dish. A delicious smell greeted me. That chicken was in a sauce, with brown rice and mixed vegetables. I checked out the fruit salad, buttered a roll, and was about to pour myself a cup of coffee when Mrs. Winchester called me. "Please . . . bring your dinner . . . in here."

I had a mischief of a time hauling all that stuff into her room and setting up at a table in there. When I got done, everything looked thrown together, but I didn't want it to get cold, so I sat down, spread the napkin on my lap, and dived in.

As I was enjoying the chicken, Mrs. Winchester wasn't touching her food. Since she was more than pleasingly plump, you would expect her to gobble down any food in sight. Chances were, she got big-bellied on chocolate candy and booze. It surprised me that she was in a talking mood; I could hardly eat for her talking to me. Not once but three times she told me, "Miss E., I had a wonderful childhood." It was the first time she had called me by my name.

I can't talk and eat at the same time, so to humor her I hurried to get through. The dessert was a lemon chess tart, just the right thing to top off the meal. *Wish I could get that recipe.*

I stacked my dishes on the serving cart, and still she had not touched her food. "Mrs. Winchester, taste those tomatoes with the cream; they look delicious!"

With a wave of her hand, she told me to take the food away. "I want to tell you . . . tell you . . ." and her voice trailed off so soft I couldn't hear her.

I rolled the cart into the hall and left it there, then locked the door again. I was about to prop a chair under the doorknob when Mrs. Winchester asked me to pull the chaise lounge closer to her bed. I was so tired I was ready to hit the hay, but I did as she asked, put my feet up, and hoped she wouldn't talk long.

That woman was no beauty, but she had a peaches-and-cream complexion. A single tear coursed down her cheek, and, looking off in the distance in a dreamy kind of way, she mumbled, "Miss E., I had a . . . I had a wonderful childhood . . . It was wonderful . . ." She fingered the sleeve of her robe, lost in never-never land.

I thought if I heard that one more time I would have to ask her, "If it was so wonderful, why them tears?"

"In my grandfather's house there were forty rooms. My nannies, my maids, my tutors . . . we all lived on the third floor—" Suddenly, as if remembering something, she stopped and asked me to bring her a little "picker-upper" from the bar.

A picker-upper? Should she pass out on me, I'm the one who will need a picker-upper! Now, I tell you, a bartender I am not, and I felt like telling her so, but she looked so sad I didn't have the heart. *Maybe she'll settle for coffee.* "Regular or decaf?" I asked.

"A martini, please."

I tried to get a smile out of her. "Wet or dry?"

"Dry," she said without a smile.

I got up from the couch, praying there wouldn't be any liquor in that bar.

Well, there was—big bottles and little bottles of all kinds of wine and liquor. While I was putting ice in the glass I could still hear her talking. "It took two rooms . . . to hold my toys . . . two rooms . . . one for dolls . . . stuffed animals . . . books . . ."

I found the vodka and sniffed it. I didn't know the first thing about mixing a martini. There were olives and slices of lemon and lime, but where was that . . . that vermouth she mentioned? *Ice—do they put ice in a martini?*

I didn't feel right about serving her a drink. The more I thought about it, the more I realized I couldn't do it. I dumped the ice in the sink, dried the glass, and put all the stuff back where I'd found it.

Going back in her room, I asked her, "Mrs. Winchester, wouldn't you rather have ginger ale? There's ginger ale in there."

She shook her head.

Well, there was no use beating around the bush. I

told her point-blank, "Mrs. Winchester, if I served you a martini I would be disobeying God, and I'm not going to do that."

"What?"

"Somewhere in the Bible it says, 'Woe unto him that gives his neighbor drink.' I can't do it. If that's what this job requires, you'll have to get yourself another companion."

Her mouth fell open. "You read the Bible?"

"Don't you?" I asked. "Don't you read the Bible?"

She stared at me for a minute and, looking downright pitiful, answered, "Sometimes I read my horoscope," as much as to say, *Will that do?*

I fluffed up her pillows. "Please, let me bring you something—a soft drink, fruit juice, whatever you like."

She turned her face away from me and gazed across the room, fingering that sleeve. I guessed she was mad at me.

"Mrs. Winchester?"

She kept looking away from me, probably wondering what kind of an oddball I was. But when she finally did speak, her voice quivered. "Miss E., let me tell you something."

I wanted to tell her, weepy as she was, that she didn't have to say anything, but she seemed determined, as if it was something she just *had* to tell me. "When I was a little girl . . . not more than six . . . maybe five years old, I asked my nanny, 'Where do babies come from?'. . . She told me . . . she told me, 'From heaven.'"

Then, right in the middle of what she was trying to tell me, she stopped talking. I waited. Tears trickled down one side of her face. I handed her tissues and waited. A clock was ticking.

I sensed that whatever it was she was trying to tell me was not yet finished, but waiting for her to go on tried my patience. I was so tired I had just about had it for one day.

Finally, choking back tears, she told me, "There was another time . . ." She took a tissue and dabbed at that good eye. "There was another time when I heard a man on the radio . . . He was talking . . . talking about Jesus . . . I asked my nanny, 'Who is that Jesus?'" Her voice was so soft and trembly, I had to strain to catch what she was saying. "My nanny . . . turned off the radio . . . She turned off the radio and told me, 'You don't need to listen to that.'"

Again she left me waiting. I thought she would go on telling me what all this meant, but she didn't. I couldn't figure out any connection between her asking where babies come from and this thing about Jesus. I couldn't make head nor tails of it, but there was no doubt that it made sense to her and that it was so all-fired important I was obliged to listen.

Mrs. Winchester lay there very quiet and seemed absolutely lost in that other world. If I had not been so tired I would have been more curious, but if she wasn't going to explain things, I wished she'd just say good night so I could go to bed. When she didn't, I spoke up. "Mrs. Winchester, we've had a long day, and tomorrow will be another long day. If you don't mind, I would like to say good night."

She kept fingering that sleeve and saying nothing.

I crawled off the couch. "Good night," I said.

"Good night," she mumbled.

I propped a chair under the doorknob and turned out all the lights except night-lights. Before I went in my room, I told her to call me if she needed me during the night.

By the time my head hit the pillow I was asleep.

7

❧

The next day we were going to Lynchburg, Tennessee, to visit Jack Daniel's grave. Mrs. Winchester slept late, and that gave me time to read my Bible and pray. I also wrote a letter to Beatrice.

Dear Beatrice,

This will come as a shock to you. I have retired from Priscilla Home. When we can talk I'll tell you more about that.

You would not believe what I have got myself into. I don't have time to tell you how I got into this mess, but to make a long story short I'm traveling across country with this rich lady to go on a cruise to Alaska. I was hired to be her companion, but they didn't tell me she was bad to drink but she is and that's why they hired me to keep an eye on her. Right now we're in Nashville staying in the Gaylord Opryland Hotel. It is out of this world!

I doubt you've heard of this woman, but she is rolling in dough. Her name is Mrs. Winifred Winchester and she's about our age or a little younger. She is a good poet but nothing to look at. Has got a glass eye and must be a size 20. At first I thought she was stuck up, but the truth is she is very shy. According to Percival, he's the showfer (sp.) who drives the car, she keeps to herself like a hermit. On the other hand she does goofy things that draw attention to herself. I can't figure that out.

By the way the car is a Rolls-Royce. Carl can tell you what them cars is like. Mrs. Winchester has two fancy dogs—one rides on the seat beside Percival and the other one is on the backseat with her and me. She calls them Lucy and Desi. Ain't that a hoot.

This Percival is so high and mighty you'd think he owned the Rolls and everything that goes with it. He looks down his nose on nearly everybody. I might add that it is some long nose he has got—I call him Nozzle Nose but not to his face. And he is one Jehu driver! On the interstates I'd say he goes a hundred miles an hour. Land sakes, Beatrice, it's a wonder we have not all been killed.

This Mrs. Winchester don't talk hardly at all, but you know me, I'm not going to put up with that even if I have to do all the talking. I started telling her about Live Oaks and she can't get enough of me telling her about things that have happened there and the people we know. Still, the only time she says much of anything is after she has got a few drinks under her belt and then she don't make a lot of sense.

It's safe to say she don't never darken the door of a church so you can see I have got my work cut out for me. As you know this lifestyle rich people has got is nothing I'm use to. When a body is rolling in dough, it's like Splurgeon says, "When the barn is full, man can live without God." Well, anyway I'll do what I can. Again, it's like Splurgeon says, "We must sow the seed on stony ground, too."

Thanks for praying for me.

Yours very truly,

Esmeralda

P.S. This is the verse the Lord used to show me that taking this job was the right thing for me to do. John 10:4.

It was after lunch before we were ready and waiting for Percival to bring the car around. Mrs. Winchester was wearing a blonde wig and was really gussied up. The top she was wearing was made out of all different colors of shaggy-looking cloth scraps. It was matched with a long denim skirt that was dark and banded with the same colors as the top. As stout as she was, you wouldn't think she could wear something like that, but she looked great.

"Mrs. Winchester," I said, "that is one good-looking outfit you have got on."

"This old thing?" She plucked at the sleeve. "It looks like they made this top out of rayon and cotton rags."

For her to be sober and talking was a welcome change.

"They call this denim a 'broom skirt,' and it does look like something they sweep with."

"Oh, I like it! Where'd you get them shoes?" They looked like leather moccasins, but the fancy stitching made me know they cost a pretty penny.

"These shoes? I think they came from Italy." A timid little smile told me she was tickled about something. "Most of those Italian shoes have spike heels and pointed toes . . . You would have to have only one toe to fit in them."

I laughed, and, unless I miss my guess, that pleased her a lot. "You'd never find that outfit or them shoes in the discounts," I told her.

"I wouldn't know," she said.

"Where do you shop, Mrs. Winchester?"

"I don't. I don't shop. I have personal shoppers at Neiman Marcus and Bergdorf Goodman. They have my sizes and send me all my clothes."

"They must be swanky stores."

"Swanky? I guess so, but some women only buy from high-fashion places in Europe like Escada. I buy American."

American? Those shoes came from Italy, and I'd bet that outfit she was wearing came from Paris, France.

The phone rang, and the maid answered it.

"Excuse me, Mrs. Win*chus*ter," she said. "Your car is waiting."

The maid fetched Mrs. Winchester's hat, a broad-brimmed straw one. I couldn't help but compliment her on that hat too—it was not only stylish, but it would also keep the sun out of her eyes—well, I mean her eye, her good eye.

"I like it too," she said. "It's a panama—you know, the kind they make out of jipijapa leaves."

We were almost at the door when I remembered the jewelry.

"Mrs. Winchester, since we're leaving the suite, don't you think it would be a good idea to put your jewelry in the safe?"

"Never mind. If it's stolen, I'll buy more."

I didn't like that one bit, but there was nothing I could do about it.

We took the elevator downstairs and found Percival waiting outside with Lucy and Desi in the car. Mrs. Winchester asked him how far it was to Lynchburg, and he said it was about seventy-five miles. She reminded him that she had to be back by 5:00.

"Yes, madam."

On the way, Mrs. Winchester surprised me by talking—telling me all about Jack Daniel. "His real name was Jasper Newton Daniel," she told me, "but everyone called him Jack. When he was only seven years old he went to work for a Lutheran minister who had a still."

"A Lutheran minister had a still?"

"Yes, that was back in the 1800s. After a few years his

congregation objected, and he sold the still to Jack. Jack was only thirteen years old when he took over."

She went on for a long time, telling me Jack Daniel's history and how he made whiskey by seeping it through charcoal, aging it in barrels and so forth. "That's what makes it Tennessee whiskey and not bourbon," she said.

I didn't have the foggiest notion what the difference was and was not the least bit interested in finding out. To me, all booze is rotgut, but Mrs. Winchester was enjoying talking about booze almost as much as she liked drinking it.

"Jack Daniel's whiskey became world famous. In competition with whiskeys from all over the world, his whiskey won the gold medal at the 1904 World's Fair."

Finally, I had to say something. "Well, I'll tell you, Mrs. Winchester, the Lord don't look with favor on bootleggers."

"Oh, Jack Daniel was no bootlegger. He was the first in the country to register his distillery. First to put whiskey in square bottles too."

Unlike her, I was not the least bit excited about Jack Daniel's contribution to the liquor industry. I had seen too much heartache come out of a liquor bottle, round or square. But I had to be polite and keep up my end of the conversation. "Since Jack Daniel is dead, do you know how he died?"

"Oh, that's a funny story." She giggled. "Early one morning he came to work and wanted to get something out of his safe, but he couldn't remember the combination. He lost his temper, kicked the safe, and broke his toe. An infection set in he could not get rid of, and six years later he died from blood poisoning."

Serves him right, I thought but didn't say so. "How do you find out so much about dead people?"

"It's very easy. My secretary goes on the Internet for information, and when she can't find enough there, she makes phone calls, goes to the library, or orders books for me."

Percival was slowing down to pull off the interstate onto a county road, and Mrs. Winchester told me we would be going to the gravesite before we went to the museum.

We turned again, this time on Elm Street. Driving slowly straight into the cemetery, Percival came to an intersection and stopped the car.

There it was, a big, square-looking tombstone resting on two stone blocks. On the top block, *Daniel* was spelled out in raised letters.

Percival opened our door, and we both got out. The Daniel tombstone was different than the others. Along one side of the tombstone face and along the top, the rock was unfinished except for oak leaves. Maybe that rough part was supposed to be a oak tree; I couldn't make it out. The rest of it was finished stone with Jack Daniel's name and dates on a plaque.

"I see he was only sixty-one years old when he died," I said. And, seeing there was no room on the stone for the name of his wife, I asked, "Wasn't he married?"

"No. Never was. Left his business to a nephew."

After she got done with the gravesite, we got back in the car to drive to the museum. Mrs. Winchester pulled out a little black book and was jotting down notes. Well, I guess if you're a poet, you get excited about stuff nobody else cares a hoot about.

At the museum, Percival let us out and started putting on the harnesses to take Lucy and Desi for a walk. Soon as me and Mrs. Winchester got out, tourists started gathering around the car, asking questions. Them Afghans and the Rolls attracted so much attention that we had the museum to ourselves.

There were all kinds of exhibits in there and a tour guide telling about the history of the still and how they made whiskey. There was this one picture of Jack Daniel, and, land sakes, he looked funny. He appeared to be about five feet tall and was dressed in a swallowtail coat that was too big for him—the sleeves hung down over his hands. He didn't look like he grew much after he was thirteen and took over the still. I reckon not. With all whiskey can do to a body, it's likely it stunted his growth.

Once the tourists started piling in the door, we left and went back to the car. We saw Percival and the dogs on the road coming back from their walk.

Mrs. Winchester had that little book open and was going over her notes. I admired the little black book with its smooth cover and elastic band. "It's moleskin," she told me. "All great writers carry one like this with them everywhere they go. We never know when we will be inspired and need to write something down before the muse leaves us."

I had never known a real writer before. I'd ask her for her autograph when I knew her better.

While she was writing, Percival put the dogs in the car and got back under the wheel. Soon we were on our way again.

When Mrs. Winchester finished writing, she handed the little book to me. I read the poem to myself.

> When Jack Daniel was born, t'was said he knew,
> That when he grew up he would learn to brew
> Whiskey that he gave his name
> And brought to him both wealth and fame.
> But an infection when he kicked his safe, poor Jack,
> Neither wealth nor fame could bring him back.

I was so impressed I couldn't say a word.

"You like it?" she asked.

"Like it? I think it's great!" I handed the book back to her. "Would you make me a copy?"

"Of course," she said, closing the book and securing it with the elastic band. She looked very pleased and leaned back with a smile on her face. "You are one of the few people I know who appreciates good poetry."

When we arrived back at the hotel, we had time to freshen up before we headed for the saloon. Once in the suite, the first thing I did was check out the valuables to see if they were still there. Of course, I didn't know everything she had, but it looked like the jewels were all there just as the maid had left them.

In the elevator going down, Mrs. Winchester told me, "My secretary has made reservations for us at the Cascades for dinner."

"The Cascades?"

"Yes. They serve seafood cuisine and there's a lovely view of the waterfall."

That sounded good, but if she got drunk we'd never make it to the Cascades. The minute we stepped off the elevator she struck out for Jack Daniel's barrelhouse. The same waiter we had the night before led us to our corner table. Once seated, Mrs. Winchester ordered a martini for herself and iced tea for me.

When the waiter served our drinks, hers looked the same as the night before, but the waiter gave me something in a tall glass that looked too good to be good. "What's this?"

"Madam, that is a Singapore Sling, compliments of the house."

I laughed. "Well, take it back to Singapore with my compliments! By the way, young man, your iced tea tastes like ditch water, so bring me a ginger ale."

Mrs. Winchester smiled. "So that Singapore Sling was no temptation to you?"

"None whatsoever."

"I wish I could say the same," she said in that soft little voice she has got. "Tell you what, as soon as I finish this one drink, we'll go to the Cascades."

8

Dinner at the Cascades had me really living high on the hog, but I wasn't eating pork! For a souvenir I took one of the menus, so I could tell Beatrice what I ate. I had something called "Chilean Sea Bass with Sake." Whatever that sake was, it made the fish taste real good. Then they had something they called "Braised Shiitakes," which to me did not sound like anything a body should put in their mouth. I reckon that's what they called them big mushrooms. The "Fresh White Asparagus, Fried Ginger, and Chile Oil" was out of this world, and the dessert was just the thing to top it off, lemon pie, which was just as fancy as the names they gave it: "Lemon Lime Meringue Tart with Mango, Raspberry, and Cassis Coulis."

Mrs. Winchester ate a pretty good meal, and maybe that kept her from drinking too much and talking half the night. Anyway, she went to bed when we got back to the hotel, and as soon as I could, I hit the hay.

But I kept waking up thinking about this and that—especially worrying about those jewels stuck in that drawer. I'm not one for taking much medicine, but I did get up and took two Tidynol. Still, I didn't fall asleep. When daylight came I got up and dressed.

Mrs. Winchester was still sleeping. Mary, one of the other maids, had come in and was putting fresh towels in the bathroom, so I asked her if she would be there a while.

"Oh yes. All morning."

"Then I think I'll go down and have breakfast."

The coffee shop in the hotel was on the first floor. It was crowded, but I found a table and was studying the menu when who should come in but Nozzle Nose himself. He walked around with a newspaper under his arm, looking for a table. Finally, he spotted me and came over.

"May I join you?"

"Sure."

He motioned for the waitress to bring coffee and then sat down. Folding his paper to a certain section, he commenced reading. Talk about bad manners!

"Good morning," I said. "What's good for breakfast?"

That jerked a knot in him; he put the paper to one side. "Good morning," he said without the "madam" before or after. *That's good,* I thought. *Maybe this morning he'll act like a normal human being.*

"What's good?" I repeated.

"I'm having eggs benedict and prune juice."

Prune juice—must be he's not regular. That could account for a lot of things, namely his disposition.

The waitress came with the coffee and was ready to

take our orders. She made me think of home. Around her waist she was wearing one of those short little aprons with pockets like the girls wear at the all-you-can-eat restaurant in Live Oaks. What was missing was a great big pretty handkerchief in her blouse pocket. That would have been cute.

I ordered eggs benedict too, although, except for the eggs, I didn't have any idea what I was ordering. I didn't need prune juice; I'm as regular as clockwork. I ordered orange juice and debated about getting toast, but since Nozzle Nose didn't order toast, I figured maybe it came with the eggs benedict.

While we were waiting to be served, Percival drank coffee and went back to reading his newspaper. Rude, that's what he was, just plain rude.

When he finished reading, he looked up. "You will be interested in this," he said and handed me the paper.

I saw an article about a big merger of companies negotiated by Philip Winchester. I read it and handed the paper back to him. "Sounds like big business."

"Oh, it is." He unfolded his napkin and spread it on his lap. "Mr. Win*chus*ter is a brilliant man—always one jump ahead of the competition." Holding his cup with his pinkie poking out, he peered over his glasses. "I presume you know that Mrs. Win*chus*ter inherited a shipping fortune from her grandfather."

I shook my head. "No, I didn't know that."

"In the years since he and Mrs. Win*chus*ter have been married, Philip has probably doubled her inheritance."

Calling Mr. Winchester by his first name did something

to Nozzle Nose—it looked like it made him feel he was right up there with the bigwigs.

"Did you say shipping?" I asked.

"Yes. Mrs. Win*chus*ter's family came to America from the Netherlands in the early 1800s. Over several generations they became the country's premier shipbuilders, operating passenger liners and an import-export business unequaled in the world.

"Much has been written about Mr. Win*chus*ter. Due to his shrewd management, the shipping business still thrives, but with the evolution of other means of transport, he had the foresight to expand and diversify. Philip—" the name did not roll off his tongue easy— "bought mines, breweries, citrus farms, hotels, and many other enterprises."

The waiter served our eggs, and I recognized the hollandaise sauce. I had made that on special occasions.

Nozzle Nose did not let up even while he ate. "As you might have surmised, theirs is a marriage of convenience." He sipped his juice. "Here I am, taking Mrs. Win*chus*ter to Alaska and her husband is aboard his yacht in the Caribbean."

"Percival, that is none of our business. We shouldn't be talking about their marriage."

"Oh, I don't know. Philip—" the name came easier—"is happy, and she enjoys her little pranks."

"Pranks?"

"Oh yes. She'll do anything to get attention."

I guess a body could think that putting her husband's picture on billboards as a missing person was a *prank*.

"Have you had much difficulty with Mrs. Winchuster's alcohol consumption?" he asked.

"I'd rather not talk about that. She might have come to breakfast with me, but she was sleeping when I left."

"Mrs. Winchuster always sleeps late, but I hope she is up before noon. Today we go to a couple more gravesites."

"Oh?"

"Chet Atkins is one of them, not far from Nashville." He was dabbing at his little mustache and gave the waitress the high sign. I drank the last of my coffee and was pulling out my wallet to pay my bill.

"No, no," he said. "All expenditures are billed to Mrs. Winchuster's account. They know me here."

"How about the tip?"

"Believe me, madam, a very generous tip is included in the bill. Put away your wallet."

We walked outside, and he left to take the dogs for a stroll. I watched a boatload of tourists floating around a bend in the river and was thinking how I'd love to be on that boat. But I needed to get back upstairs in case Mrs. Winchester needed me.

Mary let me in the door and then went back to arranging a new bouquet of fresh flowers. Mrs. Winchester was still sleeping.

After brushing my teeth, I went in my room to read my Bible and sat down wondering what the day would bring. Suddenly, I remembered that waitress and got an idea. I jumped up, told Mary I'd be back in a few minutes, and left to get back downstairs as fast as I could.

9

I spent most of the morning trying to find what I was looking for. The waitress told me where I could buy an apron like hers, but the store was some distance from the hotel. After I bought the apron, I looked all over for Velcro. I found it, then saw a Christian bookstore and bought more Gospels of John.

By the time I got back to the suite, Mrs. Winchester was getting dressed. I didn't want her, and especially the maid, to know what I was up to until I was ready, so I slipped in my room without saying anything.

I hand-sewed the Velcro onto the pockets so they could be sealed and, to make doubly sure, got out the safety pins to pin the pockets as well. *I sure hope this works.*

Once I was done with that, the next step was to see if I could fit all that jewelry in the pockets. But before I went that far, I figured I needed to ask Mrs. Winchester if what I was doing was okay.

The phone was ringing, and when Mary answered it,

I beckoned to Mrs. Winchester. "Would you like to see what I bought, Mrs. Winchester?"

She came in my room, and I closed the door behind her.

"Can you keep a secret?" I asked. "I've come up with a way I might keep your valuables safe."

"Oh, you needn't bother about that. Everything's insured. I probably have half a million dollars' worth of jewelry with me, but I don't care if it is stolen. A robbery would make headlines, and I don't mind being written up in the papers."

"Well, I do! I don't want my name splashed all over a newspaper, and it would be, because I would be the prime suspect! I would wind up in the hoosegow, and, the court system being what it is, I would probably be sent up the river for the rest of my life."

Pulling the apron out of the bag, I held it up. "Mrs. Winchester, for my own protection, I would like to use this apron to carry your jewelry on my person. Do I have your permission?"

Her mouth dropped open. "You're going to wear that?"

"Under my clothes, of course." I fitted the apron around my waist. "See these pockets? They're big enough to hold everything you've got. Don't you see? This will work, I think."

The idea tickled her. "Well, you go get the jewelry case, and we'll see."

Mary was still on the phone, which made it easy for me to slip the case out of the drawer and back to my room.

Mrs. Winchester was standing before the mirror, fitting the apron around her own waist and giggling like she was having the time of her life. She handed the apron back to me.

Between the two of us, we got all the jewelry into those pockets and sealed and pinned them securely, then I slipped off my skirt and tied the apron on me.

Underneath my skirt the pockets bulged a bit. Something made a circle impression—must have been a bracelet. Anyway, it made me look like I had a big ringworm on my stomach. I tried to pat the pockets flatter. Mrs. Winchester giggled. "Looks like you have tumors!"

I laughed. "Either that or I'm pregnant with triplets!" I turned the apron around so the bulges were in back.

"Now you have a bustle," she said, and that threw her into such a fit of laughing it looked like she couldn't stop.

"No need to get historical," I told her. "I'm used to carrying around a caboose bigger than any bustle."

Well, I could see that having the apron in back was no solution, so I said, "Let's see if we can't do something so they don't poke out so much."

Well, that worked. We rearranged the jewelry, separated the big stuff between the three pockets and spread the little stuff as flat as we could. Then I put the apron on in front of me, and it worked! The pockets were flatter, and nobody would ever guess there was anything more under my skirt than my own bay window.

Of course, I'd have to get used to wearing the thing.

Mrs. Winchester was so tickled she was practically rolling on the floor. "Of course," I told her, "if some lowlife discovers what I'm carrying, chances are I'll wake up in the morgue and the whole country will hear about the robbery."

Still laughing, she asked, "Any last words?"

"It was nice knowing you." I laughed too. It did me good to see her having such a good time.

Then Mary was calling us to lunch. When we came into the dining room, she looked at us like she wondered what was going on. "Mrs. Win*chus*ter, that was Mr. Pettigrew on the phone. He's bringing the car around and will wait for you in front."

"Pettigrew?" I asked. "Does she mean Percival?"

"Yes. My staff call him Mr. Pettigrew, but you are not staff, you are my . . ."

"Companion?"

"More than that . . ." She couldn't put it in words, so I dropped it.

We sat down at the table, and I examined my plate. "What's this we're eating, Mary?"

Mary read from the menu. "It's Belgian endive salad, with caramelized apple, frissée, St. Peter's bleu cheese, and sherry hazelnut vinaigrette."

Well, that didn't tell me much, but I figured, *If that's St. Peter's blue cheese, maybe it's okay to eat the rest of what's on the plate.* I really meant it when I bowed my head and prayed, "Bless this food."

When I looked up, Mrs. Winchester was eying me curiously but didn't say anything. I started eating, and in a few minutes, she did too.

As we were eating, I noticed what Mrs. Winchester was wearing—an orchid-colored dress with filmy sleeves and an amber neckpiece that caught the light in a beautiful way. The way her own natural hair was done up with a hair piece to fill it in looked nice, but I didn't say anything. By then I had come to realize that everything that woman wore would be gorgeous.

The food was delicious, and after we finished, I brushed my teeth, made a pit stop, and was ready to go. Mary handed Mrs. Winchester a hat made of different colors of orchid, lavender, and purple with a brim that dipped down over her forehead. It set off the outfit perfectly.

When we stepped off the elevator I could see the Rolls outside with Percival still waiting. Inside the car sat Lucy and Desi, ready to ride. Percival opened the door for us, and I asked him, "Where we headed?"

With his nose back in the air, he answered, "Madam, we will visit the city of Linton, twenty miles distant," and closed the car door behind me.

Mrs. Winchester chuckled. "It's no city, hardly a spot on the map. It's where Chet Atkins is buried."

I remembered when "Heartbreak Hotel" was popular. Chet Atkins recorded that one, as well as "Wake Up, Little Susie." Beatrice and I liked both of them, and we used to try to sing them. Beatrice was better than me at singing, but that don't mean she was, or ever would be, a threat to any star on the Grand Ole Opry.

Mrs. Winchester knew all about Chet Atkins. "He had a distinctive way of playing the guitar," she told me, "picking the strings with two fingers and a thumb."

Thinking about Beatrice, I wondered when and if she would get my letter. *She'd get a kick out of seeing me now on my way to Chet Atkins's grave and riding in a Rolls-*

Royce with a stuck-up chauffer, two stuck-up hounds,
and Mrs. Winchester, who I have not yet figured out. If
this was just me and Beatrice, I know we'd be belting
out "Heartbreak Hotel" or one of them other songs we
used to sing.

The way "Speedy" Percival Pettigrew was driving, it
didn't take long before we were turning off onto a rural
road that we followed all the way to the cemetery. We
drove through the gate under the sign that said Harpeth
Hills Memory Gardens and made a couple of turns. Then
it wasn't hard to find his grave; his marker was a big
one.

As we were getting out of the car, the jewels clinked
against one another, and I figured they were shifting
about. Well, I could fix that, pack cotton in there. That
would hold them in place.

To show some interest, I asked Mrs. Winchester what
Chet Atkins died of, and she said cancer. "He died in
2001." Of course, I could see that from the tombstone.

It made me a little sad being there at the grave of a
man who had given Beatrice and me so much fun with
the songs he played.

I guess we moseyed around there about a half hour
before we got back in the car. "Now we'll go to Tammy
Wynette's grave," Mrs. Winchester said. "She's buried
in Nashville." On the way there, she lit into telling me
all about Tammy Wynette's life.

"Tammy married a bootlegger when she was seven-
teen, and they lived in a log cabin that did not have
running water, so there was no bathroom or kitchen."
Mrs. Winchester was so amazed at that, she forgot to

plop a chocolate in her mouth. "Can you believe that? No bathroom and no kitchen! Tammy Wynette had to do the cooking over a fireplace! Can you imagine that?"

Of course, I'd heard of women living up in the mountains in cabins like that, but I guess she hadn't.

"That marriage didn't last long, and he left her with three children to support." She plopped the chocolate and took her time eating it. "In the daytime Tammy worked as a beautician and at night she sang in clubs. Have you heard her song 'Stand by Your Man'?"

"Yes, I think everybody's heard that one."

"Well, that song is the biggest hit ever sung by a female artist." She giggled. "Seems Tammy didn't stand by her man, or men, I should say; she was married five times— had five husbands."

As we tore up the turnpike, Mrs. Winchester got busy writing her Chet Atkins poem. I kept quiet so she could concentrate. Percival was weaving in and out of traffic like a football player headed for a touchdown.

It didn't take her long to finish the poem. "Here, read this," she said, and I took her little moleskin book and read to myself.

Chet Atkins was "Mister Guitar,"
Surpassed all others, a mile by far,
His style—two fingers and thumb picking sound,
Was a gift among players never before found.

There was no getting around it—Mrs. Winchester was a great poet. I told her, "One day your name will become famous, and everybody will be wanting your autograph."

My saying that must have inspired her, because she kept the little black book open to a blank page ready to write some more. I watched her out of the corner of my eye, and the minute she got that bolt out of the blue, she dashed off a poem about Tammy Wynette. She read it over once, then handed it to me and watched me while I read it.

Tammy Wynette sang, "Stand By Your Man,"
We're sure five husbands were not in her plan!
On everyone's list of country music,
She was tops in all the poll's pick.

"That's great," I said. We were taking an exit off the interstate, and when we turned onto the street, I saw a sign, Armory Drive. Percival made a couple turns after that, and we rode on Thompson Lane until we came to the Woodlawn Memorial Park.

Percival drove us right up to what must be the main building and parked. He got out and opened the backseat door for us. I climbed out and waited for Mrs. Winchester. The graveyard stretched all around, but Percival walked up two steps of the building and opened the door for us to enter. Mrs. Winchester followed right behind me as we went inside.

It was cool in there and so quiet I could hear the jewelry clinking as I walked. Our footsteps echoed off the walls and ceiling. If this was where Tammy was at, I figured it was one of those places where the dead are cremated and their remains put in cubbyholes in the walls. They call it a mossyleum.

Percival led us up some stairs and down a hallway and turned right where there were glass doors. He stopped, opened the doors, and once we entered, I felt like I was in church—in a stone church like the ones you see on TV. There were rows of vaults all alongside the walls, and it seemed like we ought to be tiptoeing down that hall. Percival had no trouble finding where Tammy was at. We stood there looking at her name and the dates printed on her tablet until Mrs. Winchester was satisfied. Then we left.

I never been inside a mossyleum before, and to tell the truth, it kind of give me the creeps.

Back in the car on our way to the hotel, Mrs. Winchester pulled a tissue out of her handbag and dabbed at her eye. "It's awful sad," she said. "Here are all these people who did so much—entertainers who made music for the whole world . . . From what I hear, they have a hard life. They work so hard, and no matter how popular they are, once they die they are soon forgotten. They all wind up the same way—a pile of bones lying in a hole in the ground or in a mausoleum."

"Oh, Mrs. Winchester, that's not where they wind up. The ones that have lived for the Lord are in Paradise. And as for their bones, one day the Lord will raise them up."

I think that was something she had never thought about before. For a long time we just rode along, saying nothing, and I wanted to believe she was thinking about what I had said.

As we were rolling into Opryland, she asked, "Is that what your Bible teaches?"

"It is. One day everybody will be raised from the dead."

She was very quiet. Then she asked me to show her where that is found in the Bible.

"Okay. When we get back to the hotel, I will."

10

Before we went to the saloon, I showed Mrs. Winchester a few places in the Bible where it teaches about resurrection—I had her read what Jesus had to say about it as well as verses from the epistles and one from Daniel. But there were verses from Ezekiel that struck us both funny. That's the chapter that talks about dead bones coming to life, and as she was reading it, we got silly imagining them bones getting up and getting put back together. I know you shouldn't laugh about Scripture, but when you think about it, that is too funny for words. Of course, Ezekiel was talking about Israel rising from the dead to be a nation again, and since the good Lord seemed to be already doing that, it didn't take much faith to believe he will raise Chet and Tammy and the rest of us too.

Well, I stuffed cotton among the jewels in my apron, and that worked fine. We got down to the saloon a little after 5:00, and I was relieved to see another bartender mixing drinks. It must have been Singapore Sling's day off. I ordered a glass of ginger ale, and even though I took my time, I finished it before Mrs. Winchester was ready to quit. She went on drinking until she was too soused to go to dinner. I managed to get her back to the suite, and Mary, the maid, took over so I could go down and eat a bite.

By the time I got back upstairs, Mrs. Winchester was propped up in bed and was all wound up talking. I let Mary go, and I settled on the chaise lounge to listen.

"Miss E., I had a wonderful . . . wonderful childhood . . . toys . . . games . . . maids and nannies who never let me out of their sight."

If I heard *wonderful childhood* one more time, I would be obliged to change that broken record one way or another.

"I had private lessons . . ." Those pudgy fingers toying with the sheet made me notice her nails; they were orchid like the dress she had worn that day. Since she had not had a manicure, it didn't take a rocket scientist to know they were press-on nails. She mumbled on. "I had lessons in art . . . music . . . dancing . . . Some of my teachers . . . most of the teachers lived with us on the third floor . . . but a few came from the outside to teach me art, music . . ."

A tear trickled down from her good eye. I put a box of tissues on the bed where she could reach them. "Miss E., I never learned to paint or sing . . . or dance . . . but I did look forward to seeing those teachers . . . the ones who came from the outside . . . They even smelled different . . . smelled of smoke . . . of food cooking . . ."

It was the liquor making her spill her guts and ramble so, but I believed what she was telling me. I was beginning to get a handle on this *wonderful childhood* she was talking about. To my way of thinking, she had been a little girl shut up with grown people who were paid to take care of her. So far she had not shown me one *wonderful* thing about that.

"The ones who lived in the house . . . they never let me out of their sight . . . They tried to teach me math . . . science . . . Latin . . . French . . . I was nine years old before I could read English . . . I never learned Latin or French."

For a minute, she stopped talking, and it was plain as day she wanted another drink, but she wouldn't ask. I felt sorry for her. Looking at her, with half her face dry and the other half wet with tears, made me realize I was seeing a picture of what was going on inside of her—one half telling me she had had a wonderful childhood and the other half crying her eye out over what was the truth. Splurgeon said, "What is in the well will come up in the bucket of speech," and that was sure happening before my very eyes.

"Mrs. Winchester, Percival tells me we drive to Chicago tomorrow. Don't you think—"

"After my accident I had . . . I had scarlet fever. They put me in the hospital for that too . . ." Her cheeks flushed, and she raised her voice. "Miss E., I will never . . . I will *never* go to another hospital as long as I live

. . . as long as I live! Do you hear? I hate hospitals! I hate doctors!"

I was glad to see that something got her dander up. "You had an accident?"

"Yes. I had an accident. A very bad accident. When I was four I fell off my pony . . . That's when I lost my eye . . . Do you know that I have an artificial eye?"

I didn't want to answer, so I kept quiet.

"Yes, you saw it, didn't you?" She looked away from me. "I spent a lot of time in hospitals . . . months . . . in one hospital after another. Two guards stood at my door . . . only my nanny visited me."

"Your nanny? Didn't your parents come?"

"Oh no. They never even knew me." A bitter little smile curled her lip.

Even though I was curious, I wished she would stop talking, considering how upset she was. But she didn't.

"I never knew my parents," she told me. "Soon after I was born they divorced." She pressed a tissue against her quivering lips; several minutes passed before she could go on. "The maids told me my mother was an actress. They told me she lived in Beverly Hills when she was not on tour . . . She's dead, of course."

I got up and brought a wastebasket to the side of the bed so she could gather up the wet tissues and get rid of them. "And your daddy?" I asked.

"My father lived abroad . . . played polo, I think . . . Had something to do with horses . . . yes, horses."

I could see how this woman could make herself sick over all this, and I didn't want to see that happen. Splurgeon says, "Raking the ashes of the past" don't do nobody good. In Mrs. Winchester's "ashes" there wasn't a single live coal that I could see. I suggested we turn in for the night. I don't think she heard me. She kept right on talking.

"My grandfather disinherited my father. I don't know why . . . Maybe he was like me . . . maybe he couldn't do the things required of him . . . I like to think that . . ."

It was pitiful, but this was no pity party. All she was doing was raking those ashes, hoping to find something good, something to make it all worthwhile. I figured those nannies and nurses must have kept telling her she had a wonderful childhood because she lived in a mansion and had all the toys she wanted. At least she was still trying to believe that, but in my mind the sooner she shucked that idea and faced the facts, the better off she would be. "So you were left to live with your grandfather?"

"You might say so. I lived in his Newport home . . . but he was never there. After he disinherited my father . . . after he did that, I was his only heir . . . He made sure nothing happened to me." She blew her nose and absently dangled the tissue over the basket before dropping it. "To make sure . . . to make sure I never had another accident . . . not another one like that one, he had my pony shot . . ."

That went through me like a knife. What kind of a man would shoot a little girl's pony? I didn't need to hear anything more; if that man had still been alive, I would have personally punched out his lights! Of course, he must have been long dead. I looked at Mrs. Winchester and thought to myself, *She could have been the poster child for all the poor little rich girls of this world.*

"They told me my grandfather was afraid I would be kidnapped . . . There had been a ransom note, they said, a note telling him . . . telling him to give them money or they would kidnap me."

"Did he give them money?"

"I don't know. All I know is, he hired two men to guard me . . . to guard his heir . . . his only heir . . . twenty-four hours a day."

If I had been her, you can bet your bottom dollar I would have run away; I would have got out of that situation. But not Mrs. Winchester; raised like she was, she couldn't have got away nor survived.

It was getting harder and harder to listen to all this misery. But when Mrs. Winchester started up again, her face lit up, and I thought she was going to tell me something good, maybe about some prank or other. "When I wasn't taking lessons or playing with my toys, there was this . . . this tiny balcony outside my window . . . I could sit out there and watch the gardeners working in the yard . . . the groomsmen exercising the horses."

Well, that sounded as pitiful as anything she had said before. But she wasn't finished. She was quiet for a few minutes then, smiling, went on. "When I was a little girl, if the hem of my dress turned up . . . they told me to make a wish . . . make a wish and kiss it . . . and my wish would come true."

"I used to do that too," I said. "What did you wish for?"

She giggled. "My wish was that somebody *would* kidnap me!"

I laughed too. "You don't mean it!"

"Yes, I do. Nobody ever kidnapped me, but they might yet. Wouldn't that be wonderful?"

"Wonderful?"

"Can't you just see the headlines—'Mrs. Winifred Win*chus*ter, Wife of Philip Win*chus*ter, Kidnapped and Held for Ransom'?"

"Well, I hope that don't happen!"

"Miss E., that would be fun, fun, fun!"

She was dead serious. *Is she wacko or what?* "Mrs. Winchester, what about your daughter, Barbara? That would worry her to death."

"Oh, she's not my daughter."

"Not your daughter!"

"No, she's Philip's daughter."

"What do you mean? He's your husband, right?"

"Oh, I guess you could call him that . . . Barbara is the daughter of one of his mistresses . . . He has full custody of Barbara, and she will inherit his estate."

"You mean—"

"Miss E., let me tell you why Philip married me."

"No, that's none of my business."

"Please, I want to tell you. You see, my grandfather knew I had no head for business . . . He wanted me to be married to a man who could manage all these businesses and things . . . somebody he trusted. He picked Philip . . . Philip was working in one of the export offices . . . He was twenty years old without a penny to his name. Philip had nothing but brains and a driving . . . a driving

99

ambition . . . My grandfather picked him and offered him my hand in marriage . . . Of course, not without attorneys and legal papers drawn up to make sure Philip never divorced me or stole my money."

This sounded like something out of an old movie, yet, knowing what I knew about that grandfather, I believed every word of it.

"I had always been a roly-poly child . . . roly-poly, yes . . . that's what they called it. At the time of my coming-out I was still overweight. Being fat, plus my artificial eye, did not make me the most desirable debutante, much less a bride. Even so, Philip agreed to marry me."

"Well, Mrs. Winchester, I don't mean to speak out of turn, but didn't you have anything to say about that?"

"Oh, I was grateful to have a husband. Philip was handsome, still is. Given time, I hoped we might have a happy marriage."

Although I knew the answer, I had to ask. "Did you?"

"Miss E., we had a wedding and a honeymoon, but we've never had a marriage."

Those words shook me to my toenails. I'd had enough of this misery. "Mrs. Winchester, it's getting late. Don't you think we better go to sleep?"

Without a word she rolled over in the bed, and I started straightening the cover over her. She caught my hand and, looking up at me with the saddest face ever I saw, asked, "Miss E., will you call me Winnie?"

Winnie? "Mrs. Winchester, I'll have to think about that."

11

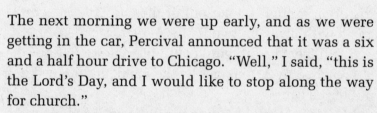

The next morning we were up early, and as we were getting in the car, Percival announced that it was a six and a half hour drive to Chicago. "Well," I said, "this is the Lord's Day, and I would like to stop along the way for church."

The way he took off his cap and slapped his thigh showed he didn't like that one bit, but before he could say anything, Mrs. Winchester spoke up. "To be sure, we will. We'll stop."

Percival drew in his breath. "Madam, may I suggest that we allow only one half hour for this delay?"

"Very well."

After about two hours on the road, when we were not far from Louisville, I saw this little country church up ahead on a side road. "Let's stop there," I said.

The church was one of those little white ones with a bell and steeple where most likely poor people worship.

The graveyard, dotted with wreaths and faded flowers, hugged the church on one side, and the rest of the yard held beat-up cars and pickups that had rolled in and stopped every whichaway.

All the women going in the door were wearing white dresses and big hats and had Bibles under their arms. Some of them wore blue ribbons labeled "Usher." The men and children were dressed in their Sunday best, and their manners matched—they didn't go running to gawk at the Rolls-Royce.

Percival parked the car at an angle, hogging space for two or three cars. I guess that was to protect it from all the other vehicles. I got out of the car. "Please, you'll come with me, won't you, Mrs. Winchester?"

She fidgeted a bit, but I could tell she wanted to go.

I reached over, took her by the hand, and helped her out of the car.

We left Percival guarding the Rolls with a book in his hand. I figured he would soon realize that these people were not the kind to do anything to his precious *motorcar* and that he would use the time we were in church to take the dogs for a walk or to read that book. According to Mrs. Winchester, Percival kept his nose in a book.

The church sign showed it was an AME Zion church like one we have in Live Oaks. I had always wanted to go to a church like that, but I didn't know how the members would take to white folks.

The people in this church could not have been nicer—ushered Mrs. Winchester and me right down to the front. Only one old lady was sitting on that front pew. She looked to be a hundred, and she wasn't wearing a white dress like the others. Hers was a cotton housedress with a crocheted shawl around the shoulders. As worn as her clothes were, they were clean and neat. Leaning on her cane with her hands folded over the crook of it, she might have been praying; she didn't look up at us.

A lady in back of us touched me on the shoulder, "This is Pastor Appreciation Day," she told me. I thanked her and took a good look at that preacher sitting on the platform. He looked like he could use some appreciation. If the woman beside me was a hundred, he was old as Methoozelah. Skinny as a rail, he wore a suit that just hung on him, and his back was bent from age, but he had a soft, good face like that on my friend Elijah.

The old pump organ commenced, and the choir filed in, women in front, men in back. Once they were seated, the organist quit playing and stood up to direct. Soon as she lifted both arms, one choir member heisted the tune, and they all began singing in different parts and harmonizing:

> Some glad morning,
> When this life is over,
> I'll fly away . . .

The music that came out of those singers would've given angels a run for their money! I do believe Mrs. Winchester enjoyed it as much as me; she was patting her foot.

Then I reckon it was a deacon who got up to speak. He talked about the years when he was a child and how the pastor had baptized him, married him and his wife, and funeralized his mama and his grandmama.

When he finished and stepped down, the choir director made a response that brought people to their feet to bring love gifts to the altar. As long as they were coming, she played "Sweet Hour of Prayer" and a couple more hymns on the organ.

After nearly every man, woman, and child had made their trip to the front, the old lady on the pew next to me raised her face toward heaven and started praying in a surprisingly strong voice.

"Dear Gawd and Father, I thank thee that you have give me the light of another day to live and breathe this side of Jerden . . . a Sabbath day to wership and rest from our labors, look one another in the face, sing your praise and pray."

The choir was humming her prayer to heaven, and the congregation was backing her up with amens.

"Lawd Jesus, high and holy, meek and lowly, walk with me, talk with me, tell me things I need to know. I am your own—your servant, your chosen one. Lawd Jesus, open the windows of heaven and pour us out a blessing that fills our cups—fills them to the brim—makes 'em spill over to bless this poor, poor world."

More amens sounded, and, to tell the truth, I felt like shouting a "glory, hallelujah!"

"Some has got hearts of stone. Lawd, give them hearts of flesh. Some follows you afar off; woo 'em back, Lawd, woo 'em with woes and whispers of love. May all o' your people here, there, and evahwhere this day take the time to be holy. With holy lives and loving hearts he'p us reach out to this pore world—to all them enemies of the cross, the fallen, the sick and suffering. Thank you, Jesus. Thank you, Jesus."

The humming grew softer; the amens were petering out.

I thought she had finished, when—"Lawd Jesus, how long must I stand on Jerden's bank a-lookin' over to the other side—a-waitin' for you to come and take me home? Oh, to look on your face—to look on your face!"

"Yes, Lawd!" came from the preacher, and the humming and amens swelled again. I glanced at my watch and whispered to Mrs. Winchester, "Our thirty minutes is up."

She shook her head like it didn't matter.

The organist played a stanza of "Sweeter as the Years Go By," and then four men moved out of the choir onto the platform to sing. You won't believe what that quartet sang! That old spiritual, "Dem Bones."

> Ezekiel cried, "Dem dry bones!"
> Ezekiel cried, "Dem dry bones!"
> Ezekiel cried, "Dem dry bones!"
> Oh, hear the word of the Lord!
> The foot bone connected to the . . . leg bone
> The leg bone connected to the . . . knee bone
> The knee bone connected to the . . . thigh bone
> The thigh bone connected to the . . . back bone
> The back bone connected to the . . . neck bone
> The neck bone connected to the . . . head bone
> Oh, hear the word of the Lord!
>
> Dem bones, dem bones gonna walk aroun'

Dem bones, dem bones gonna walk aroun'
Dem bones, dem bones gonna walk aroun'
Oh, hear the word of the Lord!

It was all I could do not to jump in singing myself! They carried the tune up one step at a time and then, repeating the words in reverse, brought it down the same way, one step at a time.

Not for one minute did I think them singing "Dem Bones" was any accident—the Lord was bringing to mind the Scripture that Mrs. Winchester and I had read. I will never forget it.

Well, I knew from experience that church services like this one could go on for half a day, and Percival was probably having a conniption fit already. As we got up to leave, I apologized to the woman behind me. "We're traveling and can't stay any longer. Wish we could." She thanked us for coming.

🦅

As soon as Percival saw us coming out of the church he hustled Desi and Lucy back inside the Rolls and held the door open for us. No sooner were we inside and buckled up but what he jumped under the wheel and gunned that car out of the churchyard like a shot out of a gun.

All the while we were flying down the interstate, all I could think about was "Dem Bones." The words kept singing in my head, and I kept singing them to myself but, for sure, not out loud.

"I liked that church," Mrs. Winchester said. "My nanny took me to church one time. We went to my grandfather's funeral in St. Patrick's cathedral, but it was nothing like this church."

"Well, as Splurgeon says, 'Going to church will not make you a saint any more than going to school will make you a scholar,' but it's the right thing to do. One of the reasons I go to church is because the Lord says we are not to forsake the assembling of ourselves together."

"I've watched religious programs on television," she said. "They have clapping music, and raise their arms a lot, but not much else."

"That's all well and good, Mrs. Winchester, but watching it on TV is not the same as going to church where you participate."

Since we were headed for Louisville, Kentucky, I thought about the Kentucky Derby. At Priscilla Home we always made it a habit to watch those races the first Saturday in May. I asked Mrs. Winchester if she had ever been to the Kentucky Derby.

"No, I've never been, but my grandfather left me a box of eight seats at Churchill Downs. Philip takes clients, people he knows. I prefer giving Super Bowl tickets to my staff. Would you like to go to a Super Bowl?"

"No, I've never had much time for sports."

We were coming into the city, and Percival was zipping right through on the interstate. Because of the time, I didn't think we'd be visiting any cemeteries in Louisville, but I asked her, "Who's buried here?"

"There's a Colonel Sanders visitor center and his

gravesite, but we won't have time to look him up today."

"Have you ever eaten Kentucky Fried Chicken?"

"No, have you?"

"Lots of times. You really should try it."

For a few minutes she didn't say anything, but then she said, "Very well, we will," and told Percival to look for a Kentucky Fried Chicken place. He glanced back at us in his rearview mirror, looking like he could bite a ten-penny nail in two.

I saw the Colonel Sanders Visitor Center sign coming up. Percival took that exit and drove on. Before long we were turning into a KFC parking lot, and he drove the car all the way beyond the dumpster to park. He did not turn off the ignition. "Madam, surely you are not thinking of—"

"Yes, Percival, we are having lunch with the Colonel."

"But, madam, we have lunch prepared."

"Never mind, go in and order whatever is necessary."

"Get the original recipe," I told him. Percival turned off the engine, got out, and trudged his way across the parking lot.

There must have been a long line or else it took him a long time to choose, because we waited quite a while before he came out lugging a bucket of chicken and a bag of who knows what. He left the stuff on the front seat while he set our tables and poured our drinks. Then, aggravated, he served our plates with chicken, biscuits, and slaw. He left what remained in the bucket for us and served himself a salad and wine.

Ours was as grand a lunch as a body could want. I was so tired of fancy meals that the Colonel's chicken made me feel like I was home again. Mrs. Winchester ate four pieces and three biscuits! When we were finished, we wiped our greasy fingers with wipe-aways, and I gathered up the trash. I was thinking Percival would feed the scraps to Desi and Lucy, but Mrs. Winchester said no he wouldn't. "He only gives them dog food prescribed by the vet."

Once back on the interstate, we headed for Indianapolis, and I asked Mrs. Winchester if we were going to stop there.

"No," she said, "the only celebrity I know buried in Indianapolis is John Dillinger, and he is famous for the wrong reasons. James Dean is buried in Fairmount, which is not far from Indianapolis but too far for us to go today."

Even without stopping again except to go to the bathroom, we were nearly 9:00 reaching Chicago. We were staying in another one of them out-of-this-world hotels, but I was too tired to pay much attention. I would take two Tidynol and go to bed.

As I was removing that apron from around my waist, I thought, *I better check this thing, make sure everything's in there.*

So far as I could tell there was nothing missing. Even so, I was thinking that with the way gangsters run wild in Chicago, to be safe, I ought not to show my face outside that hotel. Mrs. Winchester had mentioned that Al Capone was buried in Chicago, but I prayed she wouldn't want to go there. The cemetery might be in a seedy part of the city where, if we didn't run into gangsters, there'd be winos, druggies, or the like to waylay us, steal what we got, maim or murder us.

12

The next morning I was fit as a fiddle. Since Mrs. Winchester was still dead to the world, as soon as the maid showed up I planned to go downstairs for breakfast.

This Peninsula Suite we were staying in was like a mansion. Of course, I never been in a mansion, but it was a far cry from anything I ever seen in the movies. Everything about this place was made to pamper and spoil a body. Right beside my bed was a panel with buttons for climate control and for operating all the lights, TV, alarm clock, drapes—even a button to call housekeeping. All I had to do was roll out of bed and get myself dressed. I guess a body can get used to living in the lap of luxury, but as far as I was concerned, I'd never get used to it.

In addition to everything else, there was a safe in the suite. I figured I could leave my apron with her jewelry in the safe until I got back from breakfast.

I went to fix my face in the bathroom—everything in there was marble. They had a phone beside the tub and a big TV. Now, considering the way I like to soak in a tub, a small TV in my own bathroom might be a luxury I could afford, but never in a million years would I spend money like that. The night before when I was taking my time in the tub, there was this soft music playing so sweet it near about put me to sleep. Now, what if I had fell asleep in there? I'd probably have drowned before them martinis wore off and Mrs. Winchester realized something was wrong. Even if I was only half drowned, she wouldn't know how to give me artificial perspiration.

The carpet in the suite felt like it was a foot deep. And there were oil paintings on the walls that must have made many a starving artist rich overnight. The living room was so big it had room for two divans, stuffed chairs, straight chairs, footstools, a chest of drawers, tables, lamps, and, would you believe, a baby grand piano! That piano reminded me of Priscilla Home and Albert. The day he got our baby grand back in shape, he sat down and played "Twelfth Street Rag" by heart. That was one red-letter day for us.

I walked out on the terrace to have a look-see. We were so high up that I couldn't hear the street traffic below. Made me swimmy-headed looking down. I figured Mrs. Winchester would eat breakfast out there on the terrace because the dining room table was as long as a bowling alley and had these silver candlesticks with more candles than ever I saw at a wedding.

I would have give my eye teeth to know what she paid for that suite. No ordinary high flyer could afford it. It would take a supersonic high flyer and then some. *It's a sin and a shame to spend money for such as that when there's so many hungry people in the world.*

Two maids arrived, Mozelle and Tanya. That they knew my name came as no surprise; when we arrived everybody on staff knew our names—the hotel manager who made a big fuss over Mrs. Winchester, the desk clerks, bellhops, you name it. I told the women I was going to the lobby for breakfast and that if Mrs. Winchester woke up before I got back, tell her where I was at.

The lobby was on the fifth floor, and on the way I picked up two complimentary postcards with colored pictures of the hotel to send to Beatrice. They were huge cards. Glancing at those pictures I decided that if there was time after I ate, I'd take a tour of the top floors, where they have got this spa and swimming pool.

When I walked in that lobby, I felt like I was in one of them Baghdad palaces they had talked about on the news. The room was bathed in this golden light streaming through the windows. I'd say the windows were twenty feet tall, reaching from the marble floor to the gold ceiling, and there were enough tables in there to seat busloads of people, only I doubt it's the kind of place busloads come to. *Esmeralda,* I thought, *this ain't no food court!*

I could have gone for the eggs benedict again, but that cost two dollars more than two poached eggs served with peppers, onions, potatoes, and some kind of tomato coulis, whatever that was. It came with chicken, which any short-order cook will tell you is not breakfast food. I ordered the poached eggs anyway. Of course, I could have bought anything I wanted, but no matter whose money I spend, where I come from, the Great Depression is still going strong, and naturally I have got built-in principles about money.

While I was waiting to be served, I wondered where Nozzle Nose was—sleeping or reading a book. We got in so late the night before, I doubt if he took the dogs to a pet hotel. Maybe the Peninsula accommodated dogs. If not, chances are he slept with Lucy and Desi in the Rolls.

I took my time eating and watched the people coming in for breakfast. They were all well-heeled, in that big-bucks class that wear FedEx watches. Most of them looked like they were on the run, but there was this one weasel-faced man come in with a swivel-hipped girl in a miniskirt, and they were in no hurry, mainly because he wasn't up to it. One of them May and December marriages, maybe. Else he was her sugar daddy. Married or not, that bimbo kept herself busy making eyes at a businessman at the next table. To his credit, the businessman kept his nose in a newspaper and didn't give her the time of day. A man like that don't get where he got being stupid.

Percival didn't show up in the lobby before I finished eating, so I signed the bill. Glancing at my watch I figured I had time to go up to that spa they have got on the two top floors.

That was something to see! The spa was all enclosed in glass and made me feel like I was up in the clouds. People were working out on exercise machines, and according to the postcard there was a lot more than that—massages, manicures, skin care, steam baths, classes in relaxation, nutrition, you name it—even refreshments.

What bowled me over was the swimming pool. It reminded me of that picture of the Taj Mahal Beatrice has hanging on the wall of their RV. The hotel pool looked just like that one in front of the Taj Mahal. In my day I could have swimmed it from one end to the other, but not anymore. From that sun deck I got a good view of what the postcard called the "Miracle Mile." No miracle about it—just one fancy store after another, restaurants, and who knows what else. If you ask me, if you can't get what you want in a discount, hardware, or grocery store, you don't need it.

I glanced at my watch again and decided I better get back to see if Mrs. Winchester was awake. When I got back to the suite, the maids met me at the door. One look at their faces and I knew something was wrong. "What's the matter?"

Mozelle pointed to the bedroom. *Uh-oh, it's her.*

Mrs. Winchester was not only awake, she was almost historical. "Esmeralda, Percival called from the police station!" The phone was ringing. "Answer it—that'll be him."

It *was* Nozzle Nose, his voice pitched so high he was screeching. "Calm down, Percival," I told him. "Now, what's the matter?"

"It's Desi. I took the dogs to walk in Lincoln Park, and Desi's gone!"

"He just run away like before?"

"No! Desi saw this female dog and struck out after her." I didn't know a man's voice could go that high. "That female broke away from her mistress and took off with him! I tried to give chase but couldn't—Lucy refused to run after them and I couldn't leave her."

"What are you doing at the police station?"

"I've been assaulted. That female is an AKC Samoyed show dog worth a fortune, and her owner lost her mind, screaming and beating me over the head with her umbrella. Police came and took me to the police station to swear out a warrant for her arrest."

"Where's Lucy?"

"Right here with me. Please, Miss E., if that Samoyed doesn't come back there'll be the devil to pay! You'll have to find her. The police won't let me leave until they get a deposition from me and I pay a fine—a public nuisance fine."

"A deposition?"

"Yes. To bring charges against that woman for assault and battery."

"Percival, pay the fine, drop the charges, and take a cab back here."

"But don't you understand—that purebred Samoyed is a National Champion show dog! And Desi—if I don't get him back, Philip Win*chus*ter will fire me!"

"Calm down, Percival. Don't Desi always come back?"

"Please, Miss E., find those dogs or that woman's going to sue the Win*chus*ters."

"All right, now where is this Lincoln Park?" I asked him. He straightened up enough to tell me how to get there and exactly where he was when all this happened.

I don't mind telling you, I was about as scared as a body can get just thinking about going out in that strange city looking for two runaway mutts in a park that was probably full of weirdoes. I told the maids what was up and that I'd have to go, but Mozelle asked me to wait a minute. I think she called security or somebody, because when she hung up she told me, "One of the bellmen is going with you. He'll take you to Lincoln Park in one of the vans and stay with you until you find the dogs. He'll be waiting for you right in front of the main entrance."

What a relief!

That was one nice young man. He whipped through traffic like a pro and was obviously looking forward to this as some kind of adventure. "I do this all the time," he told me.

"What? Look for dogs?"

"Dogs, cats, husbands—anything that gets lost, we track 'em down."

I wasn't so sure that was the truth, but at least it was encouraging to hear.

When we reached the right place in the park, I saw plenty of weirdoes sprawled on benches, stumbling around, going through trash cans—bag ladies, druggies, winos, loonies—and there was no question who the owner of that Samoyed was. She was so historical she was standing on a picnic table screaming, "I'll sue! I'll sue!" with a bunch of them homeless people gathered around watching her. Then I saw a television remote crew was driving up. I had to do something right away or the Winchester name would be on the evening news. I jumped out of the van and hurried toward the crowd.

"Coming through! Coming through!" I yelled, and seeing I was somebody important, the crowd parted. That woman was in her pajamas and was wearing a raincoat with her feet in bunny slippers, looking about as trashy as anybody in the crowd.

"What color's your dog?" I hollered.

"White! White!" she screamed.

I turned to the crowd. "Ladies and gentlemen! Ladies and gentlemen!" Since they weren't doing much anyhow, it wasn't hard to get their attention. "Here we got two dogs missing, and there's a big reward for anybody finds the white one. Her name is . . ." I turned to the owner.

"Samantha! Her name is Samantha!" the woman screeched.

I turned back to the crowd. "There's a fifty-dollar reward for the white one—her name's Samantha, and when you find her, the other one will not be far behind. His name is Desi." I didn't have much faith that they could do anything with Desi, but knowing how much fifty dollars meant to the homeless, if Samantha could be found, they would find her. They slowly started moseying away, but one by one they must have realized what I had said, because they mustered a little more energy and commenced hollering out her name.

As it turned out, it didn't take them long to find her. Within half an hour, here come a wino holding Samantha by the collar and practically dragging her to where we were at. The dog was so dirty she didn't look very white, but that woman grabbed her, hugging and kissing her. I waited to see if she would think to pay the reward or if I would have to. Well, she didn't so much as thank me, and the man was standing there with his hand out, so I dug down in my bottomless pit and took out my wallet.

"Here, hold my pocketbook," I told the bellman, and I counted out five ten-dollar bills to the wino. He grinned from ear to ear. "Wait a minute," I said and reached for my pocketbook. "This is from Jesus," I told him and handed him a Gospel of John. Then all the homeless in earshot wanted one. I guess I passed out five or six. With one Gospel left, I offered it to that rich woman. "It's a Gospel of John," I explained.

Well, land sakes, you'd think I had offered her a rattlesnake. "No, thank you!" she said and stormed away toward the street.

The wino was tugging at my sleeve. "Fifty for the other dog?"

"Never mind," I said. "Here he comes now."

Desi was wet all over and muddy from the tip of his muzzle to the tip of his tail. There was no telling where he had been or what he had been up to, but I had a pretty good idea. If I was right about that, it was good we were traveling and would be miles away when the blessed event took place.

We got Desi in the van and headed back to the hotel.

By the time we rolled up in front of the Peninsula, Percival had arrived with Lucy. He looked terrible—his nose was all swole up, and there was dried blood on his little mustache. That lady had really whacked him good! He had a lump on his head the size of my fist. One lens of his glasses was cracked, and that made him look cross-eyed. He was so bedraggled I told the bellhop to see that his clothes were sent to the cleaners and that his glasses got fixed. I also asked the bellhop to get Desi cleaned up. He said he would and got another fellow to help him with the dogs.

"Now, Percival, you go up to your room and call for an ice pack. Lie down a while and when you feel like it, give me a call."

All that taken care of, I parted company to go up to the suite and tell Mrs. Winchester what all had happened.

13

Mrs. Winchester wanted to hear the whole story, and her mouth dropped open as I was telling her everything that had happened. Once I finished, she commenced giggling, and the more she thought about it, the funnier it got to her. I managed to get tickled too, now that it was all over.

We were still laughing when the phone rang. It was Percival, and he sounded as woebegone as a body can get, which was no wonder; he had really been put through the wringer. Even so, with good reason he was anxious to get on the road. "Ask Mrs. Win*chus*ter, if she has no objection; I would like to leave as soon as possible."

I repeated his message, and Mrs. Winchester agreed that we needed to get out of Dodge before we got slapped with a warrant or something. "Tell Percival we will leave in the morning."

I told him that, and he thanked me. "Now, Percival, did you get that ice pack?" He said he had, so I told him to take care of that lump and to call me if he needed me.

"Miss E.," he said, and I know this was hard for him to say, "I don't know how . . . how to thank you for all you did today."

"Think nothing of it," I told him. "You just take care of yourself. And, Percival, if you're not up to driving tomorrow, I can help you out."

How could I know that idea would throw him into a panic—but it did. His voice shot up so high it could have broke the sound barrier! "Oh no! No, that won't be necessary."

Without the Rolls to take us anywhere, this meant Mrs. Winchester and I had an afternoon and evening left to ourselves.

I did ask her if she wanted to go to a cemetery or something. "We can take a cab."

"No, I've been to Chicago many times, and I've seen all the graves I want to see. Al Capone's is one you ought to see. He's buried in Hillside, which is not far from here. You would understand what the epitaph on his tombstone means—'My Jesus Mercy.'" But before I could say anything, she rattled on, "I ordered a pedicure. Would you like to have one? They're coming to the suite."

"No, thank you."

"They have a lovely afternoon tea in the lobby if you'd like to enjoy that."

That sounded okay, but I told her if I ate in the afternoon it would spoil my appetite for supper. What I really wanted to do was have time alone to read my Bible and pray. "If there's nothing you need me for, Mrs. Winchester, I'll just go to my room. I have a few things I need to take care of."

It was wonderful having an afternoon free, but I hardly got settled in my room when, as you might guess, the phone rang. It was Barbara wanting to know how things were going. Since this was long distance, I gave her a short version of the excitement we'd had in the park, and she got a big charge out of that. Then she asked, "How's Mother doing?"

"She's fine. Right now she's having a pedofile," I said. "Sunday we went to a little country church."

"To church? I can't believe it. Did she like it?"

"She loved it."

"Oh, Miss E., that's great!"

"How are things at Priscilla Home?"

"Same old, same old. The new director stays in her apartment a lot, which is fine with the rest of us."

"She's not sick?"

"No. Rumor has it she's nipping."

"Now, Barbara, that's nothing but gossip; you know how I feel about that. Try to put a lid on that before it gets out of hand."

"Okay."

"How are the Ringstaffs?"

"Oh, they're great. Mr. Ringstaff still comes every day. We're studying Ephesians, and it's just wonderful. Lenora brought us a new hair dryer and gave us a concert the other night."

Barbara was pretty bubbly, which gave me a good idea

that Nancy was keeping up morale. But it worried me that the girls didn't like the new director. I wanted to ask how the money was coming in, but Barbara wasn't the person to ask.

Hearing about Priscilla Home made me blue, and the feeling stayed with me all afternoon until it was time to change and get ready for happy hour.

As it turned out, Mrs. Winchester didn't stay in the bar as long as usual. Since we were leaving early the next morning, I figured maybe she had the good sense to hold down on her drinking so she wouldn't be hungover and too bent out of shape to travel. We went to the Avenues, a restaurant next to the lobby that overlooks a park. "It's the Water Tower Park," she told me.

If I was to say what I thought of the decorating in the restaurant, I'd say it was done in very high-class Chinese art, and even though I had been turned off of everything Chinese by them Charlie Chan movies Beatrice and I used to watch, I liked what they done in the Avenues. In addition to the pretty panels and stuff, there was this out-of-this-world kitchen open to the public where you could keep an eye on the chef and everything that was going on in there. That I liked.

Even so, foreigners eat stuff we Americans don't, so I wasn't going to take a chance on ordering something foreign that would make me break out in a rash and itch for the rest of the trip. Why they don't write menus in plain English is beyond me. I spotted the word *salmon* and decided to order that. I could eat the salmon and leave off anything they served with it that I didn't recognize.

Since we had to get up early the next day, I felt it my duty to get Mrs. Winchester to eat food along with what she was drinking, because that would help keep her from getting soused. So as I studied the menu, I acted like my mouth was watering over everything on it. She fell for it and ordered everything from a sushi appetizer, which is one thing I would not put in my mouth, to a full-course dinner of Oriental seafood and some kind of red wine.

"I always stay in the Peninsula when I'm in Hong Kong or Singapore," she was saying.

"You been to China?"

She nodded, but she must have not got much out of it because when I asked her how she liked it, she said it was depressing.

Her sushi was arranged to look like a flower on the plate, and she dived right in to gobble it down. Expecting her to gag or strangle or keel over dead, I could hardly keep my mind on what she was telling me. "I read in the newspaper that Philip tried to buy into these Peninsula hotels, but they wouldn't let him."

As for the wine, she polished that off in no time flat, and the waiter swooped down on her like a vulture to pour her some more. I gave him a look that would wilt a dandelion, and he got my drift. She finished eating the sushi, but she didn't keel over or nothing.

"The Japanese must not allow foreign investors," she said.

"Japanese? I thought this place was Chinese." *So, the Japanese won't let that money-grubbing Philip buy into their business. They're smart, those Japanese.*

Well, we got through the meal okay. Mrs. Winchester

ate everything on that platter and didn't fall out from it. After I finished my salmon, I studied the dessert menu, but, like I say, it was not wrote in English. So I waited until she made her choice, banana crème brûlée with milk chocolate ice cream. That sounded okay, so I ordered that too, with coffee. Mrs. Winchester wanted Irish whiskey in her coffee. So far she seemed to be holding her liquor okay, but I never knew when another drink would tip the balance.

Even when we were back in the suite she seemed okay, but by the time we were ready for bed, she started carrying on like she did before. Only this time, she seemed to forget that business of having had a wonderful childhood. "You know, Miss E.," she said, "nobody has ever loved me . . . but that hasn't affected me in the least. I'm a well-rounded person, don't you think?"

Well, I sure couldn't agree with her about being well-rounded; that is, unless she meant her figure. She was plenty well-rounded in that department. But I know she meant her personality was not affected by not being loved. Nothing could be further from the truth, but, land sakes, I didn't have the heart to tell her she was wrong.

"Well, Mrs. Winchester, my mother always told me that love begets love. You love somebody else, and they will love you back. If nobody ever loved you, maybe it's because you never loved anybody else." I realized too late that sounded blunt, but it had just popped in my head to say it.

Mrs. Winchester stared at me and didn't say anything for a long time. I was afraid I had hurt her feelings.

As it turned out, I hadn't. I think she was debating whether or not to tell me what she finally whispered. "I love Philip."

You could have knocked me over with a feather! *How could she ever have loved a man like Philip Winchester, knowing he only married her for money?* I couldn't say a word.

That thing stayed with me long after I went in my room to get ready for bed. I took a quick bath, packed a few things, and kept thinking about it. *Love don't make no sense a-tall. It's pure nonsense. She won't never get a life if she keeps holding a torch for him. Maybe sometime I can come up with some way to help her face the facts.*

By 10:00 the next morning we were on the road going west, but we had left in such a hurry that I forgot the jewelry I had put in the safe. We had to turn around and go back to the hotel, and I tell you, Nozzle Nose was spitting gumdrops! It took a few minutes for me to put the apron on under my skirt, so, all in all, we probably lost an hour.

For the next seven days we traveled all the way to Salt Lake City, Utah, and to the Grand America Hotel. Once we got there and were settled in the Presidential Suite, I wrote Beatrice to tell her about the trip.

Dear Beatrice,

I don't have time to write you all the details about why we had to leave Chicago in a hurry. Since we left we've been on the road so much I couldn't write before now. Percival gave me a map so I could keep track of where we been. Remember that big orange geography book we had in fourth grade? Well, I'm glad we learned about the states and capitals now that I'm seeing some of them. Counting Illinoise, we been through four states, Ioway, Nebraska, and Whyoming to get to Utah. We stayed in hotels which were plenty fine but not like the one at Opryland or the Peninsula or this one. Can't tell you how many wheat fields we've passed, how many bridges we crossed, how many mountains we traveled, and how many times we ate Kentucky Fried Chicken along the way. That's right, KFC!

Mrs. Winchester has really took to the Colonel's chicken ever since she ate it for the first time. Percival didn't want to drive the Rolls anywhere near a Kentucky Fried Chicken place so he'd park around the corner and get out and go get the chicken.

While we were on the road I'll bet Mrs. Winchester ate six pounds of them good chocolates she's got, and I tell you, she might as well rub them on her hips because that's right where they're going. She got me to telling her stories about Live Oaks and it brought back memories of the good old days.

One Sunday in Nebraska I got Mrs. Winchester to go to church with me. I was wishing we could go to a church in Lincoln, Neb. You know that's where they broadcast Back to the Bible and I figured there's good churches in that town, but she said she couldn't go to any city church where somebody might know who she was. We found this nice little country church and the preacher preached the gospel, although he seemed worn out with doing it. I sat there thinking that if he knew somebody as needy as Mrs. Winchester was listening to him, he would get fired up again and preach his heart out.

After we come out the ladies stood around trying not to stare but itching to know who we were. We didn't hang around for them to find out.

I didn't ask Mrs. Winchester how she liked the sermon but she was probably disappointed that it wasn't like the black church we went to where they sang "Dem Bones." I guess I haven't told you about that, but the praying and singing in that church really blessed my soul. I can't get "Dem Bones" out of my head. Don't worry, I don't sing out loud. Ha! Ha! Now that we're in Salt Lake City it did cross my mind that if I had a mind to do it, I could throw the Mormon Tabernacle Choir into a tizzy fit. All I'd have to do would be sneak in there and when the music got soft and they were holding those low notes with all the breath they got, I'd whoop out the way I sing, and land sakes they'd go all to pieces, faint dead away, or get historical. Ha! Ha!

I tell you, this is one pretty place. There's snow-capped mountains everywhere you look so I don't have to tell you there's ski slopes, bike trails, and places to ride horses. It tickles me to see all these hikers and bikers coming in from roughing it. What sissy-britches! They head straight for the steam room or sauna, get massages, and have themselves wrapped in a cocoa butter or green tea wrap. Then they come out still thinking they're rugged as John Wayne.

As for this Grand America Hotel, I never been in a art gallery but this must be the next best thing. As well as having marble in all the colors of the rainbow and polished brass, oak wood, and ironwork everywhere, they have got statues all over the place, none naked that I have saw, and heavy antique furniture with lots of gold decoration that's sure to have come out of some palace in Europe. There's big tapestries hanging on the walls. Remember that tapestry salesman who used to come through Live Oaks going door to door? Elmer's wife went batty over them tapestries so Elmer bought her one. Well, she'd really have a fit over these they got here.

Well, Beatrice, nice as this trip is, a body gets tired of living in presidential suites and eating high on the hog. What I wouldn't give for some stew beef and rice, collard greens, cornbread, and buttermilk. I better knock it off and go mail this.

Yours very truly,

Esmeralda

P.S. That cruise will last seven days. If you're still in Seattle when we're coming home, maybe I'll get to see you.

When I dropped the letter in the mail slot and came back to the suite, I picked up the newspaper they leave at the door every morning. The maids were busy in the living room, polishing the furniture and arranging fresh flowers; Mrs. Winchester was still sleeping, so I took the paper in my room and glanced at it. I knew better than to start reading it because I'd waste the time I had for devotions.

It was the middle of the afternoon when two hairdressers, one of them a very sissy man, came from the salon to do Mrs. Winchester's hair. That's when I picked up that paper again and went out on the balcony to read. Little did I know I was in for the surprise of my life!

14

When I read a newspaper I usually don't pay much attention to the movie ads and such because I'm too busy to take in shows even if they are fit to watch. But for some reason I did take a look-see at what was happening in the entertainment department. There was this big ad about a symphony at the Abravanel Hall, and I thanked my lucky stars I didn't have to sit through a concert like that, listening to highbrow music. Albert and Lenora live and breathe that classical stuff.

However, in that ad there was this name—Dora Todd! The blood rushed to my head. Could that be our Dora? It had to be! Dora had played her harmonica in Carnegie Hall—I saw it on TV. And didn't Albert tell me she was going to be in Lincoln Center in the fall? My heart was beating a mile a minute.

Dora was at Priscilla Home when I was housemother there, and, as she put it, the Lord lit a stub of a candle inside her; her life was changed. As Splurgeon says, "Candles lit by God, the devil cannot blow out." She was a mountain girl, poor as Job's turkey, but she liked that highbrow music so much that after she went back home she learned to play it on the harmonica. None of us knew anything about that until she started sending big donations to Priscilla Home. Since we thought she was dirt poor, we wondered where she got the money to send us. Then, that night when we saw Dora on TV, it explained everything—she was making big money in the recording business.

Alongside the ad in the newspaper was a write-up about the program, and sure enough, there was a paragraph about Dora Todd, the guest soloist. It described her as "a renowned Appalachian virtuoso, a brilliant performer, a pioneer in giving the harmonica a classical voice."

I jumped up and ran back inside. "Where's the Abravanel Hall?"

The man fixing Mrs. Winchester's hair looked at me as much as to say, "The Abravanel is not for people like you," but I couldn't care less what he thought.

The lady hairdresser answered, "Madam, you would need a cab."

"Or the rail," the man added, smirking.

Mrs. Winchester, her head wrapped in a towel, asked, "Why, Esmeralda? Is there something there you would like to see?"

I was so excited I was about to jump out of my skin. "Mrs. Winchester, it's Dora! She's performing tonight with the Utah Symphony. Our very own Dora, who was at Priscilla Home when I was housemother there, she's gonna play her harmonica."

"Oh, you must go, Esmeralda. By all means, you must go. Call down to the desk. They'll get you a ticket. Percival will drive you there."

That prissy man smirked. "When I called, they were sold out."

Well, I reckon that because my call came from Mrs. Winchester's suite, they were not sold out. The desk clerk called back to tell me a ticket was reserved for me at the Abravanel box office.

When I called Percival he was anything but pleased that he had to drive me to the hall, but he said he'd have the car in front when I was ready to go.

So far, so good. Now what should I wear? I figured my suit would be okay. After I put it on, it needed a little something, so I added a big pin at the neck. Then I fixed my hair and face.

"You look nice," Mrs. Winchester said but added, "If you'd rather wear a dress, I have several you could wear for an evening like this."

I thanked her but said no. *What makes her think I'm a size 20?* It was 5:00, time for happy hour, and I was praying Mrs. Winchester would not get so loaded I'd have to stay home with her.

She chose Earl's Lounge and had only two drinks before we went to dinner. I really believe she was limiting herself on my account. I was too excited to eat and, for whatever reason, she hardly ate anything either.

We got back to the suite in plenty of time for me to get

to the concert, so I made a pit stop, messed with my hair a bit, and put on fresh lipstick.

Since I was going out in that jungle, I stashed the jewelry in the safe where it would be safer than around my waist. I took everything out of my pocketbook except a few dollars and enough identification in case I got mugged.

Percival was so cross about having to take me to the hall he did not speak all the way there. Once we got through the traffic and had eased up in front of the theater door, he snapped, "Madam, after the concert, you will find me here. Should you be detained, I will wait for you but only until quarter past eleven. Do you understand?"

"Percival, I am not deef and dumb!" Then I gave him his comeuppance. "See if you can make your way through this crowd to the box office and bring me my ticket." Aggravated, he got out and slammed the door behind him.

Expensive-looking cars were bumper-to-bumper behind the Rolls, and people—men in tuxes and ladies in evening clothes wearing jewels and fur stoles—were getting out and making their way inside the theater. I was glad to see that there were a few women who were not so dressed up. For sure, they were real music lovers willing to brave the social set.

As I sat in the Rolls waiting, I was so excited I thought I'd better make a pit stop once inside. I felt so nervous, wondering how I would let Dora know I was there. I could write her a note, but would she get it?

Percival came back with the ticket. I thanked him and got out of the car.

There was such a mob that I practically had to elbow

my way into the lobby; I didn't want to risk losing my place, so I didn't go to the restroom. Then I waited for a while before it was my turn to be ushered in.

My seat was near the front, the third from the aisle. I sat down and started rummaging around in my bottomless pit for something to write with. I found a ballpoint pen and a note pad I got at the Peninsula. Land sakes, them musicians onstage were making such a hullabaloo tuning up their instruments I could hardly think. *Looks like they would get that over with before they come on stage.* I decided I'd just write Dora that I was there, third seat, fifth row, and ask her not to leave before we got together. But when I tried to write, I discovered that ballpoint was bone dry. Frantically, I was trying to find another pen or pencil—mad at myself for not making sure I had it before I came—when here comes a couple claiming the seats between me and the aisle. I could smell his liquor and her perfume before they sat down, which told me they were not very classy. He was fat and about three sheets to the wind. While the usher waited, they fumbled around getting seated.

I said, "Psst!" to get the usher's attention. "Next time you come this way, I got a message for you."

Once the lady got seated next to me, I asked her, "Excuse me, do you have a pen?" She didn't answer, just mumbled something to the man beside her. He passed me his gold-plated fountain pen. I scribbled the note, passed the pen back to him with a thank-you, and waited for the usher to show up.

I was so nervous! And it was so noisy in there that when the usher did come back, I had to reach over the couple and nearly yell for him to hear me. "It's for Dora Todd," I said, poking the note toward him. "Please give it to her as soon as you can."

He read the note by his flashlight and frowned. "I'm not allowed to go backstage."

"Oh, but you must—how can I . . . she's a friend of mine—"

"Okay, after the concert, go to the stage entrance in back of the hall. All the artists come out that door. You can't miss her."

"Are you sure you can't give her my note?"

"No, ma'am. I'm not allowed."

"Well, who is? Is there a manager here?"

Something was happening to the lights. The usher left, and then the conductor came out on stage—his long white hair all bushy and uncombed. Everybody was clapping. The concert was about to begin.

The audience got quiet, but I was nervous and uneasy about finding Dora. I started talking a mile a minute to that lady beside me. "Dora is a wonderful girl—comes from the mountains of Tennessee—born in a holler and lived in that holler all her life. That girl can do anything—skin a deer . . . butcher it—"

The conductor bowed, stepped up on the podium, and raised his arms.

I rattled on. "If she likes you she'll do anything under the sun for you, but if she don't like you, you might as well hang it up. It's a miracle I'm here—we been traveling. No idea I'd see her here. Dora use to wear an old hunting coat, never took it off—"

The woman turned to the man, her husband, I guess,

and they started whispering back and forth. Somebody behind me went "Shhh," so I shut up.

The conductor, with his arms raised over his head and holding that little stick, looked over the players from right to left, I guess to see if anybody was missing or else warning every last one of them not to miss a note. Once he commenced waving that stick this way and that, the racket commenced.

Well, to be fair, the music did start out slow and easy, but it wasn't long before every part was sounding off at once, a racket loud enough to wake the dead.

Yet when that number ended, the people clapped and shouted "Bravo!" like they enjoyed it. Land sakes, I bet half the people sitting there didn't like it any better than me but clapped because that was the thing to do. Three-sheets-to-the-wind didn't go for it; he fell asleep during the music and slept right through the clapping.

I suffered through one number after another, each one as bad as the one before, with no time to recover in between, but that would be a small price to pay if I got to see Dora.

Finally, it dawned on me to look at the program to see when she would come on. Before I counted down to where she was scheduled to play, a man walked out onstage and started introducing her. "And now, ladies and gentlemen, here is the one we've all been waiting for, Miss Dora Todd, Appalachian recording star and harmonica virtuoso."

When I saw Dora walk out on that stage wearing that old hunting coat, I could not help myself—I jumped to my feet and commenced clapping as hard as I could. Seeing me on my feet, the rest of that crowd started getting up out of their seats and clapping. Three-sheets-to-the-wind came to and looked around.

Finally, the clapping quieted down, and we all sat down again. The conductor took his time getting the music started, but once it began, it was slow and sweet. Even so, for me it went on too long before Dora lifted the harmonica to her lips. A hush fell over the place; she began playing softly a melody that went right to my heart. I don't know what she was playing, but it was the prettiest music I had ever heard in my whole life. It just seemed to float in the air like melodies from heaven, and I am not ashamed to say, my eyes brimmed over and tears spilled down my cheeks. I could have listened to Dora playing all night.

When she got done, the applause sounded like thunder and kept on while she bowed a lot. She tried to get off-stage, but the crowd wouldn't hear to it. "Encore! Encore!" they shouted.

So she came out again and played a number that was real snappy. The crowd started clapping in time with the music, and even Three-sheets-to-the-wind sat up and took notice. I don't know when I've ever been so happy!

That was a night I will never forget as long as I live. I couldn't wait to tell Albert and Lenora I had seen Dora onstage in person. I sat through the intermission and put up with a bunch more orchestra specials, hoping each one would be the last. I couldn't wait to get out of there and get to that back entrance.

15

***

After the concert ended, that couple kept sitting, waiting for everybody else to get out before they would move. I looked at the other way out, but that long row of people was hardly moving at all. I saw what I had to do. I said, "Excuse me," and crawled over them two, blocking traffic, and squeezed into the jam-packed aisle.

Moving like cold molasses toward the lobby, I was as nervous as could be about having to find that stage entrance and getting there before Dora was out the door and gone. Pushing and shoving my way, I got past a few of them snail-paced people, but it didn't help much. I was among the last to get outside into the cool night air.

Frantic, I ran around the building. Two musicians carrying their instrument cases were coming out a door. *That's it; that's the stage door!* I hurried down there, praying I hadn't missed her. I took up a position about twenty or thirty feet from the door with my back to the wall so no mugger could come at me from behind, and watched for her, praying every minute. The two musicians were standing on the sidewalk, trying to hail a cab. Just as I was about to ask them musicians where Dora was, they piled into a cab and were whisked away.

Nobody else came out that door; the sidewalk was deserted. My heart was sinking; I must have missed her. I was on the verge of going inside to ask somebody if she had left when a big car full of men pulled alongside the curb. One man got out, and the car sped away. I wondered about asking him but then saw he was coming straight toward me. *What's this? It don't look good!* He was a big man, dressed in a suit and tie. Before I knew what was happening, he braced his arms on either side of me, his hands flat against the wall.

"Miss Esmeralda?"

"Who are you?" I demanded, my heart pounding.

"Never mind. I won't hurt you." He glanced over his shoulder, looking this way and that. Cars were speeding past, but I didn't see a single pedestrian—no use yelling. I was trapped; there was no way I could get free of him. *Oh Lord, help me!*

"I'm a businessman," he told me, "and I have your best interest at heart." *No way,* I thought. *Pinning me to the wall—he's dangerous.* He was right up in my face, I tell you, and the smell of garlic nearly knocked me over. "Miss Esmeralda, I understand you are a widow and no doubt hard up financially or you would not have taken this job as companion to Mrs. Winchester."

My head was spinning, my heart racing. *How does he know—what's back of this?*

"I have a proposition for you," he said. "It will make

141

it possible for you to retire and live on easy street the rest of your life. How does that sound to you?"

Fishy, I thought, praying somebody would show up to help me, I kept him talking. "What do you want me to do?" I asked.

Before he could answer, I saw Dora coming out the stage entrance. "Dora!" I yelled.

She stopped and looked around but not in my direction. The man saw that and grinned. "You might as well save your breath, Esmeralda. That lady don't give autographs."

I didn't yell again; out the corner of my eye I could see Dora looking my way. Seeing me, she put her finger to her lips.

The man bore down on me. "Now, Miss Esmeralda, all you have to do is keep in touch with us. We picked up the Winchester trail some miles back, and, of course, it isn't hard to track a Rolls, but we need your help."

"What kind of help?" I asked to hold his attention.

Dora was moving toward us in back of him.

"It's very simple," he was saying just as Dora reached us and dropped down on hands and knees behind him. I saw my chance; I shoved him as hard as I could, knocking him over backwards. Dora jumped up and grabbed my hand, and we lit out running to get across the street.

The light had changed, and the cars were stopped bumper to bumper. That man scrambled to his feet and was coming after us hot and heavy. Dora held on to me as we were climbing across one set of bumpers, but then our way was blocked by a cab with no passengers. I glanced back and saw the man was still coming. Dora yanked open the backseat door of the cab and pulled me in behind her. "Slam it!" she yelled. I reached back, grabbed the handle, and shut it, and she dragged me out the door on the other side.

The light changed and all the cars were spurting ahead, but one driver saw the pickle we were in and waited for us to reach the curb. Running for our lives, we kept looking back. That creep was not in sight. I don't know how or if we lost him. We kept running and didn't stop until we came to a parking garage.

As we got on the elevator, I was all out of breath and so weak my legs were about to give way. "My truck's on third," Dora said.

"How'd you know it was me?" I managed to ask.

"I thought it was you stood up when I come out on stage. I wasn't sure, because it was dark in there, but after it was all over I went a-lookin' for you but couldn't find you nowhere."

The elevator stopped; the door rolled open. "Where's your truck?"

"Third row over."

Them indoor parking lots make my skin crawl; there's all kinds of creeps lurking about waiting to waylay a body. Even that goon chasing us might somehow have got there ahead of us. As jumpy as I was, I kept looking every whichaway.

Dora opened the door for me, and I climbed into the truck. It smelled brand new.

She slid in on the other side but didn't start the engine. "Where're you stayin', Miss E.?"

I told her and explained why I was in Salt Lake City.

She had heard from Albert that I had been asked to resign, but I was too nervous to talk about that. Dora asked me what the mugger said to me.

"Oh, Dora, he wasn't just a mugger. He knew who I was and all about me and her—Mrs. Winchester."

I told her everything that had happened—so nervous I kept repeating myself. She made no comment other than to say, "You watch out, Miss E. Man like that be bound to keep on a-comin' a'ter you. You want a gun?" She reached over me to open the glove compartment. She took out a gun and laid it in her lap.

"No, Dora. I don't know nothing about guns. Chances are, before I could fire it, they'd grab it away from me." Suddenly I remembered that Percival was supposed to pick me up. I looked at my watch. It was 11:30. Too late; he would not still be waiting for me.

"Somebody gonna pick you up?"

"Yes, but I've missed him."

"I'll take you back to the hotel. Let's go back over this thing."

So we talked through the whole story again, and I was remembering little details I had left out. By the time I had went through it the second time, I was beginning to calm down a little. Dora is strong, and it helped settle my nerves being with her, having her listen. I asked her to turn on the overhead light. "Let me look at you, Dora." And in that pale light I saw a face that was far different from the careworn one she had brought to Priscilla Home. She looked ten years younger.

I told her how proud we were of her and asked about the business she was in. She told me about her agent, how he got her gigs all over the country. "He likes to arrange flights for me, but I only fly when there's not time to get there in my pickup."

Then she wanted to hear about Priscilla Home—and I was careful to put my resignation in the best light so she wouldn't stop supporting the place. There was a lot to tell her about the women she had known at the home, and we took a trip down memory lane, remembering the happy times we had there. The time slipped up on me—it was 1:00 in the morning. "I better get back, Dora. If Mrs. Winchester ain't dead to the world, she might be worried sick something's happened to me."

"Well, something did happen, now, didn't it?" she said. "Don't you fret none, Miss E. The Lord's a-lookin' out fer you." She got out the truck and looked all around the parking lot before she got back in. "I'm a-headin' out tonight for New Orleans," she told me. "Next week I'm a-gonna play in that Orpheum theater they got thar, and a'ter that I'm a-headin' back home."

"You still live the same place?"

"Same place."

We both got quiet then, hating that this visit was ending, that we would part as soon as we got back to the hotel.

"We better pray," I said, and we did—me first, then her.

Dora turned the key in the ignition, revved up the motor, and backed the truck out.

16

I tried to slip into the suite without waking Mrs. Winchester, but she roused up anyway. "Esmeralda?"

"Yes, it's me."

She was wearing a patch over her bad eye, and her glass eye was probably in that little pouch on the bedside table. "Did you see your friend?" she asked.

"Oh yes. That's why I'm so late—we've been talking."

Mrs. Winchester got up to go to the bathroom, and I went in my room to put away my pocketbook. I knew I must tell her about that man, because whatever this devilment was, it was aimed at her. I didn't look forward to telling her, because there was no telling how she would take it.

When she came back to bed, I said, "Mrs. Winchester, something happened tonight you need to hear about." I pulled up the chaise lounge, slipped off my shoes, and started telling her the story.

She sat straight up in bed, wide awake and tuned in

to every word. At first she acted silly, like it was just some kind of a lark, excitement, you know. I had to set her straight. "Mrs. Winchester, that man is not your run-of-the-mill mugger. He was *not* acting alone. Unless I miss my guess, that car he got out of was full of hoods just like him. They could easy be the mafia or a gang of them convicts the courts let loose from pens all over the country. He had to have connections; how else would he know my name and all?" I was hoping she would say we could call the cops, but she didn't. "They been following us for who knows how long, and there's no reason to think they won't keep right on. In fact, it comes to me now that he said, 'It ain't hard to track a Rolls.' They're after us, and I tell you, they mean business."

"Do you think they're after my jewelry?"

"Could be. Or they may be out to kidnap you for ransom."

"They'd be wasting their time kidnapping me. Philip would never pay a ransom for me."

"Oh, Mrs. Winchester, you must be wrong about that. Would paying a ransom put so much as a dent in that pile of money he's sitting on?"

"Oh, he wouldn't miss the money, but if I were killed he stands to gain a lot. Esmeralda, everything I own would go to him with no strings attached, and even more important than that, he would be free to marry that mistress of his. It's a wonder he hasn't hired a hit man to kill me before now."

"You don't mean that," I said to comfort her. Of course, I wasn't sure it was out of the question that he would do such a thing. From what she had told me, I wouldn't put anything past that man. "Don't you think we should call the police?"

"Yes. Call Percival. Ask him to come up here. We'll have him call the police and the FBI."

I woke Percival out of a sound sleep. When I asked him to come to the suite, he mumbled, "Jump, frog, jump."

"What did you say?"

"I'll be there," he said and hung up.

I put down the phone and sat there for a few minutes. *What if this is a plot by Philip Winchester to have her killed?* Just the thought made me shiver.

"Mrs. Winchester, maybe you need a bodyguard."

"No, Esmeralda. Ever since I was a child and had to put up with bodyguards, I promised myself I would never put up with another one as long as I lived. Desi and Lucy are all the bodyguards I need." She started getting up.

Mrs. Winchester had more confidence in those dogs than I did, but there was nothing I could say. I handed her the pouch, and she went in the bathroom to put in her eye.

Percival was not long in getting to the suite. "Esmer-alda, tell Percival what you told me," Mrs. Winchester said.

I did. The more I told him, the more fidgety he got. He wanted to know what the man looked like, was he a foreigner, did he have a gun—all the like of that. Land sakes, it had been dark. I couldn't remember what the man looked like, except that he was big, nor if he had a gun—at least I didn't see a gun.

Percival was shaking in his boots. "What do you think we should do?"

"Call the police—the FBI," I said.

Mrs. Winchester laughed. "I can't wait to see this in the papers!"

Percival protested. "Oh no, we can't do that!"

"Why not?" I asked.

"I have my orders."

"Orders? What kind of orders?"

He ignored me and spoke to Mrs. Winchester. "Madam, I suggest that you call the company for a jet to take you back to Newport or to Florida."

"Percival, I don't fly!"

"But, madam, this is an emergency."

"I'm going on this cruise to Alaska, and that's that!"

"Then fly to Vancouver."

"Must I repeat? I do not fly."

I was surprised to see Percival roll his eyes and throw up his hands; he was at his wit's end.

"Now wait, Percival," I said. "There must be a way we can throw these people off our track."

All out of sorts, he rubbed his forehead, trying to think of something. "Well, there is Sun Valley north of here. The Winchusters have a lodge there."

"Did you hear that, Mrs. Winchester? Could we go to your lodge in Sun Valley?"

"Is that what you want to do? I could call my secretary, and she could have the Sun Valley staff get things ready . . . Percival, how long would it take us to get there?"

"Eight hours or more. And, madam, we should leave right away."

She hesitated, giving the idea a second thought. "Esmeralda, I don't want to put you in danger. If these people are following us, I guess we should try to throw them off the track."

"Yes, we should, if we can."

She picked up the phone, dialed a couple numbers, and no doubt got somebody out of bed to answer. "Connie," she said, "I have had a change in plans. Is anyone staying at the Sun Valley lodge? . . . Good. Call ahead and tell the staff I am coming. There will be three in my party. But Connie, they are not to tell anyone, *anyone*, do you hear? No one is to know that we are coming. If we do not arrive by dinnertime, tell them to notify the police. And Connie, whatever you do, you must not tell anyone there in Newport or down in Florida—not anyone—that we will be at the lodge."

I was surprised that Mrs. Winchester could be so all together, especially that early in the morning.

Next, she turned to Percival. "When you go for the dogs, make sure you do not reveal anything about our departure. Bring the Rolls around, and we'll have our luggage curbside. If we can, we'll avoid a bellman."

Percival understood, put his cap back on, and left.

Mrs. Winchester went to her room to dress, and I gave her the amber necklace before I secured the apron and put it on. I packed my clothes and then went in Mrs. Winchester's room to pack her things.

"The lodge is Philip's party place during ski and hunting seasons," she told me. "He keeps his animal trophies there, and I daresay many more trophies of another kind were made there."

If that was a joke she would be giggling; she wasn't even smiling. I didn't know what to say so I just kept on working.

"I'm only a bird in a gilded cage, Esmeralda."

"Don't have to be."

She didn't say anything.

After I finished packing her things, I got out the map Percival had marked for me and tried to find Sun Valley. According to the map, the interstate would take us to Twin Falls and a state road that led north to Sun Valley. The lodge was out of the way for us; I only hoped it was far enough out of the way to escape the lowlifes chasing us.

Mrs. Winchester wanted to look at the map. "Ketchum is not far from Sun Valley. That's where Ernest Hemingway shot himself. Perhaps we can go there one day."

I couldn't believe that at a time like this she'd be thinking about dead people. I folded the map and stuffed it in my pocketbook. "I take it we're going to carry down the bags?"

She nodded. "There's a luggage cart in the hallway. Here, I'll help."

She wasn't much help, but we got my two and her ten bags on the elevator and down to the lobby without being seen. The desk clerk was reading a newspaper, and when she looked up, Mrs. Winchester told her, "Miss, we are checking out now, but you are not to record the time of our departure or anything about our leaving. Do you understand?"

The mystified clerk nodded. "I'll take care of it, Mrs. Winchuster."

We had to wait for the car. It was beginning to rain, and fog was rising from the dampness of the ground. It felt creepy standing around waiting, glancing about to make sure nobody saw us. In a few minutes, the Rolls whipped in the drive and stopped before us. A nervous Nozzle Nose apologized. "There was some delay in checking out Desi and Lucy." The Afghans were perched in their places, ready to ride.

We drove out of Salt Lake at 3:00 in the morning. Percival kept looking in his side-view mirror. Once satisfied that no one was following us, he stepped on the gas. I breathed a sigh of relief. We were in for a very long day, but so far, so good.

17

The rain never let up—broad sheets of it swept over us, keeping so much water on the windshield the wipers could not handle it. Made me nervous hearing the tires swishing on the wet pavement and Percival not letting up on the gas.

As I thought back over all that had happened, I got to wondering if maybe Percival was in on whatever this was—this devilment. At the time I didn't think much of it, but later it seemed funny that he didn't want to call the police. And what did he mean when he said he had *orders*? If he was in on this, what better place to take us than to a lodge out in the woods where there's no police nearby or anything else to keep thugs from robbing us or holding us hostage or who knows what. The more I thought about it, the more sense it made. I sat there debating whether or not to tell Mrs. Winchester what I was thinking.

Before daybreak, we stopped for breakfast. We had just come off the interstate, and Percival drove the car onto a back road and stopped. There were woods all around, and I got thinking this might be the very place where we'd get jumped. Percival got out, pulled up the collar to his slicker, and headed back toward the restaurant for takeout. I was getting nervous.

With the rain battering down, I couldn't see for sure if Percival was going to the restaurant or if there was another car parked back there. I couldn't keep my suspicions to myself any longer. "Mrs. Winchester, you don't think Percival is involved in this, do you?"

"Percival? Heavens, no. He wouldn't dare."

"What makes you so sure?"

"He can't afford to get caught doing anything illegal."

"What makes you say that?"

"Trust me. Percival can't afford to get arrested. That's the main reason he had us leave Chicago. He was afraid that dog owner would arrest him as well as sue me."

Well, I was not so sure, and if he made it back to the car without anything happening to us, I made up my mind I would get to the bottom of this.

By the time Percival returned with our ham and eggs, coffee and toast, he was a pathetic sight. After taking off his slicker, he threw it in the trunk, ran around the car, and hopped in the front seat. Even so, his uniform got very wet. Before starting the car, he got busy trying to dry himself off with a towel.

As we drove on, Percival had his breakfast on the seat beside him and ate using one hand. That made me nervous. With the rain pouring down, you couldn't see far enough ahead to know if there was a washout or mud slide on this road, a fallen tree or a stalled car. And not once did the rain slacken. If anything, it was coming down harder.

On a slow grade, Percival went around a logging truck, which scared the daylights out of me. I heard about a woman got killed when a log rolled off of one of them trucks. Percival was downright reckless. It seemed he couldn't allow anybody to be ahead of us, much less pass us. My mouth was in my throat the whole way.

Mrs. Winchester seemed not to notice. All she wanted to do was hear me talk. She wanted to know all about Dora, and when I was done telling her that, she said, "Go on." So I told her about some of the other women at Priscilla Home.

Needless to say, I was relieved when we got to the lodge and my feet were back on solid ground, even if it was muddy ground. A young man came out the door bearing a huge umbrella. We didn't need it because we were under the entryway.

One look at Percival's white face and the circles under his eyes and I thought, *That man needs help.* He looked like warmed-over death. I told the fellow with the umbrella to take care of our luggage. "Percival, why don't you get inside and dry off? This man can park the car."

I was surprised that Percival agreed to let the man park the car. By that, I knew he was plum wore out. He held the door open, and the three of us went inside.

The lobby of that place was built with huge timbers, and its walls were full of the heads of dead animals— moose, deer, elk, foxes, a raccoon, and who knows what else. Gave me the creeps. Some day all them kind of animals ought to gang up on all them bloodthirsty hunters and let them have it.

Some of the staff members welcomed us—a butler-looking man and two women in white uniforms. Supper was ready, and as soon as we freshened up, Mrs. Winchester and I sat down at the table. While I waited for her to finish her double martini I wondered where Percival was eating, so I just asked her.

"Oh, he will eat in the servants' quarters."

Here this man had knocked himself out taking care of us, driving in all that rain and getting soaked to the skin, yet he couldn't sit at the table with us? "Why?" I asked.

She looked at me kind of funny. "Well, I don't know. That's just the way it's always been."

It wasn't my place to say anything more, but I think she got my drift. I hadn't questioned it when we were in hotels because, with him being a man, I judged Percival would rather not sit with us. But here, in her lodge, it was like being in a private home.

Soon the maid came in to serve us, announcing, "Mrs. Stonewall Jackson's Stuffed Partridges."

Well, one look at my plate and I was about to say she could give them partridges back to Mrs. Stonewall Jackson. There was stuffing, a salad, and pieces of meat on little triangle pieces of toast. That's no way to serve up birds. The way I cook my quail is I pick plump ones, split and draw them, use lots of butter, some pepper and salt, maybe some bacon. I brown them on both sides, then roast them slow in a warm oven and keep basting them with butter. Soon as they get tender you got yourself some good eating. This business of serving partridges on itty-bitty pieces of toast, well, that ain't nothing I'd ever seen before.

But then I took a bite. Was that ever good! Whatever herbs they put in that stuffing made it the tastiest I'd ever ate, and as for the partridges, I right away said, "I got to get this recipe."

Mrs. Winchester smiled. "Because this is a hunting lodge, Philip thinks they should serve wild game. I like this we're having, but when it comes to elk and the like, I prefer beef or fish." The maid brought her another drink.

I didn't go so much for the aspic-asparagus mould with Roquefort dressing, but I was hungry and ate it all, as well as the chocolate mousse they served for dessert.

When we finished eating, Mrs. Winchester took her drink and went into the library. "Feel free," she said. "The maid will see after me. If you should see Percival, tell him Desi and Lucy will sleep in my room tonight."

I made it my business to find Percival. I wanted to give him a hand, if I could. I found him in the garage washing the car with his sleeves rolled up. I could see how thin and pale his arms were. He was too thin to be a healthy man. It looked like he had already downed two beers; the empty bottles were over by the washcloths. I gave him Mrs. Winchester's message.

"That means I'll have to groom the dogs," he said wearily as he sloshed suds over the back of the Rolls.

"Can't I give you a hand?"

"Would you?"

"I would be glad to."

"Here's a chamois." He tossed me a yellow cloth. "You can dry the hood and grill."

I worked for a while and then asked, "Percival, what did you mean when you said you have orders?"

He squeezed the sponge over the bucket. "Miss E., when I took this position, I was told that the day Mrs. Win*chus*ter succeeded in getting her name in the paper would be the day I'd get my notice. Those were my orders, and so far I've been able to keep the Win*chus*ter name out of the tabloids."

"So that's why you didn't want to call the cops?"

"Exactly."

That troubled me. A man like Percival shouldn't have to kowtow to "orders." And why would he want this job—treated like some second-class citizen? Of course, I probably knew the answer, but it's unnatural for a man to love an automobile and dogs the way he does.

"Percival, when you were a boy, what did you want to be when you grew up?"

He opened another bottle. "Won't you have a beer?"

"No thanks."

He drank several swallows and savored them before answering. "I always wanted to be a race car driver."

That figures.

"When I'd go in a store and see that life-size picture of Richard Petty cut out of cardboard and standing there dressed for the race, I dreamed of the day I would be that man."

I remembered seeing those cutouts in grocery stores advertising different things, and I thought to myself, *Per-*

cival, that's exactly what you are. You are a cardboard cutout with no more life than Mrs. Winchester has got. You don't have no life except driving that Rolls, tending to these dogs, and jumping when she says jump.

"Are you married, Percival?"

The question bothered him, and I was sorry I asked. "No," he said and downed half that beer. "I'm not married nor ever will be." He sounded bitter as gall. "Do you want to know why?"

"No, not really. That's none of my business." Of course, I really wanted to know.

He took off his glasses and wiped his face on his sleeve. "But you do wonder why being a chauffeur is the best I can do?"

I didn't answer. "Do you want me to dry the wheels?" I asked.

"Yes, dry the wheels."

We said nothing more until we finished washing the car and were ready to wash the dogs. I held Lucy for him. He opened another bottle and took a drink. I was getting worried; he was getting pie-eyed drunk even if he wasn't slurring his words.

"Miss E., I was born in the Ozarks," he said. "Does that surprise you? I learned how to be a chauffeur by watching old movies where actors with phony British accents put their noses in the air and serve the wealthy. I learned how to act the part, and now it comes so naturally I'm afraid I will forget who I am . . . I don't want to forget who I am."

"Percival, you've had too many beers. You don't need to be telling me all this."

"Oh, but I do—I do need to tell you. I've been rotten to you, and yet you come and help me . . . Miss E., you remind me of my mother. She was a gentle woman who worked oh, so hard. I was her only child. I grew up in the Arkansas backwoods, and it was hard making ends meet. It was biscuits and gravy that kept body and soul together. Pinto beans were a treat. At fourteen I went to work in a sawmill."

I was bowled over. This hoity-toity Percival—brought up dirt poor—working in a sawmill? He had struck me as somebody who come out of some ivy league school.

"There was an accident at the sawmill," he was saying. "I was injured, and it left me a cripple for life."

I was puzzled. He walked all right. Then it dawned on me that the injury had crippled him otherwise. This was too much; he was telling me more than I should be hearing. *Tomorrow if he remembers all this, he'll be sorry and ashamed that he told me.*

But Percival was determined. He drank the last of the beer and handed me the bottle to put alongside the others. I was getting Desi ready for washing and was trying to think of something to say that would change the subject. I wasn't quick enough.

"A few months after the accident," Percival was saying, "somebody burned down the sawmill." After combing Lucy's long silky hair, he patted her affectionately and walked around her, eyeing her looks before letting her go. "They blamed me, said I burned the mill out of revenge over my injury." He looked me square in the eyes. "But Miss E., I swear to God, I did not do it."

I handed over Desi to him and led Lucy to her pallet.

Percival straightened up and took a deep breath. "I was arrested, tried for arson, and sent to reform school. Needless to say, it broke my mother's heart. I was confined in that youthful offenders facility until I was eighteen, then I was sent to the penitentiary to finish out my sentence. About that time, Mama died . . . I don't know why . . . They allowed me to go to her funeral. In fact, the warden sent flowers. Afterward, he made me a trustee, gave me privileges. When I came up for parole eighteen months later, they let me go with five years' probation."

"Percival, I had no idea—"

"It's all right, Miss E. By the way, Percival Pettigrew is not my real name. My name is Marvin Collins. I took an assumed name, hoping none of my prison mates would be able to look me up when they got out. The name I chose fits the role, don't you think?"

"Yes, it does."

"Miss E., I tell you all this not to get your sympathy but to explain why this job means so much to me. People do not hire ex-convicts."

"But Percival, you got this one."

"I know, but only because some kind soul helped me. A social service worker put me in touch with one of the personnel managers of the Winchuster enterprises, gave him my good prison record, and persuaded him that my incarceration better qualified me for security work. The man hired me for the main purpose of keeping Mrs. Winchuster from embarrassing her husband with the publicity stunts she pulls. So far I've succeeded."

He was finished with Desi, so I gathered up their leashes to take the dogs to Mrs. Winchester's bedroom.

"Percival, I wish I had known you better sooner. I haven't been as kind to you as I should have been. If there is ever anything I can do—"

He brushed me aside. "I haven't had anybody to talk to in years, but when you came along, a down-to-earth person, unashamed of being yourself, I felt guilty not telling you the truth. You're a good woman, a Christian lady like my mother was."

"Thank you, Marvin."

He smiled. "Sounds good."

I reached for the leashes. I was too full to say anything. I felt miserable; I had treated him so bad. *How in the world will I ever make it up to him?*

18

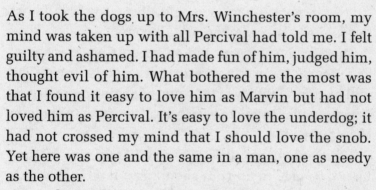

As I took the dogs up to Mrs. Winchester's room, my mind was taken up with all Percival had told me. I felt guilty and ashamed. I had made fun of him, judged him, thought evil of him. What bothered me the most was that I found it easy to love him as Marvin but had not loved him as Percival. It's easy to love the underdog; it had not crossed my mind that I should love the snob. Yet here was one and the same in a man, one as needy as the other.

I made a pallet on either side of Mrs. Winchester's bed and settled Lucy on one side and Desi on the other. They lay down and spread their long limbs as if they were used to sleeping on the floor beside her bed. There was nothing else for me to do before supper, so I went in my room. I felt so convicted I hardly had the face to ask the Lord to forgive me.

I didn't like to think about the way I had enjoyed calling Percival "Nozzle Nose." I had not given a second thought to the fact that might be a sin. Maybe I had considered it a "little" sin, but it hadn't bothered my conscience any. Splurgeon said, "It is a great sin to love a little sin," and he was right.

After I prayed I opened the Bible and read a chapter or two, but I found it hard to concentrate. I kept wondering what I might do to make it up to Percival for the way I had treated him.

It wasn't long before it came to me. Finding a note pad and a pen, I made a grocery list. Then I took it down to the kitchen. Minnie, the cook, was still there, and I asked her if there was some way I could make a meal in her kitchen.

"Not in my kitchen," she said, "but if you would like to use the bakery kitchen, it's all yours."

She took me in the next room, where there was a stove and utensils for making bread, cakes, and pastries. "This will be fine," I told her. "Minnie, one thing more, would it be possible for you to get a few things from the grocery store for me?"

"I'm going to the store right now. If you give me your list I'll be glad to do your shopping. I'll be back within an hour."

I could have hugged her!

❧

The next day after lunch, we left for Ketchum. Mrs. Winchester was in her glory and lit into telling me all about this writer whose grave we were going to visit. "Ernest Hemingway wrote a lot of best sellers," she told me. "But he was more than a writer. He was a hero in World War I. He was an ambulance driver and was badly wounded. After the war he became one of those drop-out artists—kind of like hippies, who lived in Paris. They were called the lost generation."

I was trying to remember where I had heard that name, Hemingway.

"Somewhere along the way he went to Africa to hunt big game and to Spain to watch bullfights; and one time he crashed a plane and survived. People called him 'Papa Hemingway,' but I don't know why. I think it was during World War II that he got interested in Cuba. Anyway, he lived in Cuba until Castro took over. Then he moved back here to Idaho."

"Did you say he committed suicide?"

"Yes, he did. Suicide ran in his family; his father, sister, and brother killed themselves."

"Maybe they were crazy."

"It would seem so."

As we drove into Ketchum, Percival turned on Route 75. About a half mile up the road I saw the cemetery. We drove inside, and the grave was not far. Three beautiful evergreen trees grew above the marble tablet marking his grave. That was nice. But it was sad standing there knowing a man who had the gift for writing famous books had buried himself and his talent before his time.

As at all these graves, there was nothing more to do than read the inscription and then get back in the car. Yet, in a way I was beginning to understand how Mrs. Winchester could get interested in dead people. Especially since she was a poet. Maybe she wasn't so wacko after all.

Percival turned the Rolls around, and as we headed

back to the lodge Mrs. Winchester took out her little moleskin book and a pen. Several miles down the road, she broke the silence.

"And you say all these people like Hemingway who have died will come alive again?"

"Yes, that's what the Bible teaches. No matter how we wind up—buried at sea or burned up in a fire—our bodies will be raised and changed to live forever."

"Then what?"

"Some of us will be raised to everlasting life and some of us to shame and everlasting contempt."

I was hoping she'd ask me what made the difference, but when she didn't, I sensed I had said enough right then.

I started thinking about the surprise I was planning and figured this was the time to ask permission. "Mrs. Winchester, what would you think if I had supper with Percival tonight?"

"With Percival?"

"Yes. Would you mind?"

She looked puzzled. "No. Do whatever you like."

"Thanks."

She started writing the poem. As she scribbled, scratched out words, and wrote more, she seemed frustrated. Tearing off one sheet, she started over. More scribbling, more scratching out words.

We were nearly back to the lodge before Mrs. Winchester was satisfied with what she had written and handed me the book.

I read the poem to myself:

Here lies Papa Hemingway,
Soldier of fortune in every way
This his last farewell to arms
By his own hand he bought the farm.

"That's good," I said, handing it back to her but thinking it was the saddest poem I had ever read.

When we arrived at the lodge I went straight to the kitchen. Minnie handed me an apron, and I went to work. She had the pinto beans with the salt meat simmering on the bakery stove, and I started making the biscuits.

It didn't take long before I had the biscuits ready to pop in the oven. I glanced at the clock. Percival would be coming down in half an hour, so I started making the gravy.

While the gravy simmered and the biscuits baked, I set a table for two in the bakery. I had timed it just right; I heard Percival coming down the stairs. Then I heard him talking with Minnie. In a few minutes she brought him to the door of the bakery. "Here he is," she said and left us.

He looked like a surprised little boy. "Miss E., what's this?"

I started serving our plates. "Sit down, Percival. Tonight you and I are going to have some soul food."

Seeing the biscuits and gravy bowled him over. He looked up at me. "You did all this for me?"

"For you, Marvin, so you won't forget who you are."

He smiled sheepishly. "I guess I told you everything."

"Enough," I said. "Enough to make me proud that I know you."

How we enjoyed that meal! We talked a good deal about what it was like growing up poor—the good and the bad. He would look across at me, pause, and say nothing, then he would start talking about his mother and his eyes would get misty. I brought up every funny thing I could think of to keep him from getting sad.

After he cleaned his plate, he went to the stove and helped himself to another biscuit and gravy. "I'm about to pop, but I'm not quitting."

As much as anything, he probably didn't cotton to going back to being Percival. I watched him devour that biscuit and gravy and thought about the mother who had raised him, how hard it must have been making do with little or nothing. Seeing her boy railroaded to jail surely broke her heart, and that was probably what killed her.

When he finished, we got up and were putting our dishes in the dishwasher when, lo and behold, here came one of the maids so upset she was wringing her hands!

19

"What is it? What is it?" I cried.

"Oh, Miss Esmeralda, it's the safe—the safe's been stolen!"

"Are you sure? Where do they keep it?"

"In the library."

"Show me."

Percival and I followed her into the library, where Minnie and the other staff members were huddled around a bookcase that had been pulled out from the wall. "It was in back of this," she said. "Oh, Miss Esmeralda, to think they walked right in here and walked right out with the Win*chus*ter safe! What if they come back? What if we all get arrested?"

Like I say, she was wringing her hands and tearful, which don't make for cool-headed thinking. Poor Percival, he was scared too. Actually, they were all historical, with the exception of Minnie. Cooks are used to emergencies. Of course, this was not no boiled-over pot.

All I could see was this big square hole where the safe had been. "Which one of you discovered this?" I asked.

"I did," said the same maid who had told us the news. "I was dusting."

"When did this happen?"

"We don't know. Maybe last night—maybe before, when the house was shut up. Oh, Miss Esmeralda, what should we do?" I do believe her knees were knocking. "To think a man walked right in this house and walked right out with Mr. Win*chus*ter's safe!"

She made it sound easy to lift a thousand-pound safe and carry it away. "Have you called the police?"

"No."

"Does Mrs. Winchester know about this?"

"No, we haven't told her."

"In that case, I will."

"Oh, would you?" They all seemed relieved.

"I suggest you all go back to work and I'll handle this."

After everyone had scattered, I looked at Percival. He was pale—about to become unglued. "What do you think?"

"Oh, Miss E., if the police come, it'll be in all the papers."

"I don't know that we can get around not calling them, Percival. That's up to Mrs. Winchester."

I examined the floor to see if there were recent scrapes or any evidence to tell us when the safe was took. "Percival, I don't see any reason to think this was done last night or any time recently, do you? They probably came in here when the lodge was closed."

"But what if it was last night? That could mean that whoever is following ús came in and did this."

"I hope not. But we can't take any chances. I say we ought to leave right now and let somebody else call the cops after we're gone. This is not one of Mrs. Winchester's publicity stunts. They shouldn't blame you if it gets in the papers."

"Miss E., we'll have a tough time persuading Mrs. Win*chus*ter to leave if she thinks there's any chance of making headlines."

"Well, tell me, Percival, when do we have to be in Vancouver to board that boat?"

"In three days."

"That's all I need to know. Get the Rolls gassed up in case this works."

Going up to the third floor, I breathed a little prayer that I would say the right thing in the right way to convince her that we needed to get on the road.

I found Mrs. Winchester watching TV and had to interrupt her program. "Mrs. Winchester, someone has stolen the safe out of the library."

"Oh? When did that happen?"

"No one knows. The maid found it was gone when she was cleaning in there this morning."

"Well, it doesn't matter. There's nothing in that safe. They tell me Philip only uses it to store his important papers while he's here." She reached for the remote to get back to her show.

"But it still means that someone broke in and made off

with it," I said. "We don't know who did that. What if it was done by the people who are following us? Whoever stole it may come back and do more devilment once they find it's empty."

"I see. I'll call the police—and the newspaper. Oh yes, the newspaper!" That got her excited.

"If you call the police, there'll be cops, detectives, reporters all over the place."

"Oh, I don't mind the press." She picked up the phone.

"But Mrs. Winchester, the ship leaves in three days! If you call the cops they will no doubt hold us here until they finish their investigation, catch the thieves or whatever, and we'll miss the boat."

She put down the phone. "Well, we don't want to miss the boat."

"What would you think of our leaving right now? Then we won't have to report this—we can leave reporting it to somebody else and not get involved . . ."

Disappointed, she hesitated. "Well, I guess we could leave now . . . Must we?"

"Yes, we gotta go or miss the boat."

"I hate missing the excitement."

"It's your choice."

"Well, I guess I should call my secretary and tell her to take care of notifying the police after we're gone."

"You better let someone here do that, because if your secretary notifies them, they're bound to know you were here. Let somebody here call them and tell the staff not to mention that we were here. Otherwise the authorities might hold us until their investigation is over."

"Okay," she said and moved into high gear. "I'll tell Minnie to warn the staff not to let on we were here."

So it was settled. Mrs. Winchester asked the maid to pack her things, and I called Percival to tell him to bring the car around.

We left about 10:00 and drove the rest of the night. From Twin Falls Percival said we would be crossing the Snake River Valley, but it was too dark to see anything. I tried to sleep but couldn't because Mrs. Winchester was out like a light and snoring to beat the band. We were traveling a mountain road with woods on either side, and there was construction along the way, but we were making good time.

It was still dark when we stopped for breakfast in Pendleton, Oregon. I made a beeline to the ladies' room, and Mrs. Winchester was right behind me. It was so early that we were the only customers, and Mrs. Winchester agreed that we should eat inside.

In less than an hour we were back on the road. With the coming of daylight, I could see we were traveling through hilly country with wheat farms and cattle.

Farther along, I saw a sign—Yakima Valley. That's where they grow all them fruits and vegetables we pay two prices for. Well, it was all beautiful country, but I couldn't enjoy looking, because the caffeine in that coffee had Mrs. Winchester wide awake and talking up a breeze.

"Esmeralda, how will we know if those people are following us?"

"We probably won't know."

"Aren't you excited?" she asked.

"Excited? No. If them following us took the safe, they probably thought your jewelry was in it. Since I'm the one carrying the jewels, I'm the one they'll hit over the head."

"Oh, Esmeralda, don't let them hit you over the head. Just hand the jewelry over to them."

"Don't let them? Mrs. Winchester, they won't be asking my permission to hit me over the head!"

She didn't have an answer for that, so we rode along for some time, not saying anything more about it.

When she did say something, it was on another subject. "I keep thinking about that song those people sang, 'Dem Bones.' How does it go?"

"It's easy. You start at the bottom: The foot bone connected to the leg bone; the leg bone connected to the knee bone . . ." I had to sing it to remember the words, and not wanting to blast her eardrums, I kept down my volume. I got to the chorus, and she joined in. Her voice was not a lot better than mine. "Dem bones, dem bones gonna walk aroun'; Dem bones, dem bones gonna walk aroun'—"

We wound up laughing our heads off.

"Let's do it again," she said, so we started at the top and sang down from the neck bone to the foot bone, then really belted out the chorus. Percival kept looking in his rearview mirror to see what was going on. We were having the time of our lives.

Mrs. Winchester laughed. "Once we get to the Wedgewood in Vancouver, maybe they'll ask us to sing in the Bacchus Lounge."

"Only if we can pass the hat," I said, and we laughed some more.

"We're supposed to reach Vancouver late this afternoon. The Wedgewood is one of my favorite hotels," she said. "They have good security, but I suppose criminals could find us."

She actually sounded a little wishful, like she hoped they would find us. I tell you, Mrs. Winchester was loony, all right, and didn't have an ounce of common sense, but I was beginning to understand her. I had come to believe that she was one woman who could care less about money. She was out for excitement, and you couldn't much blame her for that, seeing as how she didn't have much of a life.

As for me, I'd had all the excitement I needed for one lifetime. In my book, what she was calling *excitement* might very well turn out to be life-threatening danger, and it could happen tonight, tomorrow, or whenever we least expected it.

20

To Mrs. Winchester's delight, we arrived at the Wedge-wood in time for the cocktail hour. I was pooped, I tell you, and could have hit the hay right then. Percival probably felt the same way.

The doorman who greeted us was wearing a cutaway coat and a short stovepipe hat, which made him look like a character in one of them TV plays about England the way it used to be. So this was Canada. Here I was in a foreign country when, until this trip, I had never been outside of North and South Carolina. Never in my wildest dreams had I ever thought I would travel so far from Live Oaks.

Mrs. Winchester headed straight for the bar, but I took my time gawking at the lobby. It was so classy that I would not have been surprised to see Queen Elizabeth holding court in there. All the furniture was antiques straight out of some palace, chandeliers of cut glass, oil paintings, and big flowered carpets such as a queen might have. Whoever furnished that place sure didn't spare the shekels.

Finally, I moseyed on in the lounge and found Mrs. Winchester guzzling her martini. I ordered a ginger ale to keep her company, and we talked a bit about how grand everything was. Then I saw hanging on the wall of this Bacchus Lounge a canvas of a young man wearing a crown of vine leaves and not much else and holding a bunch of grapes and a glass of wine. Mrs. Winchester said he was Bacchus, the god of wine and revelry. Given my druthers, I'd sooner see a naked woman's picture hanging up there—the kind they had in them Wild West saloons—than a Greek god people worshiped.

While Mrs. Winchester was busy getting high, I sipped my ginger ale and looked around at all the dark wood in there. By no means was it fake, not pressed sawdust. No telling how many trees they chopped down to panel that watering hole. Would you believe, they covered the chairs and couches in there with red velvet! Drunks spill drinks, throw up, burn cigarette holes. I guess when you've got money to burn you don't have to be practical. Naugahyde would have been my choice.

It smelled good in there. Maybe they sprayed sweet-smelling stuff or maybe it was fragrance from all those big bouquets of mixed flowers that were everywhere. Now, if I was rich that is one thing I would have—fresh flowers all over the house.

Between drinks, Mrs. Winchester let me in on her favorite toast. "One martini and I am able; two martinis at the most; three martinis I am under the table; and four martinis I'm kissing my host."

Well, if you ask me, she could hold three, maybe even four martinis—it was the fifth and sixth that got her really looped.

It was some time before Mrs. Winchester had her fill, so she was not too steady on her feet as we went up to the penthouse to freshen up.

It amazed me how each of these fancy hotels was so different. The Wedgewood put me in mind of England or Greece—not America, like Opryland did. A fire was burning in the fireplace, making the living room nice and cozy. Big doors opened onto a terrace, so I walked out there and had a great view of the city. I took a good look-see before I came back inside.

There were four rooms in the suite. In the bedroom I checked out the safety deposit box and debated about putting the jewelry in it when we went to supper. There was a king-size bed in there and a studio couch in another room.

Mrs. Winchester was checking out the penthouse bar, and I had it on the tip of my tongue to tell her to lay off the booze until supper, but I thought better of it. Instead I just shook my head at her. She got my drift and muttered, "Okay."

I went in one of the two bathrooms to take a bath and found that the tub had them jets that shoot water on you. Decided I'd try it, and, land sakes, was that ever nice! I could have stayed in there hours on end.

After I got dressed, I went in to see if Mrs. Winchester was ready to go downstairs. She was zonked out on her bed, snoring like a lumberjack. "Mrs. Winchester, it's time to eat."

Hardly rousing, she mumbled, "You go on," and rolled over.

I waited around a little while, thinking she might wake up and change her mind, but she didn't, so I went on down to the restaurant.

Percival was in there, sitting alone at a table. When he saw me come in by myself, he stood up and motioned for me to join him. The waiter led the way and seated me.

"Mrs. Win*chus*ter not coming down?"

"I guess not. I left her sleeping."

"Good. It'll give us a chance to talk."

I was hungry, and Percival looked like he was about to drop, so I encouraged him to order a four-course meal. I didn't know if I could handle four courses, but to keep him company I ordered all four too. I chose an appetizer of crab, ginger, and cilantro spring roll, which had cucumber and a few other things. Percival said we should order tomato soup and goat cheese for the second course, and for the third, I picked the beef tenderloin.

While we waited, we started in on the crusty brown bread served right out of the oven with creamy butter.

Percival sipped his wine. "Miss E., what do you think?"

"About what?"

"About our being followed. Do you think we've outfoxed them?"

"It's hard to say. I hope so. At least when we get on that boat they can't follow us."

He frowned. "I don't know about that. If they found

out early on that Mrs. Winchuster was going on a cruise, they might have booked passage too."

The waiter served our appetizers, and I asked Percival what he thought they wanted.

"Money. It's all about money. Maybe the jewels, maybe they want to take Mrs. Winchuster hostage for ransom."

"Percival," I said, "you don't have to answer this if you don't want to, but do you think it's possible that Mr. Winchester has hired somebody to kill his wife?"

He thought about that a long time before answering. "I don't know. You hear a lot about that kind of thing these days. I'm reading a book now about unsolved homicides, and most of them are cases of spouse murders."

"I sure hope that's not the case here. I'm praying nothing happens. But Percival, I would feel better if you were going on the cruise with us."

He smiled. "I'm too much of a coward to be of any help. No, I won't be going with you. I have to stay here with Desi and Lucy and the Rolls."

The waiter brought our soup. Percival looked too tired to eat.

"Do you ever get tired playing this role of chauffeur?" I asked him.

"Tired? Dead is more like it." He nibbled the cheese. "I have no more life than Mrs. Winchuster has. The only thing I have outside of driving the car and tending the dogs is reading my books."

"Why do you keep on doing this, then?"

He was reluctant to answer. "The pay is good. I guess a lot of people would think the perks are great. As for myself, sharing Mrs. Win*chus*ter's luxurious lifestyle is not worth the price I pay. No matter how prestigious the job may seem, I'm still a servant at her beck and call."

As the waiter filled Percival's wine glass then removed our dishes, I looked across the table and tried to think of something that might help Percival. "After all these years—it's nearly ten years, isn't it?" He nodded. "Well, after all these years, it would seem to me that the reasons you had for changing your name and everything are no longer good reasons. You've established yourself as a good citizen. Couldn't you leave, take back your rightful name, and live a better life?"

"Miss E., I'm ashamed to admit this, but I'm afraid to try. I used to think about doing something different, but I had put it out of my mind until you came along." He smiled. "You intruded into my comfort zone and made me think about getting a life again."

"Oh, come now. It wasn't me. You had to stick with this job long enough to get tired of it. Now you can quit."

"No, I can't. You have to realize, Miss E., that since I was fourteen years old I've been isolated from society. In this job I'm still isolated. I'm not sure I can handle what it takes to live on the outside. I don't have skills of any kind."

I laughed. "You're a good actor. You could go to Hollywood and play the same role you're playing now."

The waiter was serving our main course.

"You could drive a cab, couldn't you?"

"Cab drivers are tough. I don't think I could hold my own with the public the way they do."

"How about driving a truck?"

"Truck drivers are tough too."

"Percival, where's your faith?"

He didn't answer me. I reached in my pocketbook and handed him a Gospel of John. "Try this."

Flipping open the pages, he mumbled, "My mother had a New Testament she used to read . . . I don't know what happened to it. Thanks, Miss E." He slipped the Gospel in his pocket. "What are we going to have for dessert?"

"I'll take whatever you order. Percival . . ." I was on the verge of asking him if he knew Mrs. Winchester loved Philip, but I thought better about it and didn't ask. I probably should keep that to myself.

Maybe if we get through tomorrow without any more excitement, we can settle down on the boat and then I'll try to find some way to help her face the facts.

21

The next morning the telephone woke me up. It was Barbara. "Miss E., where have you been? I lost track of you—is everything okay?"

"Yes, we're okay. How are things at Priscilla Home?"

"That's what I wanted to tell you. That war horse of a director has left, and the board is looking for a replacement."

"I'm sorry she didn't work out. Do you know if they have any prospects?"

"No, I don't know."

"This must be hard on Nancy."

"It is, but we're all trying to do everything we can to make it easy for her. How is Mother?"

"She's doing okay. We leave tomorrow, you know."

"Yes, I know. You'll enjoy that cruise. Did the dogs give Percival much trouble?"

"At times they've been a handful."

"I guess Mother has dragged you to cemeteries all over the country."

"It's not been bad. Today we're going to Port Coquitlam to visit the grave of Terry Fox."

"For goodness sake, who's he?"

"Your mother told me a little bit about him last night. He was eighteen when he lost his right leg to cancer. Then after a couple of years he decided to run all the way across Canada to raise money for cancer research."

"That's amazing."

"It is. Howsoever, the cancer came back on him and he couldn't finish the race. In a few months he died, but people were so inspired by his courage they raised a lot of money in his honor—as much as three hundred million dollars, Mrs. Winchester said."

"That's great. Well, have fun. Listen, I gotta get off the phone. Bon voyage! Take lots of pictures!"

"I'll send you a postcard. Give my love to everybody."

"I will. Bye, now."

After I hung up, Mrs. Winchester asked me who that was.

"Barbara."

"Oh."

"Mrs. Winchester, you don't have to answer this if you don't want to, but does Barbara know you are not her real mother?"

"Oh yes, she knows. You see, Philip's mistress was married to another man when Barbara was born, so everything about the pregnancy and birth was kept secret. It was prearranged that when the baby was born, Philip was to have total custody. The woman is still his mistress, at least one of them, but since Barbara grew up calling me Mother, she still does."

"Then you raised Barbara?"

"Heavens, no! I lived in Newport, and Philip brought her up in his West Palm Beach home and sent her to private schools. Our paths seldom crossed, but Philip had her call me Mother to make it appear to be on the up-and-up. When she was old enough, he told her the truth. Barbara felt bad about it and feels especially sorry for me."

"I see," I said, but I really didn't. How could any woman put up with such an arrangement? *He is one low-down, mean, stinking, trashy, common man!* But I knew better than to say anything; I'd say too much and be sorry. So I changed the subject. "Mrs. Winchester, it's late and we better get dressed if we want to have that brunch today."

"Brunch? Good. That will give us an early start to Port Coquitlam."

Traffic was heavy, so it took us a while to get to Port Coquitlam. Once we were in the town we followed Shaughnessy Street, then turned onto Prairie Avenue. Percival turned again on Oxford, and the cemetery was on the right. Mrs. Winchester and I got out and walked to the lower section of the cemetery, where we found Terry Fox's stone. It was black and about knee-high.

Thinking about that young man dying so young made me sad. So many healthy young people seem to waste their lives, but when you come across one like Terry

Fox, it makes you realize how wonderful some of them are. What courage he must have had. I hoped Mrs. Winchester's poem would do him justice.

As soon as we were back in the car she took out her pen and the moleskin book and started scribbling. After she finished writing, she read what she had written, tore it up, and started writing another one.

It took her quite a long time to finish. "Here," she said, "what do you think of this one?"

I read it to myself:

> Terry Fox was Canada's proud answer,
> To those like him who fought leg cancer,
> With artificial leg he ran the race,
> In donors' hearts he found a place.
> Great sums now in his name are raised
> A symbol of hope and courage praised.

"That says it all, Mrs. Winchester. You have a great gift."

That pleased her, and I was glad it did. If ever a body needed a little recognition, it was Mrs. Winchester. From what she had told me, that husband of hers made a doormat out of her, and I doubt if he or anybody else had ever sung her praises about anything. I was stewing inside. *All her life she's lived in a narrow rut. It's like she is dead while she is living, buried alive, you might say. Percival, too. He's in a rut, and it's like Splurgeon says, "The only difference between a rut and a grave is the depth."* I was beginning to really love them two, and I didn't want to part company with them before I saw them out of their ruts and hopefully on the road to heaven.

On the way back to the hotel, Percival stopped at a bookstore. Without explaining why, he got out and went inside.

Mrs. Winchester looked at me and I looked at her. "That's odd," she said. "He always lets me out before he goes shopping. This must be something urgent."

"He likes to read, so he's probably in there buying a book."

"Usually he gets books from the library."

We waited and we waited. Finally, he came out carrying a package.

I think Mrs. Winchester was as curious as I was, but we didn't say anything. Percival called back to us, asking if we'd like to see if the ship was in dock, and of course, we did.

The port of Vancouver was quite some distance away, but Percival was an expert at getting through traffic. He had not got lost once on this entire trip. He managed to drive us close to the pier called the Canada Place, where the *Amsterdam* was docked. From there we could see not only the *Amsterdam* but also several other ships in dock.

I tell you, it was a sight to see—big boats, little tugboats, and boxcars stacked one on top of the other. I saw another passenger liner, but it didn't hold a candle to the *Amsterdam*—that was one big boat and was so well-kept it looked brand-new.

"The *Amsterdam* is the flagship of the Holland American fleet," he said. "Beautiful, isn't she?"

Mrs. Winchester was impressed too. "Percival, how big is she?"

"She's nearly eight hundred feet long, has ten passenger decks, and twelve elevators."

"Where will we be staying?"

"You have the Penthouse Verandah Suite right up there with the captain. You'll have your own verandah where you can have lunch and enjoy the scenery as you float by."

I asked him if he had been on this cruise.

He smiled. "No, but I read everything about this ship and the cruise you're taking. You'll sail the Inside Passage to Ketchikan, Juneau, Glacier Bay, and Sitka."

As we turned to get back in the car, he said, "Oh, by the way, I read that Gospel of John last night."

"You did?"

"Yes, and today I bought myself a Bible. While you and Mrs. Win*chus*ter are cruising, I plan to start reading it all the way through."

"That's great, Percival!"

Oh, I tell you, I was thrilled to hear that, and I promised myself I would pray for him every day.

I climbed in the car behind Mrs. Winchester, and Percival shut the door. Just as he started the engine, I noticed a black car in back of us; it pulled out when we did and followed close behind. I kept looking out the back window, and that car followed us until we were on the freeway. Somehow a truck cut in between us, and after that I lost sight of the car. It might be nothing, but I didn't like the looks of it.

22

The next day as we were boarding the ship, I kept a sharp lookout for anything suspicious. As far as I could tell, everything and everybody seemed to be on the up-and-up. White uniformed officers and crew welcomed us like we were royalty, and I breathed a sigh of relief now that we were safely aboard.

A white-gloved, foreign-looking steward took us up on the elevator to the Penthouse Verandah Suite. When I walked in, the first thing I noticed were the windows; they went from the floor to the ceiling. What a view we would have once we were out of the harbor! I couldn't wait to see those snow-capped mountains and green forests pictured in the brochure.

The penthouse had four rooms—a living room, dining room, bedroom, and dressing room, as well as a pantry, half bath, and a bathroom with whirlpool bath and shower. I was all agog as I walked around checking out everything. For Mrs. Winchester there was a king-size bed and for me a sofa bed. If they had put a stove in there, a body could set up housekeeping, because it had a refrigerator, a minibar, a VCR, and almost everything needed to keep house.

I walked out on the terrace, where there were chairs and tables. I had read all the brochures about the cruise, and there was so much to see and do on that ship I was anxious to take it all in. Howsoever, I knew Mrs. Winchester would not take in much of it, because when we were in those fancy hotels she didn't take advantage of the spa, the pool, or shops. As for me, I didn't want to miss a thing.

I got busy unpacking our things, and when I was done we went down to a promenade deck, looking for a place to eat.

Before we found the Lido, our cruise was getting underway. It was nothing less than a thrill to feel that ship easing out in the water. Gliding out of the harbor, heading toward the big water really got me excited.

I finally found the Lido, but we didn't have time to eat before a whistle sounded and somebody came over the loudspeaker telling everybody to gather on a deck for a lifeboat drill. Because Mrs. Winchester is slow, we were the last to get where we were supposed to be. An officer in a crisp white uniform issued each of us a life jacket. It was a struggle, but I got mine on, then helped Mrs. Winchester.

After the drill was over, Mrs. Winchester and I went back to the Lido. What a spread they had! Everything from soup to nuts. Seeing so much food, my eyes are always bigger than my stomach, so I tried to be careful. One of those little foreigners in a white jacket was in back of the buffet, and I told him, "It's a wonder this ship don't sink with all the food you have to bring on board."

"Excuse me, madam. I will get you that information." And he disappeared into the kitchen. When he came out again he handed me a sheet listing the pounds of beef, lamb, fish, etc., brought on board.

Once we were seated, I took a minute to glance over the list. "Mrs. Winchester, listen to this: 3,234 pounds of beef, 2,859 pounds of poultry, 1,014 pounds of pork, 2,859 pounds of fish. It goes on and on like that, and then they list hundreds of bottles of wine, beer, and soft drinks. I can't get over this. Don't you know a lot of this food is wasted, left on people's plates or is left over and can't be used? Think how many hungry people in the world could be fed with just what's wasted!"

"I never thought of that," she said.

I felt guilty eating as much as I did, because I really didn't need it. But of course, there was no way I could send it overseas to starving people.

After lunch, we took deck chairs and sat outside. Even though Mrs. Winchester was as usual wearing a hat and sunglasses, I could see that some people standing at the rail were recognizing her. One would tell another, and that one would look over her shoulder to stare at Mrs. Winchester. One of the women broke away from the huddle and brought her husband over to introduce themselves.

"Mrs. Winchester, we are the Williamses of the department store chain. My hus—"

"I am Mrs. Win*chus*ter," she said in a voice as cold as a cucumber.

"Forgive me. To be sure, Mrs. Win*chus*ter, we would like to have you join us later for cocktails."

"No, thank you," Mrs. Winchester said and looked away from her.

"Perhaps another time," the woman said, and she and her husband walked away.

I looked at Mrs. Winchester. "They look like nice people," I said. "The Bible says if you want friends you have to be friendly."

"Miss E., people like that gravitate to someone like me for all the wrong reasons. They think they can get to Philip through me or they want to climb the social ladder by telling people they know the Win*chus*ters. Women fawn all over me, but I know they talk about me behind my back."

I couldn't deny that she was probably right. I was glad that for some reason she didn't feel that way about me.

"Wait until dinner and you'll see," she said. "We'll be assigned to a table with other passengers. They'll find out who I am and will fall all over themselves trying to make an impression."

The gulls were circling all over the ship, mewing and swooping down to pluck things from the water. It was breezy out there, and I needed a jacket, but I knew if we went back to the penthouse Mrs. Winchester wouldn't want to go out again. I was beginning to smell what I hoped was sea air, so I asked her if it was sea air.

"Not yet, but tonight we'll be out in the ocean for a while. After that we'll be on the Inside Passage."

A steward was coming on deck bringing blankets. I

took one and thanked him, and after he left I said to her, "All these stewards look foreign."

"They are; the stewards and dining room employees are Indonesian."

I sat there wondering where Indonesia was . . . I knew we sent missionaries to Indonesia. *Now look here—I have got that mission field brought to me on board this ship. I wonder if these Indonesians speak English?*

Here came another couple heading our way. Lo and behold, they stopped too. The woman was about as homely as a mud fence, but diamonds were dripping from her ears and fingers, and she spoke in a highfalutin, cultivated voice. "Mrs. Win*chus*ter? I believe we met in Stockholm, didn't we?"

Mrs. Winchester didn't give her the time of day, but the woman persisted. "Perhaps you remember? We are the Baileys from Bailey and Scholl, the New York brokerage firm."

"Never heard of it," Mrs. Winchester snapped.

Talk about a cold shoulder!

"But you do remember us from Stockholm?"

"No, I don't remember you."

That woman would not give up. Looking at the chair between Mrs. Winchester and me, she asked, "Is this chair taken?"

"Yes, it is," Mrs. Winchester said.

"I see." Finally miffed, she took her husband's arm. "Excuse me, Mrs. Win*chus*ter, we must hurry on; we're meeting the Rothschilds for tea."

After they left, I asked, "Who are the Rothschilds?"

"About the richest people in the world. Believe me,

there are no Rothschilds on board this ship. They keep to themselves in Europe."

I laughed. "No Rothschilds, eh? What about this deck chair between us—you said it was taken."

"It's where our pocketbooks are, isn't it?" That tickled her. "Give that pushy woman a chair and we'd be stuck with her the rest of the afternoon."

I was enjoying watching the people strolling around on deck. There were women on that boat who looked like Miss Americas, and there were other women who looked like something the cat drug in, but there was one man who was the funniest-looking thing on board. Wearing shorts and as duck-legged as they come, he must have thought we were going to Hawaii, because the shorts were orange polka dot, and the shirt that bulged over his paunch was purple with flowers like a tropical garden. Ruby red in the face, he was trying to jog around the deck. The woman he was with made no effort to keep up; she was dressed all in black, the nearest thing to widow's weeds, and had a cigarette in a long holder. Puffing away, she was looking for a place to sit down. Seeing the chair between me and Mrs. Winchester, she aimed for it, uninvited. I scrambled to snatch our pocketbooks before she flopped down on them. Making herself comfortable in the chair, she held the cigarette to her mouth with one hand and dangled her other hand beside the chair. The breeze carried a whiff of alcohol my way.

"It's a bore," she said looking out over the water. "These

cruises are all alike. There's nothing to do but sit and wait for them to open the casino. I prefer Atlantic City."

Mrs. Winchester ignored her. The woman went on talking, as foulmouthed as a sewer, cursing her husband and criticizing the food, the crew, and everything she could think of. When she had said all she could think of about them, she lit in to telling one dirty joke after the other and laughing so loud you could have heard her all the way to Alaska. It didn't take long for me to have a bellyful of that. I reached in my pocketbook and took out a Gospel of John. "Here, would you like to have a Gospel of John?"

She looked at the book in my hand and, taken aback, swore. "What are you, a Jehovah's Witness? I have my own religion, thank you!" She was about to pop out of that chair when Mrs. Winchester spoke up.

"I am Mrs. Win*chus*ter," she announced in a voice as commanding as some general. "And this is my friend Esmeralda."

"Winchester?" the woman repeated. "You don't mean—"

"The name is Win*chus*ter."

"You're not related to Philip Win*chus*ter, are you?"

"I am his wife."

"His wife?"

"Yes, his wife."

The woman snuffed out her cigarette. "Pardon me. I had no idea—"

Mrs. Winchester motioned to me. "Hand me the book, Miss E."

I passed the Gospel over to her, and she poked it in the woman's face. "Here, you need to read this."

"Oh, thank you. Indeed, I will."

Her jogging husband in the "what not to wear" sports outfit came huffing and puffing around the deck, and the woman yelled to him, "Yoo-hoo, Melvin, come see who I have got here!"

The man was red in the face and out of breath.

"It's Mrs. Win*chus*ter—*the* Mrs. Win*chus*ter—Philip Win*chus*ter's wife!"

Mrs. Winchester was struggling to get up.

"Help her, Melvin, help Mrs. Win*chus*ter."

"No, thank you. I can manage."

By then I had got up out of my chair and had gone around to help her. Without any further conversation, we left the two of them standing there with their mouths open like they had seen the Queen of England.

As we were going up in the elevator, Mrs. Winchester fumed. "That was one crude woman."

"She was that, all right. But I reckon you can't make a silk purse out of a sow's ear."

"What? Say that again? A silk purse out of a sow's ear?" That struck her so funny. "What's a sow's ear?"

"A sow is a mother hog."

She was still laughing when we got off the elevator.

Mrs. Winchester went in to take her bath, and I went to the closet to find something to wear to dinner. I decided to wear my navy suit. Dressing for dinner was not the easiest thing for me, and I hoped I would look all right. I held the blouse in front of me and looked in the mirror to see how it looked. *Well, it won't be as fancy as what Mrs. Winchester will wear, but it ought to do.*

I put the suit back in the closet. I was going to get comfortable, slip off my clothes and put on my robe. I would read my Bible a while and maybe take a nap.

I was sound asleep when Mrs. Winchester woke me up; it was time to go to dinner. One look at her and my heart sank. She was wearing a beautiful, floor-length mauve dress decorated with seed pearls and tiny feathers. She looked like a million dollars!

23

I wore my navy suit but dressed it up with a strand of pearls. We ate in the LaFontaine Dining Room, which had seating on two decks; we were on the Upper Promenade deck. In a room with a beautiful stained-glass ceiling and also views of the sea on three sides, a body could not ask for anything better.

After taking in my surroundings, I happened to see who was coming in the door. It was none other than the couple Mrs. Winchester had given the cold shoulder to. That Mrs. Bailey was decked out in a silver sheath with a slit in the skirt to her thigh. Wearing bracelets nearly to her elbows and silver chains and earrings, she would be a prime target for any jewelry thief that might be roaming these decks.

As for her husband, he was wearing a white dinner jacket, ruffled shirt, black tie, and dark slacks. There was something about him that reminded me of that bartender back at the Jack Daniel bar; maybe it was his big belly.

"How charming that we are seated here with you, Mrs. Winchuster," the woman said.

Huh! She probably asked to be seated at our table.

In addition to the Baileys, there was a suntanned young man in his thirties, I'd say, with slick black hair, dark eyes, and the whitest teeth I'd ever seen. Flashing a smile that could bowl over most women, he introduced himself. "I am Lionel Listrom, of the Rodeo Modeling Agency." Dressed in black leather and sporting a pleated shirt open at the neck to reveal chest hair and a gold chain, he looked for all the world like some flamenco dancer you might see on TV. Because there was no woman with him, I figured he was single, divorced, or otherwise on the loose.

Fortunately, there was a fortyish woman, dressed no better than me, who told us she was Mildred Peterson, a high school librarian from Milwaukee, Wisconsin. She looked as self-conscious as the wallflower at a senior prom. I thought that if I had the opportunity, I would take her under my wing and try to show her a good time.

Our table had one oddball—an Indian from India, wearing a turban, a Nehru jacket, and a jade medallion. I don't think he spoke much English, because he had to repeat his name, Alphonso Pasquali, three times before everyone understood what he was saying. In my book, that name didn't fit him. Neither did his fair skin and handlebar mustache—not for an Indian. He was fifty if he was a day, a tall man, more stout than fat, and I wondered, *Why would a man like that be taking a cruise to Alaska alone?* I never caught what he said his line of work was. He kept his head down, serious as a judge, and didn't look like the type who would be interested in the shows, the spa, or the scenery. *He's probably a gambler,* I thought. Of course, a body can never tell about foreigners.

Our red-coated waiter had gone around the table taking orders and was at my elbow waiting for me to make up my mind. As I turned my wine glass upside down, I decided to skip the appetizer and go for the cheddar and broccoli chowder, a green salad, and prime rib.

Mrs. Bailey was talking as I ordered my food. "What do you plan to do in Ketchikan, Mrs. Win*chus*ter?"

"Enjoy myself."

"I mean, will you take the flight over the Misty Fjords or visit the Native Village?"

"We haven't decided."

"I see."

The waiter served the appetizers. My chowder was delicious.

Mrs. Bailey sipped the wine and hardly touched her shrimp. "My husband, Raymond, is interested in the canoe safari, but I thought, Mrs. Win*chus*ter, if you were planning to go on one of the land excursions, I would tag along with you."

Lionel spoke up. "Oh, by all means you should take the canoe safari. It's the only way to see the backcountry."

Unsmiling and sounding irritated, she replied, "I take it you've been on that one?"

"Oh yes. I often travel the Inside Passage and have enjoyed most of the excursions. The canoe trip is exciting." He leaned over to speak to the librarian. "And, Miss Peterson, what do you plan to do in Ketchikan?"

"I'm going to visit some of the shops."

"Oh, come now, there are shops everywhere. Come with me and we'll take a jeep and a canoe and explore the country. You'll see breathtaking sights, maybe a bear or some wild goats."

Flustered, her cheeks rosy, she murmured, "I don't think so."

The waiter served our dinners.

The prime rib was tender and juicy, and the serving was small enough to be just right. In a restaurant they often overload my plate, and I feel I have to eat it all, which only goes to make me uncomfortable around my middle, and after that it plumps up my rear.

As for Mrs. Winchester, she left off eating and just kept drinking wine. I should have kept track of how many glasses she downed.

Talking up a storm, Mrs. Bailey didn't come up for air. "Raymond and I flew to Vancouver from Dulles—we live in Westchester when we're not in Europe or Asia. Raymond's business takes him all over the world, because most prominent foreign investors depend upon the Bailey brokers for the best investment service. My Raymond manages portfolios for the Saudi royal family as well as many other heads of state, don't you, dear?"

He did not comment; neither did anyone else. Alphonso never looked up from his plate except to turn up his glass and drain it dry. The waiter made sure no glass stayed empty and was quick to pour his full again.

Lionel was carrying on a conversation with the Peterson woman while the rest of us ate and Mrs. Bailey talked. "We were in Monaco last winter and saw the princesses

Stephanie and Caroline. What a tragedy that Grace died in that accident. Her daughters are as beautiful as she, but unfortunately, their scandals have besmirched the royal family name. What a pity."

If anyone was interested in what she was saying, they didn't show it, particularly Mrs. Winchester. I was curious about the Indian, so I said to him, "Mr. Pasquali, what part of India are you from?"

He waved his fork at me, and I was given to understand that he didn't hear me. When I repeated my question, he still didn't understand. I gave up. I don't think that man spoke six words during the whole time we were at the table.

Frankly, I was glad when we finished eating the meal and had ordered dessert. It meant we could soon leave the table and be done with that motor mouth. I had ordered the French chocolate chambord with chocolate sauce, although I didn't have the foggiest idea what chambord was. I had learned that when you order from one of these menus that is not totally wrote in English, what you do is pick what you do recognize, as in this case, chocolate, and go with that. Usually it's edible if not scrumptious.

I never tasted anything as good as that dessert. My curiosity got the better of me, and I had to ask what chambord was. Right away Mr. Bailey explained, "It is a raspberry liqueur, Miss Esmeralda."

Liquor or not, I figured it was nothing more than flavoring. After all, vanilla extract is about 90 proof. I enjoyed that dessert so much I wasn't going to spoil it by feeling guilty over a little alcohol. But as good as it was, I wanted to finish it so we could leave.

But wouldn't you know it, Mr. Bailey came up with something that would keep us at the table no telling how long. He was studying the wine list, which was a yard long, when he frowned and beckoned to the waiter.

Practically beaming, Mrs. Bailey explained. "Raymond is such a connoisseur of fine wines that he is never satisfied with the common selections offered on lists."

Raymond Bailey looked up at the waiter. "See if you can't find us a bottle of Chateauneuf du Pope."

Mrs. Bailey turned to Mrs. Winchester. "As you see, my husband is quite reserved, aloof, you might say. Raymond is never one to flaunt his knowledge, wealth, or prominence, which I understand is true of your husband as well, Mrs. Win*chus*ter. Only the nouveau riche calls attention to their wealth. We both come from first families of Virginia and are proud of our heritage. Gentility is, of course, the mark of a blue blood, wouldn't you say, Mrs. Win*chus*ter? Raymond's family tree goes back to James Madison, and my family is rooted in the aristocracy of land-grant planters."

Huh! Planters, my eye. I bet they were dirt farmers.

I had finished this chocoholic's dream dessert when, finally, here came the waiter with that bottle of wine.

"The Chateauneuf du Pope is from the captain's private stock," he explained as he was filling all the glasses except mine.

Still bending Mrs. Winchester's ear, Mrs. Bailey was saying, "Both our families go back to the highlands of

Scotland. Raymond is of the Campbell clan and my family is of the MacDonald clan."

That gave me something to ask her. "Do you go to the Highland Games on Grandfather Mountain?"

"No, we've never been there."

In my book, how could they be Scotch if they'd never been to the Highland Games? Any Scotchmen worth their salt would go to the celebration on the Grandfather at least once in their lifetime.

"You really shouldn't miss it," I told her. "All the clans are there with their men in skirts blowing bagpipes."

"Are you Scotch?"

"I don't know. Maybe Scotch-Irish."

"Then I don't suppose you have been?"

"Oh yes. Several times. I like to watch the border collies rounding up ducks, putting them through hoops. And I like to watch the Scottish games. As for the bagpipes I'd just as soon hear donkeys braying."

Mrs. Winchester and the men laughed at that, but I think Mrs. Bailey might have been taken aback; at least she was stumped long enough for Raymond to stand up and get a word in. "Gentlemen, I see that we have enjoyed the last drop of this magnificent Chateauneuf du Pope. Shall we retire to the smoking lounge for cigars and brandy?"

Lionel begged to be excused. "Miss Peterson and I are going to the Ocean Bar where we can dance. Perhaps we'll see you later when the show begins in the theater."

We all got up, and to my surprise, as the men filed toward the lounge, Mrs. Winchester followed them.

"Mrs. Winchester," I whispered, "the men are going to smoke cigars."

"I know," she said, as tipsy as all that wine had made her.

There was nothing for me to do but go along with her. Once inside the lounge, she said in too loud a voice, "Anything to get rid of that woman."

A dozen or more men were coming into the room, and, seeing two women in their ranks, they all looked surprised. A few of them found it funny and nudged each other, chuckling. The steward whispered, "Madam, the ladies room is down the corridor on the left."

Mrs. Winchester brushed him off. "I'll have a brandy . . . thank you . . . a brandy . . . and a cigar."

The look on that steward's face was one to behold. He quickly began serving her first and offered brandy to me, but I declined. Then he passed her the humidor of cigars, and when she took one, he offered her a light. The men were really getting a kick out of this, but not Raymond Bailey. He cleared his throat to say something. "Ah, Mrs. Win*chus*ter, how nice of you to join us. Gentlemen, this is Mrs. Win*chus*ter, the wife of Philip Win*chus*ter, whom you all know for his highly successful financial acumen and his phenomenal exploits in the world of business."

He didn't bother to introduce me. What did he think I was, a pinch of snuff?

He turned to Mrs. Winchester, who puffed a cloud of smoke in his face. "We are indeed delighted to have you join us," he said.

There was no way in the world he could mean that. He was much too flustered to be delighted.

Mrs. Winchester did not acknowledge his welcome with so much as a nod. As she sat drinking and smoking, the room was awfully quiet. Cigar smoke drifted in the air, rising to the ceiling. I guess those men didn't know what to say or think—at least not while Mrs. Winchester and I were present. They made sidelong glances at us and then faced the other way, chuckling. I'm sure they'd have a rip-roaring good time over her and me once we were gone; this was something they would never forget and their wives would never stop talking about.

"What's the matter . . . what's the matter with this crowd?" Mrs. Winchester hollered. "I've seen . . . I've seen better parties at a wake."

The men busted out laughing.

"That's better," she said and swirled the brandy in her glass before taking another sip. But she wasn't done. Hailing Mr. Bailey in a loud voice, she bellowed, "Mr. Raymond . . . Raymond Bailey." She waved the glass at him. "That wife of yours . . . that wife of yours never stops running her mouth . . . never . . . She has no . . . has no terminal facilities . . . What she needs . . . sir . . . what she needs is a muzzle—that's what she needs, a muzzle!"

The room exploded! The men were laughing so hard that some of them had to wipe away tears. All except Mr. Bailey, that is. Red in the face, he sputtered, "Thank you, Mrs. Winchuster. Now, may I help you to your feet?"

"Indeed not! I am not ready . . . not ready to leave."

I was so embarrassed I could have crawled under the

rug. If she kept on drinking and smoking, she'd be getting sick off that cigar, probably upchucking all over the place.

Thankfully, she shut up, snuffed out the cigar, drained the brandy glass, and showed no signs of throwing up.

"Aren't you ready to go?" I whispered.

She did not answer. I was helpless to do anything but wait.

She tried to stand up; I propped her up with both hands on her back. Wielding the empty glass, she waved it around, announcing, "I am Winifred Win*chus*ter . . . and I am here to tell you . . . to tell you . . ." She stopped, unable to remember what she wanted to say. Looking at me, she mumbled, "What is it . . . I want to say?"

"I don't know, Mrs. Winchester. Since you've finished your brandy, maybe you want to say good-bye."

"Ah, yes . . . Yes. Gentlemen . . . I take my leave of you . . . Good-bye, good-bye . . ."

She was weaving sideways and still waving the glass; I reached for it and handed it to the steward.

"Here, may I help you?" he asked.

"You take her other arm," I told him and together we managed to steer her, wobbling, toward the door.

Just outside the lounge, Mrs. Bailey was waiting, either to listen at the door or to witness our exit. She whispered to me, "Did she smoke a cigar?" I ignored her. "Brandy—did she drink brandy?"

Mrs. Winchester called a halt. "Mrs. Bailey," she said, "I would thank you . . . thank you to get out of my way . . ." She gave a horselaugh. "And take your mouth with you."

"Please excuse us," I said.

I was worrying that in the state she was in we would never get her back to the penthouse. The steward was looking at me questioningly as much as to ask, *What are we going to do with her?*

"The show," Mrs. Winchester said. "I want to see the show."

I looked at the steward, silently telling him, *You don't argue with a drunk,* and told him, "There's nothing to do but try to take her to the theater."

Mrs. Bailey was following right on our heels. I felt like spitting in her eye.

Mrs. Winchester stopped, turned around, got right up in Mrs. Bailey's face, put her finger to her lips, and said, "Shhhh!"

Chances were that little gesture would only fan the flame of that wagging tongue. The news of this episode would spread like wildfire all over the ship. Of course, knowing Mrs. Winchester, nothing would please her more.

It was an ordeal getting her to that theater, but the steward was a most obliging young man. Without his help I could not have done it. Fortunately, only a few people were there, and we were able to get seats near the front. Mrs. Winchester sat down heavily and started fanning her face with a tissue. "It's too hot in here."

It wasn't the room that was too hot—it was all that booze steaming her up. For the first time on this trip, I felt disgusted with Mrs. Winchester.

24

❧

The music was nice, from the fifties, I guessed, and as they were playing, Lionel Listrom and Mildred Peterson came in and sat nearby. I smiled to myself. *When they were dancing, I wonder if he dipped her. That would have made her heart flutter.* From the way it looked to me, I wouldn't have to show her a good time; Lionel was taking care of that.

I don't think we had been sitting there more than ten or fifteen minutes when Mrs. Winchester's chin dropped down on her chest. I sure hoped she wouldn't fall fast asleep, because her snoring could wake the dead.

Well, the show started with a bang, but Mrs. Winchester slept right through it. They brought on the first act, a row of skimpily clad women in a chorus line, singing and kicking up their legs. I tell you, none of them had the figure to be showing so much skin. They'd of looked a lot better in muumuus.

Mrs. Winchester was leaning forward and would have fallen out of her seat if I hadn't caught her and pushed her back. I decided that it would be better if she leaned against me, but at about that time she roused up and looked all around, probably wondering where she was. "The show's started," I told her.

The second performer was a man who impersonated the singing of Elvis, Neil Diamond, Andy Williams, and a few other crooners. He was good and sang songs I was familiar with. The crowd was mostly senior citizens, so they liked him too.

Mrs. Winchester was looking for a waiter to bring her another drink. *Oh no, not another one!* The waiter didn't see her and left before she could get his attention. I breathed a sigh of relief. Given more time, maybe later she'd be in better shape for me to get her back to the penthouse.

After the impersonator finished, Katarina Zigova, a gypsy girl, came on, dancing barefooted and shaking a tambourine. Dressed in a skirt that reached the floor and wearing a dark red blouse with baubles around her neck and bangles jangling on her arms and ankles, she danced down off the stage, whirled around on the floor, singing and flouncing her long shiny hair to wild applause, hand clapping, and whistling.

There was no doubt in my mind that she was a real gypsy. Gypsies used to come through Live Oaks and camp out at the clay pit. They would steal chickens and clothes left overnight on a clothesline. Everybody locked their doors when the gypsies were in town, and children were warned not to go outside because gypsies would steal them. Even so, we kids used to sneak out near the clay pit and lie in the tall grass to watch what they were doing around their campfire and to hear them making music.

Sometimes, during the day, a gypsy man would go around to the farms and shoe horses. Another one was a tinker who would repair holes in kitchen pots.

One day a gypsy woman came in the variety store where Beatrice and I worked. Beatrice was trembling from head to foot, so I waited on the woman. She bought the brightest-colored rayon and broadcloth piece goods we had, as well as needles and thread, some grosgrain ribbon and buttons.

Another time one of the gypsy children got sick and had to go to the hospital. The whole tribe descended on the hospital and would not leave until the child was discharged.

The only time they bothered me was one night when they put a dent in a door of my Chevy. I didn't hear them until it was too late, but I saw them running away. The next morning here come two gypsy men offering to fix that dent for cheap, but I didn't fall for that. I gave them a Gospel of John and told them they needed to get right with the Lord.

When Katarina finished her act and went backstage, I saw the steward again making the rounds with drinks, so I decided I better try to get Mrs. Winchester upstairs before she could get another drink. I stood up. "It's time to go," I said firmly.

"Oh?"

I took her arm and helped her out of the chair. Far from steady on her feet, she leaned against me, and I'll tell you, she felt like a bale of cotton. Lionel came to my rescue—took her other arm and had her lean on him. Over his shoulder, he told Miss Peterson, "Wait for me, Mildred, I'll be right back."

We made it out of the theater and to the elevator okay. Lionel held up Mrs. Winchester while I punched the button. Zooming upward, we didn't have to stop for people getting on and off, so we went straight up to the navigation deck. I got out the key and unlocked the door, and together we got Mrs. Winchester to the bed. I pulled down the spread before we rolled her onto the middle of the bed. I thanked Lionel and saw him to the door. I also thanked the Lord, who must have been looking out for me when Lionel came to help.

I removed Mrs. Winchester's sunglasses, hat, and shoes, but I didn't try to undress her. I straightened that beautiful mauve gown as best I could, hoping it wouldn't get too wrinkled, and pulled the spread up over her. She was mumbling about something, but she was half asleep. Once she was dead to the world maybe she would sleep it off before morning.

I went in my room, undressed, and took a bath. Later, as I was getting ready for bed, I could hear her snoring loud as a foghorn. This had been the worst day I had spent with Mrs. Winchester, and it looked like I was not making any headway with helping her. I had a lot to pray about, so I read a while and also poured out my heart to the Lord.

I don't know how long I prayed, but before I settled in for the night, I looked in on her to make sure she was all right. She hadn't moved an inch, and judging by the way she was snoring, I'd have to put a pillow over my head if I expected to get any sleep myself.

I fell sound asleep. Then—it must have been the middle of the night—the bed started rocking. I woke up and lay there wondering what was going on. Whatever it was, I hoped it wouldn't wake up Mrs. Winchester. I listened, and her snoring was keeping time like a buzz saw. The rocking motion went on for some time, and I kept listening to hear if something would fall off a shelf or something, but nothing did. I was tired and figured it was nothing to worry about. I turned over and went back to sleep.

🌿

The next morning at breakfast, everybody was talking about the rough sailing. Some of the passengers had got sick from it, but Mrs. Winchester and I had no complaints. An officer told us we traveled rough seas when we were crossing ocean water, but now the ship was back in the Inside Passage and there would be no more of that.

We traveled all day on the Inside Passage, and the scenery was like one calendar picture after another. To avoid the crowds on deck, Mrs. Winchester and I went up to the Crow's Nest, which was a bar that was almost deserted during the morning hours. As we glided along we passed forests that reached down to the water's edge with waterfalls a mile high and with eagles in treetops or soaring high in the sky. From where we were seated, the fishing boats on their way to the sea or anchored in the channel looked like chips floating in the water. Prettiest of all were the snow-capped mountains with the morning sun shining on their slopes. Traveling this way was like watching a moving picture changing from one scene to another. I kept looking, hoping to see wildlife, but without binoculars I didn't spot any.

Lo and behold, about lunchtime, Mrs. Bailey found us. "Oh, there you are!" she said and sat down beside Mrs. Winchester. "I've been looking for you! This is a wonderful view. It's lovely from up here."

"We were just leaving," Mrs. Winchester said and got up.

With that we took the elevator down to the main dining room, the Rotterdam. "Do you think she'll follow us?" I asked.

"If she does, we'll lose her—we'll go up to the penthouse and order lunch."

That Rotterdam Restaurant was like nothing I had ever seen before. Everything looked so expensive—the linens, the delicate stemware, and the china. No one came in that we knew except Mildred Peterson, and since it didn't look like Mrs. Bailey was following us, we sat down.

Seeing us, Miss Peterson came over, and I asked her to join us. I tell you, she had stars in her eyes! She was so excited she lit right into telling us. "I've decided to go with Lionel tomorrow on that backcountry trip. He seems to be such a nice man."

The way she said it, I think she wanted our approval, but neither of us said anything.

"I didn't say I'd go right away, but last night we had such a good time, I decided to go."

"You went dancing?"

"Oh yes, but that's not all. Last night, Lionel took me backstage to meet Katarina Zigova, the gypsy, and guess what? She asked me if I would like to have a personal consultation! Of course, I jumped at the chance, and she asked me to meet her backstage this afternoon at 2:00."

"What for?" I asked.

"I don't know yet. Maybe she'll read my palm, tell my fortune. I can't wait!"

I didn't say anything, but I figured that gypsy knew a sucker when she saw one.

After our soup and salad, Mrs. Winchester wanted to go up to the penthouse. "I've called for a hairdresser and manicurist," she told me. "After that a masseuse is coming to give me a massage. I'll be busy all afternoon, so feel free."

I decided to sit by the pool a while. I saw that foul-mouthed woman with some other women walking toward me. They were all looking amused. "Hi," she said. "We just heard about Mrs. Winchuster drinking brandy and smoking a cigar with the men. Is it true?"

"Where'd you hear that?" I asked.

"Mrs. Bailey. Mrs. Bailey told us."

"Excuse me," I said and got up. I left them laughing.

After that I ducked in one of those duty-free shops and lost them. I didn't buy anything except some cards. Then I saw that a movie was about to begin, so I went to the theater.

It was just what I needed. The movie was a Debbie Reynolds film, and it was funny—I got some good laughs.

After the movie, I still had time to kill before I had to get ready for dinner. I went in the library to write my cards. I had picked the one with a picture of the ship for Beatrice because she and Carl would both like that one. The other card had a picture of the captain and officers in their sharp-looking uniforms, and I knew the Priscilla Home girls would get a kick out of that one.

That done, I started back to the penthouse. While I was waiting for the elevator, I heard someone calling me. "Miss Esmeralda! Wait up!"

It was Miss Peterson. She was all bubbly. "Oh, you won't believe what Katarina gave me!"

"Gave you?"

"Well, I paid her for it. But it's worth more than the seventy-five dollars she charged." The elevator arrived. "Let's go up to the Skyroom. I doubt that there are many people there now. What I have to tell you is not for any-one else's ears."

The elevator carried us to the Sports Deck, and we walked to the Skyroom. We had our choice of seats.

"First, let me tell you how amazing Katarina is. She knew all about me—knew I lived with my parents in Milwaukee, that I love to read and travel. Said my career had something to do with books. She knew I was single, but she said that will change soon."

"Really? How does she know that?"

"Oh, I hope you won't think I'm silly." Fumbling in her purse, she took out a slip of paper. "I wrote it down. It's a love potion, Miss Esmeralda. She gave me a love potion."

"A love potion?"

"Yes. Listen to this: 'In a bottle of water from a running spring, place three hairs from the tail of a red mare, stir with the feather from a bluebird's wing, seal the bottle, and place it in the fork of a tree when the moon is on the rise, and soon your lover will find you.' Oh, Miss Esmeralda, I know it's probably foolish of me to think this can work, but what have I to lose?"

That's about the silliest thing I ever heard of. Where's she going to find a running spring in Milwaukee, much less a red mare? Well, I won't rain on her parade.

"Oh, but one thing more," she said. "Katarina warned me that Mrs. Winchuster is in grave danger."

"What?"

"Just that. That Mrs. Winchuster is in grave danger. She didn't say what it was—maybe it's because she drinks so much. Who knows. Maybe you shouldn't tell her. There might be nothing to it."

I didn't know what to think. Maybe I should let it pass. On the other hand, if Katarina knew something we didn't, I needed to find out what it was.

25

***

I kept thinking about what the gypsy told Mildred about Mrs. Winchester being in danger. I did not have the slightest faith in any of that crystal ball, hocus-pocus stuff, but what if Katarina had overhead something, or saw something we weren't aware of?

Should I tell Mrs. Winchester?

I was looking in the closet for something to wear and decided on my navy suit. Wearing that apron full of jewels around my waist, I was more comfortable in the suit; the jacket was loose and even hid my bay window. I would save the blue dress for the night we were to eat at the captain's table. I swept up my hair in that French twist that Bud liked, wore the silver earrings he gave me, and said to myself, "They can like it or not; this is me."

Mrs. Winchester came out of her room wearing a soft leather jacket and pants. Large as she was, I was surprised that she would wear pants. "You look great!" I told her.

"Oh, this? Well, I do like it." She held out her arm so I could feel the leather of the sleeve. "They wash this Italian leather to make it soft," she said.

"That crewneck looks soft too."

"It is. It's silk and cashmere. I think the pants are brushed cotton, something like that."

"Mrs. Winchester—"

"For heavens sake, when are you going to stop calling me Mrs. Winchester? I really wish you would call me Winnie."

"No, that wouldn't be right. I'm your hired companion."

"Tommyrot!"

"Well, maybe I'll think about it . . . Now I have something to say. I hope you won't mind my saying it."

"Say whatever you like."

"It's about last night. You really went overboard."

She laughed. "If you hadn't taken care of me I might have done just that—fallen overboard."

"Well, I hope tonight you'll not put us through what we went through last night."

"Okay," she said. "But it was fun, wasn't it?"

"Maybe for you, but not for me."

"Esmeralda, set your mind at ease. I have already decided to skip cocktails before dinner; there's plenty of wine served at dinner to satisfy me. I'll be good. Let's go."

"Mrs. Winchester, do we have to sit at the table with the Baileys?"

"Oh, I wouldn't miss it for the world. I can't wait to see if she keeps her mouth shut. Besides, if he shows off again tonight, ordering wine that's not on the list, I'm going to give him tit for tat."

No one was on the elevator when we were riding down, so she asked me, "Did you happen to hear anyone talking about me today?"

"Yes, I did. That foulmouthed woman and her friends asked me if you smoked a cigar and drank brandy with the men."

"Good. I don't suppose it made the papers, but tomorrow when we go ashore, we'll find a newspaper and see."

Alphonso Pasquali, the Baileys, Lionel, and Mildred were already seated at our table when we arrived. I had too much on my mind to pay much attention to any of them. If what the gypsy said was true and Mrs. Winchester was in danger, it would be up to me to try and protect her.

I heard enough of the table conversation to know it was all about politics and the world situation. Raymond Bailey had made himself the star of that show, and Mrs. Bailey couldn't get a word in edgewise.

I ignored them and concentrated on the danger we might be in. There might be no truth in what Katarina had said. It could be nothing but a ruse to make Mrs. Winchester curious enough to pay big bucks for gypsy flapdoodle.

On the other hand, my being pinned to the wall by that guy in Salt Lake City, the Winchesters' safe being stolen out of the lodge, and our suspicion that we might have

220

been followed—well, there was good reason to think we were in danger.

Since we would be going into Ketchikan the next morning, I knew I must see Katarina that night and find out what, if anything, she knew.

After my herring appetizer I concentrated on eating the lobster I had ordered. I had always wanted to find out what lobster tasted like, since everybody raved about it being so great, but it cost more than I'd ever pay myself. Since I wasn't paying, I took a chance and ordered it, knowing I might make a fool of myself trying to eat it, cracking that shell and digging out the meat.

Fortunately for me, the lobster was served with the shell cracked open and the buttered meat in pieces, making it a breeze to eat. One taste and I was hooked for life!

By the time I had finished eating it, everyone was through and waiting for dessert. I ordered a peach sundae. Well, the desserts came, but, wouldn't you know it, Raymond tells the waiter to bring us all something not on the menu—cherries jubilee!

I had finished my sundae when the cherries jubilee arrived, brought in with a lot of hoopla, the dish in flames and creating quite a stir among the diners.

Mrs. Winchester had said that if he ordered something not on the menu, she was going to give him tit for tat.

Well, nothing happened.

Once we were done with the cherries jubilee, we left the table and headed for the theater.

With ringside seats and Mrs. Winchester not so soused as to embarrass me, I looked forward to the show. Katarina Zigova was on the bill but not the first entertainer.

The first was a magician with a shapely female assistant. Billed as an "illusionist," he caused the woman to float in the air. After that, he cut her in half. Then he shut her in a box and pushed swords through the box at different angles, only to have her step out totally unharmed. Those were tricks I had seen on TV, but frankly, I don't care for magic.

I was anxious for Katarina's act. Maybe there'd be some way I could get her attention and arrange to see her later. I had to get to the bottom of that warning.

The next entertainer was a comedian who sang as well as cracked jokes. He reminded me of Victor Borge. He would sing something pretty, get a body listening, then stop and say funny things.

During his act I was thinking that maybe if Katarina got offstage and danced near us, I could get her attention—pass her a note or something.

At long last, the band gave a big fanfare. Katarina came onstage, playing her violin fast and furious.

"She's playing 'Flight of the Bumblebee,'" Mrs. Winchester told me.

That was exactly what it sounded like. I loved it! I could just hear bumblebees busy about my hollyhocks then streaming back to their hive.

Katarina brought down the house with every number she played. Along with the music, she danced, but not offstage where I might get her attention.

Maybe after this was over, I could get Mrs. Winchester back to the penthouse right away, then make some excuse to come back down here and catch Katarina in her dressing room.

26

We got up to leave the theater, and I purposely left my glasses on my chair so I'd have an excuse for coming back down there. Lionel tapped me on the shoulder, and I was afraid he was going to hand me my glasses. Instead he whispered, "Need any help?"

I thanked him but said I could manage.

Mrs. Winchester was really in good shape. We got on a crowded elevator and there were stops on the way up, but I heard not a peep out of her.

We were hardly inside the penthouse when she said, "Now, Esmeralda, you saw what Bailey did tonight ordering cherries jubilee, which was not on the menu. Now, I want you to be thinking about what we can order tomorrow night that will top anything he can imagine. Let's try to think of something that will stump even the chef!"

So anxious to get back down to the theater, I was hardly listening. "Okay," I said, "but right now I need to go back downstairs. I've left my glasses somewhere."

I got out of there as fast as I could. As I waited for the

elevator I prayed I wouldn't have any trouble finding Katarina.

The maintenance people were already in the theater cleaning. I hurried to my seat to pick up my glasses. Lo and behold, they weren't there! I looked all over. Finally, I went over to one of the cleaning men. "I left—"

"You looking for your glasses?"

"Yes. I was sitting right there." I pointed.

"I turned them in to the purser."

"Where's he?"

"His office is just beyond the front office on the right."

I ran out of the theater and hotfooted it down to that purser's office. He handed me my glasses, and I asked him, "May I go backstage? I need to see Katarina Zigova."

"I'm sorry. Backstage is off-limits to guests."

"You must be mistaken. Last night two people at my table, Lionel Listrom and Mildred Peterson, went backstage."

I don't think he heard me. "Perhaps you would like to leave a note for Miss Zigova asking for an appointment?"

"No, I need to see her right now!"

"Well, I am sorry, madam." He was about to turn away and then must have had second thoughts. "Tell me, madam, aren't you a member of the Winchuster party?"

"That's correct."

He pondered that for a minute. "Perhaps something

can be arranged. Miss Zigova will be performing in the Crow's Nest at midnight this evening."

I couldn't wait that long. "No," I said. "I need to see her right away."

"It's that urgent?" He looked off across the deck like he was thinking. Then he began writing a number on a piece of paper. "Madam, this is highly irregular, but under the circumstances, I am going to allow you to go to Miss Zigova's room. If she is not there, you will have to wait and see her in the Crow's Nest. Go down to the Dolphin Deck. This is the number of her room."

I thanked him and ran to the elevator and waited impatiently. As soon as it arrived and emptied, I jumped on and punched the button for the Dolphin Deck.

Finding the room was easy. I hesitated at the door and listened. I could hear voices. I prayed Katarina would let me talk to her, and then knocked.

Almost immediately the door was flung open. It was Lionel!

His mouth dropped open. "Miss Esmeralda!" He was in his undershirt and had a razor in his hand; he'd been shaving.

I glimpsed Katarina on her way to the door. "Who is it?"

Lionel was so bamboozled he couldn't answer.

She opened the door wider. "Oh, I thought it was the steward." She looked at him, her eyes flashing.

Finally, he mumbled, "It's Miss Esmeralda."

"Oh." Her eyes softened. "I've been expecting you," she said. "Mrs. Winchuster sent you?"

"No. Mrs. Winchester knows nothing about this."

"Please, come in," she said.

Katarina led me to a couch, where I sat down across from her. Lionel went back to the bathroom.

"My brother," she explained.

Brother, husband, lover, I didn't care. Whoever he was, it didn't take a rocket scientist to figure out he was her partner in her psychic schemes. There was no doubt in my mind that he was the one who supplied Katarina with all those personal details about Mildred Peterson.

"Miss Esmeralda," she was saying, "you are a most resourceful, persuasive person."

"I did not come here for myself."

"I know, but no one, absolutely no one, is allowed to visit ship personnel in our quarters. I can understand your desperation. Mrs. Winchuster is in grave danger."

"How do you know that?"

"Oy!" she cried. "We dare not speak of it."

"Did you see something—hear something?"

"Oh yes! Oh yes!"

"Then tell me."

"I dare not. My knowledge is only for Mrs. Winchuster's ears."

I didn't know what to think. If this was only a ruse to get at Mrs. Winchester and her money, I might as well leave.

Lionel walked in the room fully dressed. He and Katarina started talking in a foreign language. She jumped up from the couch, furious—beating on his chest with both fists, following him around the room, and screaming. He stopped, grabbed both her wrists, and got right up in her face. "Katarina!" She hesitated, and he lit into her, yelling rapidly in that foreign tongue. He kept on and on, his voice getting lower. Finally, when she seemed to be hearing what he said, he let her go.

He stopped talking and turned to me. He sat down while she stood, arms folded and her dark face unsmiling.

"Miss Esmeralda," he began, "forgive me for speaking in our Romani tongue, but there was something I had to explain to Katarina. I suppose you understand that Katarina expected to engage Mrs. Winchuster in some profitable magic arts in exchange for what we know."

He took a deep breath. "We gypsies have a difficult life, Miss Esmeralda. Some say we are the lost ten tribes of Israel. If that is so, perhaps that is why our people have been hounded, jailed, beaten, and murdered all over Europe. We are a different people who hold to our traditions any way we can. If you were one of us, you would understand. But you are not one of us. I am fond of you, Miss Esmeralda. You are a good woman, an honest woman who cannot understand why we must live by our wits. Yet I beg of you, forgive us our ways and means of making a living."

He sighed again. "Miss Esmeralda, the only way I can give you the information you are looking for is by making a deal with you."

"A deal?"

"Yes. Our livelihood depends on our keeping this work on cruise ships. Miss Esmeralda, if you will promise not to give us away, to tell absolutely no one from the captain on down, I will tell you all that we know."

"What about Mildred? It wouldn't be fair of me to know the truth about you and not tell her."

"There will be no need to tell her. What is done is done. It will not happen again. Katarina will not charge Mildred for any further services, and I will see that Mildred enjoys herself for the remainder of the cruise. Is it a deal?"

"How can I believe you'll keep your word if you are in the business of deceiving people?"

"It is the chance you will have to take if you want to know what we know."

I didn't know what to do. Then I got an idea. "All right. I'll promise on one condition. I am going to keep in close contact with Mildred Peterson. I will make it my business to find out if you continue to dupe her for money. If you do, I'm going straight to the captain and tell him how you have defrauded her."

"All right. It's a deal."

"Now tell me, what is it you know?"

He stood up and paced the floor. "The man at our table pretending to be an Indian is not an Indian. He says he trained helicopter pilots, but that too may be false. Everything about him is as phony as the magic you saw tonight. He might be Italian. If so, I might add that he is a stupid man to use his real name, Alphonso Pasquali. I don't know what his game is, but whatever it is, there is no doubt in my mind but that Mrs. Winchuster will be his victim. She is the wealthiest passenger on this ship; why would he target anyone else? He may be a jewel thief. Whatever jewels Mrs. Winchuster has should be secured in the purser's safe."

"Is that it?"

"That is all, but Miss Esmeralda, beware of him. Katarina was not lying when she said Mrs. Winchuster is in grave danger. She and I are keenly sensitive to clues that betray the motives of men who design evil. A disguise is a telltale clue. By choosing to sit at our table where he can observe what you and Mrs. Winchuster say, he can learn your plans and make his plans accordingly."

"It's strange that we never see him except at the table."

"He claims he plays poker all day. There is no telling what he's doing—what he's up to. Tomorrow, when you go into Ketchikan, be sure Mrs. Winchuster's jewelry is secured."

"Thank you, Lionel. I had suspected Alphonso was not an Indian, but I was busy and didn't give him much thought. Are you sure this is all you can tell me?"

"Yes, but take this warning seriously. That man is a thief or worse, so beware of him."

"Thank you. I better go now. Mrs. Winchester expected me back right away."

He walked me to the door. "Thank you," I said again and left him to Katarina.

As I went up the elevator, I thought about all Lionel had told me. *Jewelry thief! What if that man knows I am wearing half a million dollars' worth of jewels around my waist?*

27

The next morning we took the tender, the small boat that went from the ship to shore, to Ketchikan and boarded the bus for the Native American Village. I had never heard of the Tlingit Indians, but that's not surprising; the only Indians in my neck of the woods were the Cherokee. The guide said that *Tlingit* means "thundering wings of an eagle." I'd been seeing eagles flying now and again, but, land sakes, I hadn't heard them making a sound, certainly nothing like thunder.

As we were gawking at all the totem poles, I wondered what they were all about. The guide explained that the Tlingits did not have a written language, and that's why they carved totem poles. By what was carved on the poles they could tell stories of their past to their children. As we watched, two men were chopping out another totem from a cedar log. An old man had a carving knife and was carving the details and smoothing the faces of the figures.

Mrs. Winchester said her feet were bothering her, so

I suggested we go in this big lodge where we could sit down on benches and hear all about the Indian culture. People drifted in, and in a few minutes the guide began talking. He told us there were two tribes of Tlingits, the Eagles and the Ravens, and that the only way they could have a good life was by going through all this rigmarole to live in harmony with each other. "Ha!" I said. "The UN should take a tip from the Tlingits!"

When we came out, Mrs. Winchester remarked, "I don't think there'll ever be peace in the world, do you?"

"Yes, I do. When Jesus comes, there'll be peace."

"I thought he had already come."

"He has, but he's coming again."

"Oh."

I guess we moseyed around more than an hour, watching craftsmen doing wood carving, working with leather, making beaded bags and silver bracelets. I bought a souvenir for Priscilla Home—a seal carved from a kind of soil they have in Alaska.

Once we were back in town, we walked along Canal Street, which had been the red light district before prostitution was outlawed, or so we were told. The boardwalk was damp and slippery, and I had to hold on to Mrs. Winchester to keep us from falling and maybe dumping both of us in the canal.

Dolly's House was where the most famous madam had run her business. Of course, I had never been in one of those houses and didn't know what to expect, but I was surprised by all the fancy furnishings they had. It meant

Dolly had made big bucks from the kind of sin carried on in her house.

When we came out, I asked Mrs. Winchester, "Do you care that people call you madam?"

"No. Do you?"

"Yes, I do. To me, a madam is somebody runs a bawdy house. I am not, never have been, and never will be a madam."

She laughed. "Esmeralda, when somebody calls you madam, they don't mean it that way. They mean it as a mark of respect."

"I know, but I'd sooner they use my own name."

"Isn't it time for lunch?" she asked.

"Yes. We can go back to the ship if you like." That's what I would have done, because, after all, our food was already paid for. But no, she wanted to find the best restaurant in town.

I asked the same bus driver who brought us into town, and he recommended the Heen Kahidi Restaurant in the Cape Fox Lodge. He told us how to get there, and when I told Mrs. Winchester we'd have to take a tram up the hill to the lodge, she was tickled pink.

Well, riding a tram was something I'd never done before, and I enjoyed it. The view from the tram of Ketchikan and the harbor was something I'd never forget.

We were running late and must have missed the lunch crowd, because there were no other customers in the restaurant. That restaurant was Class A in my book. It had a pine-beamed ceiling and a river-rock fireplace as well as beautiful windows with views of the harbor. Our table was by a window.

The menu listed all kinds of fancy seafood. I turned my glass upside down and waited while the waiter poured Mrs. Winchester's wine.

After we ordered and the waiter left, I whispered, "Are you going to be good today?"

"Oh yes," she said. "One glass of wine with my lunch and a drink or two later, that's it."

In a few minutes we were served our salads. Believe it or not, Mrs. Winchester wanted me to ask the blessing.

I did, but the moment I opened my eyes, I saw none other than Alphonso Pasquali with two other men being led to a table in a far corner. My heart started beating like a trip hammer. *Had he followed us here? Are those his poker buddies? Does he know I'm wearing these jewels?*

"Isn't that Alphonso?" Mrs. Winchester asked, then answered her own question. "Who else would be wearing a turban? He looks like a maharajah or something."

"Yes, it's Alphonso Pasquali, all right."

Almost as soon as they sat down, Alphonso must have pointed out Mrs. Winchester, because both men turned around and looked our way, turned back around and nodded their heads. I did not like the looks of that!

They made me so nervous. I wondered if Alphonso and those men had been anywhere around us when we were at the Indian village. I had been so caught up in all the things we were seeing there, it hadn't crossed my mind to be on the lookout. Even so, that turban would have made him stand out in the crowd; I wouldn't have missed him. I knew if he had followed us onto Canal

Street I would have seen him, because there's only a narrow boardwalk and few places to hide.

Mrs. Winchester finished her salad then needed to go to the ladies' room. I didn't know if I should go with her or not. Since there were no other women in the restaurant, we would be in there all alone, unless a woman on staff was in the bathroom too. If the men knew I had the jewels on me, a ladies' room would be an ideal place for them to jump me. I decided it was best to let Mrs. Winchester go by herself while I kept watching to see if any of them got up and left the table. I didn't think they would jump her since I had the jewelry, but who knows what a criminal mind is thinking?

Mrs. Winchester always takes her time in the bathroom, but that time I thought she'd never come out. I took a deep breath. It always helps my nerves to remember that Jesus said, "I am with you always." And I know Splurgeon was right when he said, "The sheep are never so safe as when they are near the Shepherd."

By the time she came back, the waiter had removed our salad plates and was serving our lunch. Since we had been told that Ketchikan is the salmon capital of the world, I had picked salmon with chive sauce, braised cabbage, and corn crepes. I was so nervous I ate like I was starving. Knowing it wouldn't be very long before supper, I should not have eaten so much, but I couldn't help myself. Mrs. Winchester even ordered us a delicious little pastry for dessert, which I wolfed down.

After we finished eating, my problem was deciding whether or not we should wait for those men to leave before we left. Mrs. Winchester and I planned to visit the fishery after lunch, but if I had my way, we would skip the fishery and take the next tender back to the ship. Of course, if I changed my mind and said I didn't want to go, Mrs. Winchester might ask me why, and I sure didn't want to explain.

I decided we would sit there until Alphonso and his friends were gone. Then I'd give them enough time to take the tram down before we left. Mrs. Winchester had already signed the bill and was ready to go, but I wasn't finished with my glass of sweet tea. To keep us sitting there, I started in talking. She loved my Live Oaks stories.

I began telling her all about Maria, the woman with AIDS who I took into my home and nursed until she died. I started at the beginning, telling her about how Maria lived in a boxcar with her three children and how, when she was deathly sick and had no hospital insurance, I bluffed her way into the hospital by saying she was a celebrity, Carmen Miranda.

It was a long story, and I dragged it out even longer; I thought those men would never leave. They had finished eating but were drinking coffee. *They're waiting for us to walk out of here and maybe jump us on that tram.* The waiter kept refilling their cups. Once I saw Alphonso glance our way, and I did not like the looks of that.

I kept on talking, adding on to that story, telling Mrs. Winchester everything I could think of.

Finally, Alphonso got up, and the three of them filed out of the restaurant. Seeing that they had left, Mrs. Winchester started getting up.

"Don't you want to hear the rest of the story?"

"There's more?"

"Oh yes."

She settled back in the chair. "Do go on."

I told her about the Osbornes adopting Maria's children and how I was renting my house to them. On and on I went, giving Alphonso plenty of time to take the tram down before we left. I don't think Mrs. Winchester suspected a thing. After I ended the story, I made a trip to the restroom, and by then the tram had been down and up again a couple of times.

As we boarded the tram, I didn't see those men anywhere, and when we reached the bottom, I made sure they weren't waiting around a corner for us. Mrs. Winchester was saying, "From what I hear the fish hatchery is fascinating."

Well, when we got to the fish hatchery and could see the salmon leaping up falls and swimming, it was interesting, but I was in no frame of mind to be fascinated. The guide was telling about the way the hatchery harvests the eggs and produces more salmon than could be done the natural way.

It looked like Mrs. Winchester was going to hang around there the rest of the day, but I reminded her that we didn't want to miss the last tender. She agreed, and we took the next bus back to the pier.

"You haven't forgotten to think up something to order tonight that will top Bailey, have you?" Mrs. Winchester reminded me.

To tell the truth, I hadn't given it another thought, but as we were riding back on the tender I did come up with something I knew the ship would not have on board. "What about clabber?"

"Clabber? What's that?"

"It's sour milk that has clotted. You eat it with nutmeg, sugar, and milk."

"I never heard of that."

"It's not likely anyone at the table has heard of it either, and I know the chef won't have it."

"You're sure?"

"As sure as rain. Milk aboard ship is pasteurized, and milk that is pasteurized won't clot."

She liked the idea, so that was settled.

That night it seemed everybody was dressed fit to kill. I wore a skirt and blouse with my cardigan sweater and told myself I was comfortable being who I am. I thought of Percival saying he didn't want to forget who he was.

One of the staff was doing an ice carving, and I stopped to watch him. Even though he was not far along with the carving, already I could see it was going to be a swan. I wondered why that ice didn't melt.

When I made my way to the table, I saw that everyone was already seated and that Alphonso was already sipping his wine. After eating that big lunch so late in the day, I was not hungry and I wondered what to order. Looking at the menu I saw the name of a dessert that looked interesting—"Mudslide." For the fun of it, that's the only thing I ordered. Nobody seemed to notice. Everybody at the table had their head down, poring over the menus, but the minute Mrs. Winchester told the waiter to bring her two slices of bread, a banana, and some mayonnaise, every head popped up openmouthed.

"Are you unwell?" Mrs. Bailey asked.

"I'm perfectly well," she answered. I could see Mrs. Winchester was getting a charge out of all their attention.

"There's a physician on board," Mrs. Bailey insisted but got no response from Mrs. Winchester. "When I travel, and we do travel all the time, I make sure that the medical facilities available are of the highest standards. One never knows when one might fall ill or be indisposed for one reason or another."

After everyone had ordered, Mrs. Bailey took the floor again. "What a lovely day we've had on the canoeing safari. My husband is such an expert with the paddles, aren't you, dear?" But giving him no time to respond, she asked, "And, Mrs. Winchester, did you enjoy your day?"

"Yes."

Seeing she was not going to get anything more out of Mrs. Winchester, she looked to me. "Did you two stay aboard ship?"

"No," I said. "We toured the town."

Seeing as how I was not going to satisfy her curiosity, she had an edge in her voice. "How nice. Bought little trinkets, I suppose?"

Lionel spoke up. "Miss Peterson and I had a great day. We took a jeep and rode through the forest first, then joined a rafting party to ride the rapids."

Mrs. Bailey didn't bother to ask Alphonso what he had done. He was slurping his soup and saying nothing to nobody.

"Now, about tomorrow," Mrs. Bailey began. "We'll be in Juneau. What do you plan to do there, Mrs. Win*chus*ter?"

I was surprised that Mrs. Winchester told her. "We're going to the Mendenhall Glacier."

"Wonderful! We are too. Raymond has us going by helicopter. We would love to have you come along with us."

"We will go by bus," Mrs. Winchester said, lathering mayonnaise on a slice of bread.

"Oh, nonsense. I know you would rather fly."

"You know nothing of the kind."

"Oh."

28

I knew we would see plenty of glaciers when we traveled to Glacier Bay, but then we would be on the ship, whereas at the Mendenhall we could actually walk on the glacier. As we were traveling on the tour bus and enjoying the scenery, I suddenly saw a rainbow that was absolutely round! "Look, Mrs. Winchester! Did you ever see a rainbow like that—wide as that one and in a circle?"

"Oh no, I haven't. It's beautiful. Maybe it's a good omen."

I didn't say nothing, but I have never put no stock in omens. I changed the subject. "They sure fell for that clabber joke last night, didn't they?" We both laughed.

When the bus arrived at the Mendenhall, we waited until everybody got off so Mrs. Winchester wouldn't block traffic in the aisle and could take her time getting down them steps. A soft, drizzling rain was falling, and I was glad I was wearing my parka with the hood. Mrs.

Winchester was wearing a beautiful ivory-colored parka that came down to her knees and had a coyote-trimmed hood. It looked great, but *coyote*? Who'd want to wear something come off a coyote?

By the time we got off the bus, everybody was already out on the ice. A helicopter was parked nearby. "I hope that's not the Baileys' helicopter," I said. "Wouldn't they just fly over the glacier but not land?"

"Who knows? I hope we don't run into them."

"That woman can talk the horns off a billy goat, can't she?"

Mrs. Winchester was so unsteady on her feet that I debated about taking her onto that ice. Out of the corner of my eye I saw a couple men getting off the helicopter and thought I might ask them to help me. One of them hailed me to wait up, so I figured they saw I needed help. I waited as they were coming our way, glad there was somebody friendly enough to lend me a hand.

But as they reached us, they didn't look at all friendly. One of them said, "Ladies, come with me."

"What?" I said. "Why should we come with you?"

He grabbed Mrs. Winchester by the arm and at the same time poked a pistol at me from under his jacket. Before I could scream, the man in back of me slapped his hand over my mouth and pressed the barrel of another gun in my back. "Come quietly or you will die," he said.

With both hands I was trying to pry his fingers from my mouth and kicking him as hard as I could but getting nowhere. He kept pressing that gun in my back and swearing.

The other guy was hustling Mrs. Winchester toward

the helicopter. I knew she was terrified. Even if I could get free, I couldn't let them take her away by herself.

The chopper blades were rotating as that goon got me to the helicopter. He pushed me inside, and I fell against Mrs. Winchester. Climbing in after me, the goon slid the door shut and bolted it. Mrs. Winchester was terrified; her heart palpitating in her neck. A third man, taller than the other two, sat at the controls and did not turn around to look.

"Where are you taking us?" I demanded.

Nobody said a word.

"Who are you?" Still no answer. "What do you want? Is it jewelry? If it is . . ."

Those men just stared straight ahead and said nothing.

Mrs. Winchester clutched my arm, shaking all over. I worried that she might be in shock. "I don't know what they're up to," I told her, "but just hang on." Over and over I was telling myself, *What time I am afraid, I will trust in thee.* But I was scared stiff.

The way that helicopter leaned sideways as it swept away from the glacier gave my stomach a turn. In no time we leveled out and were flying over open water.

Hoping to keep Mrs. Winchester from passing out, I reached my arms around her. I held her as best I could, telling her, "Don't worry. There's nothing going on here that the Lord can't handle." Her whole body was shaking.

It wasn't long before I saw a forest of trees growing down to the water's edge—then a house built on stilts alongside the water. We passed over the house, and I saw no signs of life the rest of the way.

We were flying overland close by the water and must have flown for another ten minutes before the helicopter began slowing down. Finally, it was hovering over a clearing. "Where are we?" I demanded. Nobody answered.

Once we landed, the pilot cut the engine, and we sat there while the chopper blades whacked slower and slower. There was nothing to see outside except that bare spot of ground we had landed on and dense trees all around.

One of the men opened the door and crawled out. The other man nudged me with his gun. "Get out."

I had no choice. Once on the ground I reached up both hands to help Mrs. Winchester. She was in such bad shape that it took both of them goons to help me get her out. After we got her down on the ground, the man inside climbed out and the pilot followed.

The pilot led the way on an overgrown path leading through the trees toward the water. Mrs. Winchester and I were herded in back of him by the other two men bringing up the rear. The ground beneath our feet was soggy, and I slipped once but didn't fall. I was holding on to Mrs. Winchester, and it's a wonder we both didn't wind up on top of each other. Her teeth were chattering, and I had to keep talking, trying to calm her down.

That path led to a house built on stilts over the edge of the water. I saw two boats docked underneath the house and a slippery gangplank that led up to the back door. I doubted that Mrs. Winchester could make it up there in the state she was in, but one of them hoods took her other arm. With her teeth chattering and trembling like she was, we had to take it slow and easy. Taking one step at a time, we did manage to get her all the way up without a mishap.

At the door a stringy-haired woman in a shabby coat and big boots met us and let us inside. A young man holding an assault rifle stood in back of her, looking like he was ready to shoot at the drop of a hat.

The pilot held a straight-back chair for Mrs. Winchester to sit on, and I sat on another one beside her. He told the woman, "Get Mrs. Win*chus*ter a drink." And the woman went in the next room. From what I could see, it was a tiny kitchen. The boy with the weapon sat down by an open door that led to a porch. Didn't look like he relaxed one muscle.

Finished with getting us settled, that pilot pulled up a chair right in front of me, straddled it, and looked at me with a big smile. "We've met before," he said.

I had never in my life seen anybody that even looked like that beetle-browed goon. He sure wasn't the suspicious guy on the ship Lionel had warned me about. *He can't be that so-called Indian; he's not wearing a turban or a Nehru jacket. In fact, he don't have a mustache.*

Seeing I didn't recognize him, he leaned over and got right up in my face. I smelled garlic on his breath, and the wheels in my head started spinning. In no time it dawned on me who he was.

"I know you!" I yelled. "You're the one who pinned me to the wall!"

"Right," he said and backed off, grinning from ear to ear. "You should've listened to me that night, Esmeralda.

You could've saved us a lot of time and trouble. All you would've had to do was let us know when we could take Mrs. Winchuster without interference. As it is, we had to take you too. Now, instead of being a hostage, you could've been in on the ransom."

"Ransom?"

"Three million, in fact. A million for each one of us."

"You'll never get it. Philip Winchester will never pay a ransom."

"You better hope he does. If he don't pay, you two better prepare to meet your God."

"I am prepared!" I told him.

"That so? Esmeralda, I understand you are religious. For whatever it's worth, you better start praying Philip Winchester forks over that three mil."

The woman came with the drink and handed it to Mrs. Winchester. The pilot turned aside to introduce the woman and the fellow with the assault rifle. "This is your hostess, Daisy LeGrande, and your host, Willie Miller." He laughed like that was funny. "Willie is a fisherman, but he won't be doing any fishing until we finish this job."

Seeing the pilot wasn't ready to leave, the other two men sat down, and he introduced them. "This here is Tony and that's Pee-Wee." Both of them had beady eyes like them serial killers you see on *America's Most Wanted*.

"You haven't told us who you are," I said.

"No, I haven't, have I?" Grinning like a Cheshire cat, he was enjoying this game he was playing. "How unmannerly of me. Let me help you ladies guess who I am. Mrs. Winchuster, I got to hand it to you. You played a good game of one-upmanship on that world traveler Bailey, didn't you?" He laughed. "You beat him at his own game, ordering that clabber—something he never even heard of before."

He *was* the Indian! "Where's your turban?" I demanded.

The other two men snickered.

Alphonso pulled the turban out of his jacket pocket along with the fake mustache. "I'll be glad when I can get rid of this stuff for good, but I'm bound to wear it until this cruise is over. You have to admit, Esmeralda, I had you fooled."

"Oh, I don't know about that. I figured you were a phony from the word go."

"Did you? Esmeralda, I have to hand it to you. You are one gutsy woman."

The other two men were getting jittery. The one named Tony said, "We better get out of here, Alphonso. Once these women are missed, the law'll be all over the place."

"You're right. But first, I got to take care of a little business. Hand me that tape recorder, Pee-Wee." Pee-Wee handed it to him, and Alphonso started messing with it. "Mrs. Win*chus*ter, have you settled down enough to give us a sweet little message for your husband? He'll want to know you're all right before he shells out the dough, so tell him you are both fine and that we're taking good care of you, okay? Tell him the sooner he pays up, the sooner he can get you back."

She had calmed down a bit, even though I knew she was still scared out of her wits. She nodded.

"Okay, now speak up; we want Mr. Win*chus*ter to think

we can deliver you alive and well as soon as he comes through with the cash."

She looked at me for help. "Do as he says," I told her. "Just speak up and say that you and me are okay. I guess you better tell him they're treating us okay and for him to pay the ransom."

Her voice was a bit shaky, but she gave the message almost word for word. Alphonso played it back and was satisfied that it would do. "Well, we gotta go," he said. "I got to get the chopper back to the rental agency. I'll catch the tender back to the ship while you boys take care of the rest of this business." The three got up to leave. "Daisy, take care of these ladies, and you, Willie, see to it they don't go no place." He laughed. "If they do, you'll not see the light of another day."

Wide-eyed and sweating, Willie was tense and nervous, which is not a good combination when there's a finger on a trigger. He didn't say a word.

The three goons left, and once they were down on the ground, Willie told Daisy to pull up the gangplank.

"There's no need of that," Daisy said. "You want it pulled up, do it yourself."

"Takes both hands, and I got to hold on to this gun."

"I'll hold the gun for you," she said. Seeing as he was not willing to let her touch the gun, she looked disgusted and said, "All right, I'll pull it up. Esmeralda, I'll need your help."

Together we got the thing up off the ground and fastened the cable to hold it there. "I don't hardly never pull it up," Daisy was saying. "It's too much trouble and not a bit o' use doin' it way out here. There's bears and moose, but it ain't likely they would ever take a notion to come up it."

She shut the door behind us.

Willie looked like he was frozen to that chair and was gripping the assault gun so hard his knuckles were white.

"What's got you so uptight, Willie?" I asked him. "We can't go nowhere."

He didn't answer.

Daisy went in the kitchen and turned on a radio, saying we sure didn't want to miss the news. I heard some static, and Daisy fooled with it until she found a better station. Coming back in the narrow room, she sat down and started talking.

"Having womenfolk to talk to is a treat for me. It ain't often I go downriver far enough to stop in at the next house, where Granny Sparks lives. It's easy twenty miles or more."

I heard the chopper engine starting up.

"Willie here, he don't got the nerve for what he's doin'. It's his first time signing on with crooks. He don't have sense enough to know what he's got hisself into, and I tell you, he's 'tween a rock and a hard place. The law catch him holdin' you two at gunpoint, and he'll spend the rest of his life in the pen. Not do what them plug-ugly hoodlums give him to do, and they'll blow out what few brains he has got. They'll most likely do that anyway to make sure he don't talk."

I could hear the chopper taking to the air. I listened until I could no longer hear it.

So this is it. We're kidnapped.

29

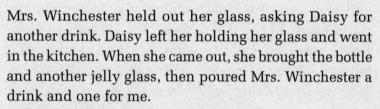

Mrs. Winchester held out her glass, asking Daisy for another drink. Daisy left her holding her glass and went in the kitchen. When she came out, she brought the bottle and another jelly glass, then poured Mrs. Winchester a drink and one for me.

"No thanks," I said. "I don't drink."

"If you lived in Alaska, you'd have to drink." She sat down and started drinking the one she had poured for me. "Mrs. Win*chus*ter, where you from?"

"Newport, Rhode Island," she said.

"And I'm from Live Oaks, South Carolina," I told her.

"Well, I'll be! I'm from Mississippi—sixty miles outta Jackson."

"What brought you to Alaska?" I asked.

"That crazy husband I married. I had a few husbands, but he was the craziest. This fool Billy Tyson showed Tom a gold nugget. Said he found it up here and that there was buckets more where that come from. The only hitch was, Billy needed money to sink a shaft to get at where the gold was at. Said any man willin' to put up two or three thousand dollars, he'd take on as a partner to share and share alike in the mining business.

"Fool that he was, Tom was in a fever pitch to sell out and move up here, sure he'd make a killing in gold. He wouldn't listen to a word I said. The next week we pulled up stakes and flew up to Juneau.

"Turned out, Billy Tyson wasn't nothin' but a drunk. They dug a shaft but never found a speck of gold. Once Tom's money was spent, Billy took off, and we never saw hide nor hair of him after that.

"Crazy as he was, Tom wouldn't give up workin' the claim. I warned him that with all this rain coming down nearly every day and night, one day the dirt above that mine was gonna give way and that shaft cave in on him. But, like I say, he wouldn't listen to me.

"Sure enough, one day Tom didn't come home, and when I went lookin' for him, I found the shaft not only caved in but a good ten feet under dirt. I could have dug Tom out, but why bother? He had done buried his-self."

"Willie your son?" I asked.

"Heavens, no! He took up here 'bout a year ago when his motor give out on him. Drifting on the big water, like as not he would have drifted clean out to sea, but he saw my light up here and started hollering. I heard him and put out to rescue him. He don't usually stay here, but he's in and out."

"How'd you get mixed up with Alphonso?"

"It's Willie. He was down in Ketchikan, and Alphonso

asked him if he knew where there was a hideout some-
place where a man would be safe from the law. That
right there should have told Willie this was something
he don't want no part of, but not Willie. He plays the
big man and tells Alphonso there's no better place than
mine for a hideout. Tells him where it's at and how to
get here.

"Then Alphonso asked him if he would like to make
a thousand dollars and, of course, Willie don't think
to ask questions, he just said yes, and that sealed the
deal. Alphonso told him he'd see him in Juneau about
the plans."

"But Daisy—why did you go along with Willie?"

"Had no choice. Before I knew anything about Willie's
big deal with these crooks, that Tony and Pee-Wee come
up here in a chopper to check out my place. Said they
were looking for real estate to buy. I asked how they
found out about my place, and they said they met up
with Willie and he told them.

"Well, that sounded okay. Willie knows I want to get
back to Mississippi, and if I could sell this place I would
be on my way. But before I know anything about this
Alphonso gang, this morning Willie shows up. And I'm
glad to see him, thinking he had sent them two buyer
prospects. Then he asks me if I would like to make five
hundred dollars. Pore as I am, I can't look five hundred
dollars in the face and walk away from it, so I said, 'That
all depends; what would I have to do?'

"When Willie told me they would be bringing you two
up here for us to hide, I coulda killed him! It was too
late to do anything but stay put. You get in the way of

men like Alphonso, and they'd sooner shoot you dead as hear you out." She got up from her chair. "Now I got to go help up the beans."

I followed her to see if there was anything I could do to help. She filled a plate with beans and handed it to me. I took it in to Mrs. Winchester and went back for Willie's plate. Then we served ourselves.

We ate balancing the plates on our knees. After all the rich food we had been eating on the trip, those beans tasted mighty good. Even while Willie was eating he didn't put down that gun. I was wondering if what Daisy had said was true, that he was doomed either way, if the law caught him or if the gang killed him to keep him from testifying against them. He'd be better off throwing in with us, helping us escape and get back to civilization.

"Willie," I said, "you heard what Daisy said. If you get caught holding us this way, they'll send you to prison. What's worse, knowing you can identify them, those crooks ain't likely to let you live to testify against them."

"I heard what she said."

"Your best bet is to help us get back to Juneau. You'd be a hero, plus Mr. Winchester will pay you a big reward."

Daisy pitched in to help out. "That's right, Willie. You got nothing to lose and a lot to gain by doing what Esmeralda says."

"Leave me alone! I can handle this."

"Well, just think about it, Willie," I said.

That night Daisy put up two cots in the room where we had sat all day, and she showed me a chamber pot in the kitchen in case we had to go in the night. Daisy was going to sleep in the kitchen on a pallet with the radio on so as not to miss the news.

I asked her where Willie would sleep, and she said he wouldn't sleep, he'd stay put sitting up in that chair.

How stupid can he be? "How does he think we could get away from here?"

"He don't think straight, Esmeralda, and it's no use arguing with him. That boy is scared of his own shadow. He's mortally afraid of lightning, passes out at the sight of blood, and now that he has got hisself beholden to Alphonso, he'd sooner shoot us as get shot by them. Willie's so nervous, the least little thing could set him off."

❦

Well, needless to say, that night I didn't get much sleep—and neither did Mrs. Winchester. With that radio going and no bedding on those army cots, comfort was out of the question. Only once during the night did Willie leave that chair—and that was to go out on the porch to relieve himself.

Daisy had given me a lot to think about, but Mrs. Winchester wanted to talk.

"Esmeralda, do you think they're going to kill us?"

I had to be honest. "I don't know," I whispered. "The best that could happen is they'll get the ransom and make a quick getaway, and we'll never see them again. It'll be up to Daisy or the FBI to get us back to civilization. But on the other hand, even if they get the money and take off, since we know who them three are, they might come back themselves or send somebody else to kill us."

"Esmeralda, I'm not prepared to die."

"Well, I can help you with that."

Hesitating as she did, I had started to say something more when she spoke up. "Do you remember my telling you about when I was a little girl—how my nanny told me where babies come from?"

I had to think on that one. "Yes, I remember that. She told you babies come from heaven."

"She did. And do you remember that time when I heard somebody talking about Jesus on the radio and I asked her who Jesus was?"

It was easy to remember that one. "Yes," I said, "I remember. She turned off the radio and told you you shouldn't listen to such as that." *Where is she going with this?*

"Esmeralda, when I was lying in the hospital after my accident, I had a dream . . . I have never told anyone in the world what I dreamed. It was sacred—something special for me only . . ."

"Do you want to tell me about it?"

"Yes, I do . . . In my dream I saw this platform, which to me was heaven, because there were babies in baskets on the railing around the platform. Coming down from the platform were steps that ended on the brink of a rushing stream. Jesus was standing on one of the lower steps, reaching out his hand to me. He wanted me to take his hand and swing round onto that bottom step and go with him to heaven."

I could see in my mind's eye what she was telling me. "Were you afraid?"

"I wasn't afraid, but I didn't want to leave and go with him . . . Esmeralda, I said no."

I didn't know what to say.

"All through the years, ever since, I have regretted that I said no. Do you think Jesus will ever forgive me for that sin?"

"Yes, I know he will." I thought of something Splurgeon said. I told her, "Winnie, it would take an angel's tongue to describe Jesus's love for you."

"But it was awful of me to say no."

"I've done worse than that. When I was a little girl, I knew I should become a Christian, but I didn't. I think I always believed Jesus suffered on the cross in order to forgive sin, but I thought I had plenty of time to decide about that. Then my mother died. My heart was broke, and I had no one to turn to. One verse kept coming to my mind, and I knew the Lord was reaching out to me."

"Do you remember the verse?"

"How could I ever forget it? 'The blood of Jesus Christ, his Son, cleanses us from all sin.' Like all children, I wasn't perfect, but I realized that the worse sin of all is refusing the love of Jesus. That's when I must have become a Christian. I don't know the day nor the hour when, but I know Jesus has saved me because that burden of guilt is gone."

"You mean he didn't give up on you?"

"No, he didn't. And the Lord was seeking you back then when he gave you that dream, and he is seeking you now."

"Do you really think so?"

"I know so. Splurgeon said, 'No sinner was ever half as eager for Christ as Christ is eager for the sinner.'"

"What do I do?"

"Just ask him to forgive you, and he will."

"But Esmeralda, it's more than the dream bothering me. It's my drinking. I can't stop drinking."

"I know you can't, but if you come to Jesus, he will change you. He will give you power to stop drinking. Don't you have a lot of other questions you need answered?"

"I suppose so. But I'm not smart like you, Esmeralda. I'm only a simple woman who needs forgiveness and needs help to live the kind of life you live."

"Then, Winnie, just bow your head and tell him what you want."

She was quiet for a while, and then she whispered, "I will."

30

The next morning, I was folding up the cots and Daisy was in the kitchen frying fish when the news came on the radio.

"Two passengers have been reported missing from the cruise ship *Amsterdam* and are believed to have fallen overboard in the Juneau harbor. Missing since dinner last night are two women, Mrs. Winifred Winchester, wife of Philip Winchester, the well-known financier, and her companion, Mrs. Esmeralda McAbee. It is thought that one of the two women fell overboard, and in the effort to rescue her, the other one drowned as well. Search teams are searching the harbor, hoping to recover the bodies."

The newscaster turned to other news.

"Would you hear that!" Daisy exclaimed.

"It never crossed my mind they'd think we fell overboard," I said.

Willie's eyes were about to pop out of his head. "What if they don't never know no better?"

"Don't worry, Willie, you'll get your money," I told

him. "Once news of the ransom note comes out, they'll call off the search for our bodies, and then we'll see what happens."

We ate breakfast, then I went in the kitchen to help Daisy with the dishes. I mainly wanted to talk with her. "Daisy, we got to think this thing through or we are all going to wind up dead as doornails."

"I know it, but with Willie like he is, there ain't no way to get around him. He's got no more sense than to think that once that ransom is paid, he'll get his money and that'll be all there is to it."

"I hate to say this, but Mrs. Winchester told me her husband won't pay the ransom. It's a long story that I'll not go into, but you know how these rich men are. It ain't above any one of them to be in back of something like this, hiring somebody to murder their wife. If that's the case here, there is no way you and me will be left alive to testify. On the other hand, if this is truly a kidnapping and Winchester don't pay the ransom, them three goons will see to it that we're bumped off."

"I know that's the truth, but what can we do?"

"Daisy, you know Mrs. Winchester is filthy rich."

"Yeah, I heard that."

"Well, lemme tell you something—she is mighty careless about jewels; won't put them in hotel safes or nothing. When I found out she leaves them any old place, I knew sooner or later somebody was going to help themselves to every diamond and ruby she has got, and when that happened, I'd be the prime suspect."

"That's right. They'd sooner pin it on you than get to the bottom of a case like that."

"Well, now, if Mrs. Winchester would be able to offer Willie half a million dollars in jewels, don't you think that would change his mind and he'd go along with helping us get away?"

"I wish I could say yes, but there is no way under the sun that he would. In the first place, he don't value nothin' but cold cash. Give him rubies and diamonds and he'd think no more of them than what comes out of a Cracker Jack box. Besides, he wouldn't know what to do with them."

We finished the dishes and went back to sit in that little room. Well, I tried. I knew it was a long shot, but I was awful let down. All them jewels around my middle but not worth a dime.

Mrs. Winchester asked Daisy to turn up the radio so we would be sure to hear if there was more news. I thought Mrs. Winchester looked pretty calm considering what we were going through. I got out a Gospel of John, and she asked me to read out loud. I was glad to do that, because then Willie and Daisy would also hear some of the things Jesus said and did.

By midday a talk show was interrupted by a news flash. "Today the Associated Press has learned that Mrs. Winchester and her companion, who were reported yesterday to have fallen overboard from the cruise ship *Amsterdam*, did not fall overboard but have been taken hostage. A ransom note was delivered to Mr. Philip Winchester at 8:00 last night, Eastern Standard Time. We will keep you posted as developments occur."

That announcement meant we were moving that much

closer to whatever fate was in store for us, and I knew we had to do something soon or we would die.

I got up to go out on the porch. Willie jerked up the gun. "What's the matter, Willie, do you think I'm going to jump or something? Mrs. Winchester, you stay inside and keep listening to the radio. Willie, you guard her good, now."

Daisy laughed and followed me onto the porch.

It was raining hard, and with the radio blaring, I was sure Willie couldn't hear us talking. "Daisy, what are we gonna do?"

"I don't know."

I knew Daisy was on our side, but getting Willie to join us seemed impossible. Without him and that gun, it would be simple for us to crank up one of those boats under the house and go by the water down to Juneau.

As I thought on it, I finally did get an idea. I thought it all through before I shared it with Daisy. Then I explained all the details and what part she would play in the plan.

When I finished, she said, "It might work. When the rain lets up I'll tell Willie I'm going fishing. I'll catch enough fish for our supper and come back. Then I'll gas up my boat and fix his so it won't run. That way we'll be set to go if we get the chance."

We heard Mrs. Winchester calling us, and we ran inside. The radio was sputtering, but I could hear that Philip Winchester had offered a five-hundred-thousand-dollar reward for information leading to the safe return of his wife and her companion.

I can't tell you what that meant to Mrs. Winchester. She just fell apart sobbing. I hugged her and let her cry her heart out.

31

❦

Having stayed awake all night, Willie looked like a zombie, but he was no less trigger-happy. Daisy spoke to him as she was putting on her slicker. "This rain ain't never gonna let up, but if we want something to eat for supper, I got to go fish."

I helped her get the gangplank down, and she left. I could hear her under the house working with the boat, and it wasn't long before the motor started. Soon it was humming across the open water.

I was anxious to fill Winnie in on our plan, so I said, "Excuse me, Willie, but I got to go in the kitchen and use the chamber pot. I'll have to close this door." No sooner did I go in there but I opened the door a crack, caught Winnie's eye, and beckoned to her. Right away, she caught on that something was up. "Mrs. Winchester," I said for Willie's benefit, "I'll be in here a while. If you want to hear the radio you'll have to come in here too."

Once inside, I turned up the radio to make sure Willie couldn't hear us. I took considerable time explaining all the details to Winnie and her part in the plan. She got all excited. I put my finger to my lips to caution her. "Don't let on we got anything up our sleeve."

While we waited to hear Daisy coming back, Willie had a hard time keeping his eyes open. Jerked awake, he sat up bolt upright and asked me to make him a cup of coffee, which I did.

About an hour later, here comes the sound of Daisy's boat heading home. I don't know who was the most excited, me or Winnie, but I'm proud to say we both kept our cool.

Daisy spent considerable time under the house, messing with the boats, but finally she came up the gangplank. I met her at the door, and, sure enough, she had a great big fish. "Halibut," she said. She was dripping wet. "Did more bailin' than fishin'."

We left the gangplank down. "Any news?" she asked.

I shook my head and followed her into the kitchen. She put the halibut in the sink and poured herself a cup of coffee. "You ready?"

I nodded.

I left Daisy drinking the coffee. When she came out the kitchen, she looked at Winnie, and Winnie nodded slightly. They were both ready to put our plan into action.

Winnie got started. "Is that all we have to eat—*fish*?"

"Ain't that good enough for you, Miss Got Rocks?"

"We had fish for breakfast! I'm accustomed to better meals than this. I have a delicate constitution and do not tolerate beans and fish."

"Oh, you don't? Well, listen to me, lady. If you're so high-and-mighty you can't eat what I eat, you need takin' down a notch or two!" Daisy flung off her parka and rolled up her sleeves. "And I'm just the one to do it!" she said. "Outta my way, Willie!"

"Esmeralda! Do something!" Winnie screamed.

I stayed put.

Daisy was dancing around with her fists balled up. "Git up, Miss Got Rocks, and I'll show you a thing or two." How she did it, I'll never know, but she yanked all two hundred pounds of Winnie out of that chair.

"Now, see here!"

With that, Daisy hauled off and hit her hard with an uppercut. Winnie's glass eye popped out and bounced on the floor. Willie saw it, freaked out, and fainted dead away. I grabbed his gun and picked up that eye, and the three of us hightailed it outta there!

I hit that gangplank running, but my feet went out from under me and I slid all the way to the bottom. Daisy hung on to Winnie, and them two got down without no trouble.

Winnie's foot got stuck in the mud, and it took both of us to get her in the boat. I handed her the assault rifle. "Hold this, Winnie, while we untie the boat." We shoved off, and Daisy eased us out from under the house. We chugged out a ways, then speeded up.

With the rain coming down like it was and the motor going full blast, we couldn't hear each other talk, but I could see them two were happy the same as me. I couldn't get over it. We had pulled it off! We were on our way back to Juneau!

Daisy sat in the rear of the boat with me on the other end and Winnie in the middle. In that pouring-down rain the boat would have soon got full of water, but there were a couple of cans in the boat to bail with. Winnie and I were working like crazy bailing out the water. With all our weight, it wouldn't take much to swamp the boat. Of course, we were all getting drenched, but that was the least of our worries.

It seemed like forever before the rain let up and the gray sky lightened a bit. Winnie and I kept bailing for fear the rain would start up again. It was all I could do to keep dipping out the water and throwing it over the side, and I was amazed that Winnie, who had probably never used them muscles before, didn't give up and quit.

At last, it seemed the rain would hold off, so we slacked up on bailing. It was then that I noticed how bedraggled we looked. Not only had we not had a bath in three days and had slept in our clothes and not changed our underwear, but we were muddy and wringing wet. Any bag lady would have been more presentable than we were.

Winnie wiped her runny nose on the sleeve of that ivory parka, which was too wet and dirty for even a runny nose. Something had snagged the sleeve in such a way the armhole was almost ripped out, and the coyote trim looked like a slick dishrag.

I knew I looked as bad as or worse than Winnie, but as for Daisy, she looked about the same as before. I had never seen her but what her stringy hair was falling down in her face. And she never laced her boots. They must have been full of water; my feet were sloshing in my shoes. But if ever I was face-to-face with an angel, it was Daisy LeGrande. That Mississippi woman, poor as a church mouse, could have saved herself and claimed a big reward—or run off to Juneau and left me and Winnie to die by Willie's hand. I wondered how many women would have done that. All the good people are not sitting up in church, you know.

❦

I have no idea how long or how many miles we traveled before Daisy swung the boat inland. "Auke Bay," she hollered above the roar. In the distance I could see some boats. *Must be a harbor.*

As we drew nearer, I could see it was a marina with all kinds of small and big craft anchored there. Daisy cut the motor to a slower speed and let the boat cruise the rest of the way. A bunch of people were on a pier. One man was standing on his houseboat fixing something. I was happy we had escaped, but meeting people, as bedraggled as we were, was something I could do without.

Daisy steered the boat toward an empty slip, then cut the engine to an idle. On the dock several men stood watching. Like a pro, she eased our boat into place slick as a whistle. I climbed out to get it hitched up, and a couple of the men came to help me. "Looks like you been on the water for some time," one of them said. "You weren't lost, were you?"

I didn't answer him. "Sir, will you help me get Mrs. Winchester out of the boat?"

"Winchester? You mean—"

"That's right. We been kidnapped."

"Hey!" he yelled. "It's Mrs. Winchester!"

Boy, did them men hop to it! The people piled off that pier like a bunch of grackles swooping down. "Just help Mrs. Winchester," I said.

Three or four men practically lifted Winnie out of the boat and carried her onto level land. They set her down, one shoe on and one shoe off and her clutching my pocketbook so full of water that the water was pouring out. That bottomless pit would never be the same, but I took it out of her hands, hoping that later I could salvage something out of it. I told a man in a mackinaw, "We need to get to the police station."

"Of course! Of course! I'll take you there," he said.

"No, we'd ruin your car; our clothes are sopping wet. Just tell us where we can get a bus or a cab."

"No, lady! My truck's parked right up there next the light pole. You're coming with me." The people were pressing in from all sides, anxious to see or help us, but they were too nice or too dumbfounded to ask questions. "Now get outta my way, folks," he said.

People wouldn't let go of us—escorted us all the way to the truck and, anxious to help, offered to take one or two of us in their cars because the truck had only a narrow space for a backseat. "No," I said, "we'll stay together." Daisy and I crawled in the back, then several men practically picked up Winnie and put her in the front seat.

No sooner were we inside and the doors shut than our knight in shining armor told us, "My name is George. Call me George." With the motor running, he dialed his phone. "I'm calling the chief," he said.

While he was talking on the phone, he eased his way through the gawking crowd then turned the truck onto the road. I thought we were in the clear and on our way until I glanced out the back window. "Daisy, look at that—they're all following us." It looked like every vehicle in that parking lot had pulled out behind us.

George finished talking and hung up the phone. "Ladies, the chief says you got company down at the station."

"Who could that be?" I wondered.

"Reporters, photographers, you name it! You ladies have been on TV and in every newspaper in the country—around the world, in fact. Last night, my wife sat up until 3:00 in the morning watching the news on TV, hoping they'd find you."

That's all we needed—a bunch of reporters. I leaned over to the front seat. "Well, Winnie, you always wanted to be kidnapped. How did you like it?"

She shuddered. "Like it? I was terrified! I must have been out of my mind ever to imagine it would be fun."

I laughed. "It's over now, and you can enjoy all the attention we'll be getting."

"Attention? Looking like this? Esmeralda, can't you do something about avoiding those reporters?"

"Winnie, I don't know that I can."

"Hey, lookee there!" George exclaimed. We were coming up on a patrol car catty-cornered across the street. "They got the streets blocked off both ways!" He rolled down the window and hollered to a police officer. "Let us through, buster. I got Mrs. Winchester and two other women in here."

I didn't like the looks of what lay ahead—a bunch of

people waiting with microphones and cameras. "George, is there any way you could get us inside without getting mobbed?"

"I sure can," he said and gunned it. That truck sped forward and took a fast left turn on a service road that took us around in back. Before the crowd realized where we were headed, we had stopped. George hopped out, ran around to open the door for Winnie, helped her out, and ushered her toward the back door of the station as Daisy and I crawled out. We had to run—the press people were hotfooting it around the corner of the building. The man holding the door open for us looked like the chief of police. We three had just got inside and shut the door when we heard the chief telling the reporters, "That's all for now, folks. There'll be a news conference later."

George had come inside and was still holding onto Winnie's arm when the chief came in again. "Thanks, George," he said. "Thanks for bringing them in, but I'll handle it from here."

George was reluctant to leave. The chief thumbed toward the door. George looked at the three of us. "Ladies, if there's anything I can do for you, you just give me a call. Chief knows my number." With that he left, and the chief shut the door behind him.

"Now, ladies, if you will come in my office, the FBI is on their way to interview you. In the meantime, I can bring you up to date on how matters stand at the moment. But first," he opened an office door, "there's someone here waiting to see you."

I couldn't believe my eyes—it was Percival!

32

Both of us, Winnie and me, burst into tears, grabbed Percival, and hugged him for dear life. It's a wonder we didn't break him in two the way we were squeezing him. "Winnie, we better let go, we're getting him all wet."

We both let go of him, but Percival put his arm around Winnie, and she leaned against his shoulder. "Oh, Percival," she cried, "I was never so glad to see anybody in my whole life!"

"The feeling is mutual," he said, taking off his glasses and wiping his eyes on his sleeve.

"Percival," I said, "this is Daisy LeGrande. She rescued us. When there's more time, we'll tell you the whole story, but right now we want to hear about you. When did you come up here?"

"As soon as I heard you were missing. I chartered one of those small planes and flew out as soon as I could, but by the time I got here, it was dark, and the search for your bodies had been called off. I checked by the police station, but they didn't know anything more than I had already heard on the news. I rented a jeep, took a room in a motel, and kept the radio on all night, but it was not until the next morning while I was shaving that they broadcast about the ransom. It was then I knew you'd been abducted, and, bad as that was, at least it meant you were alive.

"I jumped in that jeep and rode all over the place asking questions, hoping to find an eyewitness. But, tell me, who kidnapped you—do you know who they are? Where'd they keep you?"

"It's a long story, Percival," I told him, "but right now we need to get out of these wet clothes and get cleaned up before we can face those law enforcement people."

"Okay," he said, "I'll call the motel where I'm staying." He picked up the phone and made the reservations for the "Smith sisters, Mary, Martha, and Magdalene."

We got a laugh out of that. He had the presence of mind not to give our real names, but that's Percival for you—always on top of things.

"This place is nice, the Country Lane Inn," he said, "but not the exceptional accommodations you're accustomed to. For that reason, reporters won't look for you there. You should be safe from the press, at least for a little while. Nice restaurant, room service, and it's near the airport."

"Let's go," I said.

"Okay. I'll drive you there. And, Esmeralda—" He handed me a pad to write on and a pen, "on the way, write down the sizes you ladies wear and I'll see what clothes I can find. In the meantime, I'll ask the man at the desk if he can't send up some bathrobes."

He turned to Winnie. "Mrs. Win*chus*ter, about your luggage. What shall I tell the *Amsterdam*?"

"Where is the *Amsterdam*?"

"After Glacier Bay it was scheduled to visit Sitka."

"Well, Percival, I don't know what to say. We want to get out of here as soon as we can, but we don't know how long the authorities will keep us."

"I hope we can get out of here tomorrow or the next day. What would you think of asking the purser to hold the luggage until the ship gets back to Vancouver and then deliver it to the Wedgewood?"

Winnie agreed to the idea. I wasn't so sure. I thought we might be in Juneau much longer than that, but I didn't say anything.

As we came out of that little office, Percival told the receptionist where we would be staying and the phony names we would be registered under. She looked startled. "You're not *leaving*? Chief Kline wants to question the victims, and we expect the Alaska Bureau of Investigation momentarily."

Percival answered for us. "Tell the chief these ladies will be available as soon as possible but that right now they need to get cleaned up and have a hot meal."

The chief must have overheard because he came out of his office right away. "Now, see here—the ABI is on its way . . . Oh, that's right, you do need to get cleaned up. Did I hear you say they'll be staying at the Country Lane Inn? Well, okay, but ladies, once you get there, stay put. Patrolman Norton here will drive you there."

"Chief," Percival said, "don't you think it might be better if I take them? If they go in a patrol car they'll be spotted right away, and the newspeople will pose problems we don't need right now."

"You got something there. Okay. Let's see, the press is swarming all over in back. Where you parked?"

"In front."

"Good. Now, ladies, once you are safely inside the Country Lane Inn, do not show your faces outside your rooms. We don't know where your abductors are nor what intentions they might have. In a little while, I'll drop by and have each of you give me a statement. The ABI will also come to where you are for their interview. In the meantime my officers will keep the motel under twenty-four-hour surveillance.

"Now, ladies, if you should need anything, give me a call. My entire force is on the alert ready to respond at a moment's notice."

He rubbed his chin, thinking. "Now, let's see . . . Tell you what. I'll send Norton out back to tell the press I'm on my way to hold the news conference. That'll hold them there while you people go out the front door, give you time to get away.

"Norton, you follow the jeep in the patrol car, make sure they get where they're going without any interference."

Chief Kline led us through the office and held the front door open for us. Daisy and I ran to the jeep while Percival brought Winnie.

On the way to the inn, we traveled the Glacier Highway, retracing the route George had brought us from Auke Bay. The patrol car was following us but lagged behind a few vehicles that came between us.

When we arrived at the motel, we were still pretty

much wet to the skin. Percival asked us to wait in the jeep until he was sure the coast was clear. He jumped out and ran inside.

A plane was zooming over our heads, aiming to land. After it passed, I commented, "If that kind of noise keeps up all night, we probably won't sleep much."

"Not sleep?" Winnie repeated. "Esmeralda, bailing out the boat was the most work I've ever done in my life. I have got aches and pains from muscles I never knew I had. Sleep? You better believe it, I could sleep through the entire Air Force landing and taking off!"

We all laughed.

Daisy peeked out to see if Percival was coming. "What's keeping him?"

"Well, he said he'd check to see if the coast was clear," I reminded her. But it was taking him quite some time.

"There he comes!" Winnie said.

Then I realized what had kept him so long—he was bringing bathrobes, which probably meant it took the desk clerk time to round them up.

Percival handed the robes to me and helped Winnie out of the car. Daisy and me got out after her. "Coast is clear," he said.

If anyone saw us, I did not see them. It was a good thing; anybody see us they'd be liable to think we had walked the plank and been fished outta the deep! At least the way we looked was a perfect disguise for Winnie. Nobody would ever guess that the woman wearing only one shoe, a muddy pantsuit, a bedraggled parka, and leaving a wet trail behind her was Mrs. Philip Winchester, one of the richest women in the world.

Percival saw to it that the elevator didn't stop to let anybody on until we reached the top floor. He gave Daisy the key to her room, and I followed Percival taking Winnie into our suite. "Mrs. Win*chus*ter," he said, "you'll want to make a quick call or two. Everybody's worried sick about you, and they'll be anxious to hear that you're safe."

I handed him the phone, and he dialed a number. "Who're you calling?" Winnie asked.

"Philip. I'm calling Philip Win*chus*ter."

33

Percival called Winnie's secretary, and she told him there was no way to reach Philip Winchester. He handed the phone to Winnie, and the secretary told her that the day Philip heard the news about the two of us falling overboard, he headed for the mainland but was forced into port by a tropical storm. The news of the kidnapping reached him later, there in Guadeloupe. Right away he authorized his attorneys in the States to negotiate the terms for delivering the ransom and to post the rewards. No sooner had he done that than the tropical storm turned into a hurricane and island communications shut down and were not yet up and running.

Hearing that, Percival said he'd run along and see what he could do about getting us some clothes. To me it seemed too late for any store to be open, but summer days in Alaska are long, and store hours could be longer too.

Winnie took one of the robes and went in to take her bath. I decided to call Priscilla Home.

Nancy answered the phone, and as soon as she heard my voice she shouted, "It's Miss E.! It's Miss E.!"

Hearing somebody calling me "Miss E." was like music to my ears. I could hear the women running downstairs, sounding like a thundering herd and yelling, "Is she all right?" "Where is she?" "Is she coming home?"

After all we'd been through, I felt like the prodigal son, once lost, now found. "They sound historical, Nancy."

"They are! I tell you, we've been so worried about you, Miss E. We couldn't do anything but stay glued to the TV, watching the news and praying. Where are you? Are you okay? How's Barbara's mother?"

"We're fine. We're in a motel in Juneau, and Percival is taking care of us. Nancy, we've been through quite an ordeal, but the Lord was with us all the way—tell the women their prayers have been answered. Tell Barbara I'd put her mother on the phone but she's in taking a bath. Maybe she'll call later, but right now we're trying to get ready to meet with law enforcement officers. They're coming to ask us a lot of questions. When things quiet down, maybe I can fill you in on the details. As soon as we can, we'll leave Juneau and head for home. I'll keep in touch."

"Oh, Miss E., don't hang up. Give me your phone number. Even before all this happened, the Priscilla Home board was trying to get in touch with you. And your friends Beatrice and Carl have been calling here trying to find out anything they could. Beatrice said that if we heard from you to tell you they're camping in Seattle and will stay there until they hear from you. She said Carl bought a cell phone just so you can call them. Here's the number," and she gave it to me.

Well, at last, I said to myself. *Beatrice has got a phone.* "Nancy, call Beatrice and tell her I'm okay. I gotta go. Here's the number of the motel and our suite number." I spelled it out for her. "You got that?" She had it. "Now, don't give out that number to anybody you don't know. Reporters and cameramen are all over Juneau looking for us. We had to register under phony names in this motel, and we aren't allowed to leave our rooms until the law tells us we can. When you call, ask for our suite number. If that don't work, just ask for the Smith sisters."

"The Smith sisters?"

"That's right—Mary, Martha, and Magdalene."

She laughed. "What a hoot!"

"Okay, I've got to go. Give my love to everybody and thank them for praying for us. Be sure to call Albert and Lenora and anybody else who's been anxious."

When I hung up the phone, I tucked Beatrice's number under the lamp for safekeeping. I would call her later.

I grabbed a robe and dashed in the bathroom to take my bath. As I stripped off those wet clothes, I wanted to chuck them for good, but my better judgment told me to hang on to them in case I needed them later. The apron with the jewels was soaking wet, but it had held up good. I needed to rinse it out and hang it up to dry. I hurried back in my room and put the jewels in a pillowcase.

There wasn't time for anything more than a quick shower, but I had to take the time to wash my hair. I had just started blow-drying it when the phone rang. I went in to answer it.

It was Chief Kline. The ABI investigators were with him, and he wanted to know if they could come up. I near about panicked! None of us were fit to be seen barefooted in bathrobes, and with wet hair to boot. I tried to put him off. "Chief, we're not presentable. We're also exhausted and haven't had a bite to eat. Can't this wait?"

Of course, I should have known the answer. "No, this is urgent," he said. "Tell you what I'll do; I'll check into this restaurant they have here and bring you takeout dinners."

"Thanks, Chief, but I think a better idea would be for us to order room service while you men stay in the restaurant and have a cup of coffee or something. Give us about an hour and maybe—"

"Well, I don't know about that. Let me ask Rollins. Hang on."

I turned to Winnie. "It's Chief Kline. He wants to bring the ABI up here to question us."

When he came back on the phone, he said they'd give us half an hour.

Did I ever fly into action! "Winnie, you heard what I said—I told him we weren't ready, but all he said was they'd give us thirty minutes!"

She was combing her wet hair and trying to get out the tangles. "They can't come up here. We haven't got on any clothes."

"They're the law, Winnie, and they're coming." I walked in her bathroom. "What's more important than anything—we got to get our heads together. They'll be asking every question under the sun, and we have gotta make sure we say the right thing. The way we answer can make a big difference."

"We'll just have to do the best we can, won't we, Esmeralda?"

"No, listen. If we don't handle this right, they could very well decide Daisy is a suspect—that she was in on the whole thing—and arrest her. What we have to do is convince them that Daisy was not in on it—that those creeps tried to use her but failed. We have to make them understand how she could have saved herself if she'd been willing to leave us stranded, but she didn't, and how she helped us escape. Daisy deserves all that reward money, but she won't get it if we don't stick up for her. You know how things like that go."

"Okay, Esmeralda. You do the talking, and I'll back you up."

I called Daisy, and she came to our suite. In that white terry cloth robe and all nice and clean, Daisy looked downright cuddly. "Daisy, I got to dry my hair. Winnie will tell you what's up."

Somebody was at the door. I glanced at my watch; our thirty minutes were not up.

Daisy called in to me, "It's Percival."

I went in the living room, and there stood Percival holding an armload of clothes, a couple of big plastic bags full of who knows what, and a smaller bag. "This is the best I could do," he said and opened the smaller bag. "I went by a drugstore and got some makeup and toiletries." He handed Winnie a pair of sunglasses. "There's a big exclusive department store in town, but it was closed. I had to go to the Salvation Army for these things. The lady in charge looked through several racks of clothes trying to find your sizes but finally decided on three jumpsuits that should fit you."

He laid the beige jumpsuits on the couch and handed me one of the big bags. In it were some underthings and sleepwear.

"I told the lady at the Salvation Army that I didn't know how to shop for ladies ready-to-wear but that as soon as the stores opened tomorrow I would have to buy whatever else you needed. She was so nice; she offered to go with me. In the morning I'll come by to get your list of what you need, your shoe sizes and everything else.

"Now, I've got to get out of here. I saw Chief Kline downstairs with the ABI agents. He said they're waiting to question you. Want me to go down and tell them you need a little more time to get dressed?"

"Oh, thank you, Percival," Winnie said. "Thank you, thank you! I don't know what we would have done without you."

He looked plum worn out, so I told him, "Now, Percival, you have a nice dinner and then take it easy, get a good night's rest. If we need you, we'll call you."

"Miss Esmeralda, I haven't heard your story yet. If Chief Kline will let me, I'll come up and listen while you go over everything with them."

After he left we got dressed as best we could. Sorting out the underwear, we found a set for each of us. There was not much fit to the jumpsuits, which was a good thing; loose as they were they covered all our bulges. All the bedroom slippers were alike—blue mule type.

Once we got dressed and had our hair combed, we

three stood before the bathroom mirror looking at ourselves. "You know what?" I said. "If we had parachutes we could join the 82nd Airborne!"

There was a knock at the door; I went to answer it. Percival was standing there with Chief Kline and two men. I let them in.

Before they sat down, the chief introduced the two inspectors from the ABI, Dixon and Rollins, who looked for all the world like J. Edgar Hoover G-men: dark suits, shirts and ties, and shoes polished to a patent-leather shine.

Then we all sat down—we three women on the couch, with the three officers and Percival sitting across from us on chairs.

"Ladies," the chief began, "we have good news for you. Inspector Rollins will explain."

Rollins cleared his throat. "About an hour ago the ABI received word that two suspects have been arrested and are now in custody. Seattle authorities made the arrests when the suspects attempted to pick up the ransom money. Arrangements had been made for the ransom to be delivered to an abandoned barn in a field outside the city. Officers had the barn under surveillance when the suspects arrived. One suspect remained in the vehicle with the motor running while the other one went inside the barn. As the suspect was coming out of the barn with the briefcase containing the ransom money, officers arrested him and the one in the car at the same time. They offered no resistance."

They had to be Pee-Wee and Tony, I thought.

"In the interest of justice," the chief said, "we've

got to find all the evidence we can to convict these criminals when they go to trial. Your positive identification is, of course, vital to this case, but we need to know all the details concerning your abduction and any additional information you can give us that will aid the prosecution."

He placed a tape recorder on the coffee table, and the ABI men took tablets and pens from their pockets.

The room fell silent.

Rollins cleared his throat again. "Perhaps, Miss Esmeralda, you should begin. Just start at the beginning and tell us where and how you were abducted."

Well, I did start at the beginning and did the best I could. But when the story came to our being held hostage in Daisy's house, I had to make sure Daisy was not incriminated. I asked Daisy to tell them how she got involved.

Of course, that brought up Willie. They didn't know about him, and this bit of information put the ABI agents on the edge of their seats, scribbling like crazy.

"Well," Daisy said, "that Willie, he don't lack much of being feebleminded. He knows right from wrong, everybody does, but the trouble is, what he thinks is right is mostly wrong. In this case, he got drawed in by thinking gettin' a thousand dollars was right. In his mind, anything go against that—anything come between him and gettin' that money had to be wrong. We couldn't talk no sense into him. He's what you might call a blockhead."

Officer Dixon pressed her. "But you went along with Willie, didn't you? You expected to get some of that thousand dollars, didn't you?"

I jumped right in. "No, sir, she didn't!" I said. "She was one with us from the day we set foot in her place."

Then between Winnie and me, we told them the whole story about Daisy saving our lives.

"Now," I said, "the third man we told you about, the one who piloted the helicopter, he's still on the *Amsterdam*. I don't know as you can call a stupid man a *mastermind*, but, be that as it may, Alphonso Pasquali strikes me as being the leader. I'd say them other two, Tony and Pee-Wee, went along with anything he said and carried out his orders."

"Excuse me," Officer Rollins said and flipped open his cell phone.

His call must have been to ABI headquarters, because he told them to get warrants for the arrest of Alphonso Pasquali and Willie Miller.

"Now, mind you," Daisy said, "Willie is not the sharpest knife in the drawer. He won't think nothin' much about gettin' arrested, but he will make hisself sick thinkin' about that money he ain't gonna get."

Winnie spoke up. "Speaking of money, Chief Kline, you tell the authorities Daisy here deserves both of those rewards. She's told you more than you knew about Willie and those other two, Tony and Pee-Wee. But more important to Esmeralda and me is the fact that she made it possible for us to escape. I have no doubt Daisy saved our lives."

"Yes, thank you, Mrs. Winchester, we'll pass on that information," the chief said.

Rollins turned to Daisy. "Do you think Willie will still be at your place?"

She grinned. "He can't go no place. I disabled his motor—took out the spark plugs. Matter of fact," she reached in her pocket and showed them the spark plugs, "they got wet and ruint."

"Does he have a gun?"

"Not anymore. We turned his assault rifle over to Chief Kline."

"Are there any more guns in the house?"

"There's a no 'count, rusty Winchester rifle without no bullets."

He wrote all that down. "Now, tell me, how can we get to your house?"

"If you know the way, you can fly over there by seaplane or helicopter, but the way I go is by boat. My boat's right down here at the Auke Bay marina."

Rollins and Dixon walked over to the window to talk. When they came back, Rollins said, "All right, Mrs. LeGrande, what say Agent Dixon and I rent a boat in the morning and follow you back to your place?"

"Fine with me."

"Then I guess this is all for now, ladies," Rollins said. "Chief Kline will have your statements typed up and will bring them here sometime tomorrow for you to sign."

The three men stood up to leave.

"How much longer must we stay here?" Winnie asked, so tired her voice broke.

"Mrs. Winchester," Robbins said, "we won't hold you here any longer than is necessary. As soon as we've apprehended these other two conspirators, Chief Kline will notify you. However, when you are released, it will be vitally necessary that you keep us informed as to your whereabouts and that you be prepared to assist us further in this investigation if that becomes necessary."

He turned to Daisy. "Mrs. LeGrande, we'll meet you at the marina first thing in the morning—no later than 9:00."

The three thanked us for our help and left in a hurry.

Winnie sighed. "Percival, will you order dinner for us?"

"Certainly, madam. What would you like?"

"Anything—anything at all." She was awful shaky trying to get up off the couch; he and I had to help her. "Percival, I need a drink." Winnie was falling apart.

34

The next morning, Daisy came to our suite ready to meet the ABI agents at the marina. She was wearing the clothes she had on the day before, and although she had dried them overnight, her boots were still wet. I suggested she try using the blow-dryer on them, and she did that while we were waiting for room service to send up our breakfast.

Winnie was still asleep, and we didn't want to wake her. The ordeal we had been through had just about done her in.

Room service sent up waffles and sausages, juice and coffee. "Daisy," I said as we were eating, "I want to thank you again for helping us escape. I believe with all my heart that you saved our lives. You truly earned the reward money you're going to get."

"You think I'll get it? What if—"

"No 'what ifs' about it. If need be, Winnie and I will see to it that you get it. What will you do with all that money?"

"Ha! I'll be on the next plane outta Juneau, get back to Mississippi as fast as I can. And as God is my witness, the next time I leave Mississippi I'll be bound for the Promised Land."

"Daisy, are you sure you're going to heaven?"

"No. Is anybody sure?"

"I am." And I tried to explain to her how she could be sure too, but that didn't seem to interest her. "Daisy, have you got a Bible?"

"Had one back in Mississippi."

"Well, when you get back there, promise me you'll read it."

"Okay, if you say so."

"You promise?"

"I promise. When I get back, I will."

The TV was on without the sound so as not to wake Winnie, and we watched the pictures showing Chief Kline's press conference. Then they showed a picture of Country Lane Inn, so I guess everybody knew where we were staying.

Daisy finished eating, gulped down the last of her coffee, and got up from the table.

"Wait a minute," I said and went back to the telephone stand to write the address of Priscilla Home on a slip of paper. "Daisy, once you're settled, would you send me your address? I don't know where I'll be, but I used to work at Priscilla Home and they'll forward your letter to me."

"I ain't much for writin', but I like to get a letter once in a while. Say you'll write me back?"

"I promise I'll write you as soon as I get your address."

We said our good-byes. "You take care of yourself, Daisy."

I watched her until she got on the elevator, then I closed the door. I felt a little sad about Daisy. *Maybe she will read her Bible. Maybe she'll write to me.*

With Winnie sleeping, there was nothing I had to do until the chief or Percival arrived, so I spent a little time going through my pocketbook and seeing what I could salvage. Anything plastic was still okay, but the Gospels of John and all the other stuff I had to throw away. I hung the bottomless pit on the showerhead, thinking it might dry, but I had my doubts.

After that, I went in my room and sat down to read and pray.

Winnie and I had eaten lunch before Percival came. As he came in the door with boxes and packages stacked one upon another, he looked about as frazzled as ever I had seen him. "They're all out there now," he told us. I took the pillows off the couch to make room for the packages.

"Who?" Winnie asked.

"The press. They're all over the lobby—in the dining room—everywhere you look."

"How do you suppose they got wind of our being here?" she asked.

"Maybe they followed Chief Kline to this motel yesterday, or maybe somebody working here got suspicious that the Smith Sisters were you two and tipped them off. I sneaked in by taking the freight elevator . . . Well, here's what that Salvation Army lady and I bought." He opened one of the boxes. Inside was a broad-brimmed hat for Winnie, which she put on her head. It looked like a perfect fit. "And here's this," he said, opening another box and pulling out an elegant pantsuit. The material was the kind that won't wrinkle and packs easy. Winnie held it up to her, and we could see that it would fit her. To go with the pantsuit was a matching ocean blue cashmere coat with wide collar and deep pockets. It reached to the knees and was just what Winnie and I needed to hide our double-decker busts.

Percival looked relieved that what he had bought for Winnie was okay. "For you, Esmeralda, we picked this denim jacket and jeans."

The jacket had looped brass buttons, and the jeans also had looped brass buttons down the side of the legs—much too stylish for my taste, but they were my size and I was glad to have anything to wear.

Percival was showing us several pairs of shoes with pocketbooks to match. Out of the lot Winnie and I each found a pair we could wear, and I was especially glad to have a new bag to replace my bottomless pit. "We'll leave what we can't use for the maids," Winnie said.

"When do you think they'll let us leave?" I asked Percival.

"Tomorrow. The captain of the *Amsterdam* has Alphonso Pasquali in custody ready to be turned over to the authorities in Vancouver, and Chief Kline said as soon as Rollins and Dixon return with the other fellow, we'll be free to go. The only thing he asks is that you keep him informed of your whereabouts in case he needs to get in touch. I took the liberty of buying our tickets for a flight out of here tomorrow at 11:41."

I gathered up all the empty boxes and bags and stacked them in a corner. "Percival, you must be tired. Why don't you stretch out on the couch and rest a while?"

Well, he wouldn't do that, but he did sit in a chair and put his feet up on the coffee table. Winnie and I, dressed in our comfortable jumpsuits and bedroom slippers, sat down to talk.

"About letting Chief Kline know where we are," I said. "Right now I don't know where I'll be."

"Oh, you'll be with me," Winnie said confidently.

"No. Once we get back, I want to see what I can do about getting work like I had before—housemother in a ministry for women."

"Oh no. I want you to come with me. Do you know where I'm going? I'm going to move to Live Oaks, South Carolina. I want to make friends with all those nice people you've told me about."

I nearly dropped my teeth. I couldn't imagine the wealthiest woman in America fitting in with my friends—not with Clara and them other Willing Workers. They would think Winnie was too strange to be living on the same planet, much less in Live Oaks. "What in the world would you do there, Winnie?" I asked.

"I have it all planned. I'm going to go into business there. I've learned all about it from TV. There used to be this show that took place in a diner, and the way the waitresses called out the orders—you know, they'd yell,

'Shipwreck,' meaning scrambled eggs; 'BLT,' for bacon, lettuce, and tomato; 'Big boom booms, make 'em cry,' meaning big burgers with onions; or 'Hold the mayo!' All of that fascinated me. There was this cook in a big white apron and wearing a chef's hat working behind the counter, and even though there was this order wheel full of tickets, never once did he look at the tickets; he kept all the orders in his head. You'd see him pouring waffle mix onto the waffle iron, popping toast in the toaster, slapping hamburger patties on the grill, minding the waffles, scrambling eggs, flipping the patties, tending the deep fryer, slapping the meat onto hamburger buns, putting cheese on this one, tomato and lettuce on another—all in a kind of steady rhythm. How he kept all the orders in his head is beyond me, but he did. With a burger he'd add fries hot out of the grease, quick wrap the bun in paper, and then you'd hear this *ding-ding*, which meant, 'Pick up order.'

"I'm going to buy a diner and hire you, Esmeralda, as the short-order cook. It'll be fun, I tell you!"

I rolled my eyes at Percival. "I don't think so, Winnie." The more Percival and I thought about that, the funnier it got. We laughed so hard Winnie realized her dream of having a Live Oaks diner was out of the question.

"Well, if not a diner, could you and I just live in Live Oaks? Esmeralda, I really need you to help me get over my drinking problem, and I think living in Live Oaks away from drinking people would help me more than anything else. I would build a big house, but if you wanted your own place, I would build you a cottage next door."

"No, Winnie. Unless the Lord made it clear that he wanted me to do such as that, it wouldn't work. As for your drinking, only Jesus can help you, and what Splurgeon said is true, 'He will never cease to help us until we cease to need.'"

Percival took his feet off the coffee table, leaned his elbows on his knees, and asked, "Esmeralda, how'd it come about that you started calling Mrs. Winchuster Winnie? Never before have I ever heard anyone call her Winnie."

"That's because no one ever has," Winnie said. "I always wanted someone to call me Winnie, but even Esmeralda took a long time coming around to doing it. Percival, I'm sick and tired of being looked up to as someone important. I've never done anything in my life that was worth a dime."

"Well," he said, "you're not by yourself. I'm sick and tired of being Percival. I want to go back to being me, if you know what I mean."

"You want us to call you Marvin?" I asked.

"Yes," he said, "but there's more to it than that. This role I've been playing is not for me. A man ought to be able to be himself—to live in the real world without pretense or shame."

"You're not going to resign, are you?" Winnie asked.

"I don't know for sure. I don't think taking care of you and the dogs is what I want to do for the rest of my life. You can understand that, can't you, Mrs. Winchuster?"

"Winchester," she repeated. "Yes, I do understand, but Percival—"

He corrected her. "Marvin."

"Okay, Marvin. I do understand, but I don't know how I can manage without you."

"You've been good to me, Mrs. Winchester, and I will always be grateful, but . . ." He placed his hand over his heart. "I don't feel good in here living this lie. Do you know what I mean?"

"Yes. I think I do. Have you been reading the Bible you bought?"

"I've read the Gospel of Matthew, but it's raised more questions than it's answered."

The phone was ringing. I answered it.

"Hello, Esmeralda? It's Roger Elmwood."

"Oh, hello Roger. How are you doing?"

"I'm doing well. Esmeralda, Mabel wants to speak with you a minute."

Mabel was so excited she could hardly talk, telling me how happy Live Oaks was that I was safe—how Pastor Osborne had held special prayer services for my release, etc., etc. I thanked her—told her I'd tell them all about it someday.

Then Roger got on the line again. "Esmeralda, yes, we are all thankful that you're okay. We want to hear all about it later. Right now I have some important business to discuss with you. Are you free to talk?"

"Yes, I'm free."

"The board has asked Nancy to be the director at Priscilla Home."

"Oh, that's fine. You couldn't have picked a better person."

"Yes, but she will only accept our offer on one condition."

"What's that?"

"Nancy said she will take the job only if you agree to be the resident manager."

"You mean housemother?"

"Well, whatever. The same job you had before. Now, I know these younger board members let you go because they thought you were too old for the job, but you know me well enough to know I never thought that." He chuckled. "After all, I'm about your age, and I'm still going strong."

I was quiet, but what was welling up inside of me was pure joy! I could have danced a jig!

"Well, Esmeralda, you don't have to give me your answer tonight, but—"

"Roger, count me in. I'll be back in two weeks, maybe in ten days."

"Thank you, Esmeralda. I'll call Nancy right now and give her the good news. In the meantime, keep in touch and if there's anything we can do for you, let us know."

"Okay, thank you, Roger. Good-bye." And I hung up.

"What was that all about?" Winnie asked.

"They want me back at Priscilla Home."

"Are you going?"

"Yes, I am."

Her face fell.

"Winnie," I said, "I'm taking you with me. Priscilla

Home is where you need to be. With Albert teaching the Bible, you'll find all the help you need in Jesus."

She stared at me. I don't think she could believe what I had just said.

"I mean it, Winnie. You're going with me."

She got up out of her chair, came over to me, and hugged the breath out of me!

Marvin smiled. "What about me? I'd like to study the Bible. Do they take men?"

"No, but I think I know a way to get you what you're looking for."

"How's that?"

"Albert Ringstaff, our Priscilla Home Bible teacher, lives up the road from us. He and his wife, Lenora, have a large house and another small guesthouse. The last time I talked with him he asked me to be on the lookout for a man who can drive and who can also do the yard work. Would you be interested in that?"

"You say he's a Bible teacher?"

"Yes, and a very learned one, I might add. You two would get along good."

I could practically see what was turning over in his head. "What will we do with Desi and Lucy?"

"I think the Ringstaffs would welcome them. The women at Priscilla Home also need a dog; two would be even better. Lucy and Desi will be no problem."

"Then you call him. Ask him if the job's still open."

I did call, and Albert remembered meeting Marvin the day he came to Priscilla Home and showed Albert all about the Rolls.

"Bring him on," Albert said. "We really need him."

"And he needs you, Albert."

❦

So, it was settled. The next day we flew out of Juneau for Vancouver. There was not a peep out of Winnie about being afraid of flying. She and I were in big seats up front, and since there were no other passengers sitting up there, I was humming. Winnie heard me, and she started singing the words. "Dem bones, dem bones . . . Now hear the Word of the Lord . . ."

Acknowledgments

I am indebted to Tod Benoit, author of *Where Are They Buried? How Did They Die?*, for information on deceased persons and burial sites, and to John Heilig and Reg Abbiss, coauthors of *Rolls-Royce: The Best Car in the World*, for descriptions of the Mulliner Park Ward Touring Limousine. Dr. Bradley Bethel of Laurinburg, NC, shared his personal experience as an owner of a Rolls-Royce.

The following individuals graciously corresponded with me concerning the *Amsterdam*, flagship of the Holland American line: Christopher Wilson, Erik Elvejord, and Hilda Cullen.

Of the four five-star hotels visited in this novel, explanations of facilities and services were given by Mike Gregory, Karen Hunter-Lowery, and Jeffrey Zimmer of the Gaylord Opryland Hotel, Nashville; Kate Duffy of the Peninsula, Chicago; Shannon Short of the Grand America, Salt Lake City; Ms. Joanna Tsparas and Lisa Irwin of the Wedgewood, Vancouver, Canada.

The greeting card poet, Arthur Reimer, wrote the poems

attributed to Mrs. Winchester. Nancy Daughtry, one of my former students, served as research assistant.

My longtime friend, Alvera Mickelsen, critiqued the manuscript and improved it immeasurably. My sister, Jennie Free, an avid reader, helped by giving me a reader's viewpoint on this story.

Joyce Hart, my agent, and the hardworking professionals at Baker Publishing Group have done more for Esmeralda and me than words can tell. Thank you, one and all!

Margaret A. Graham is the author of seven nonfiction books, one work of juvenile fiction, and five novels. She conveys her deep love of the Scriptures as a speaker, Bible teacher, and newspaper columnist. Graham resides in Sumter, South Carolina.

Guts, gumption, & *grace*

Enter the charming world of a feisty Southern widow whose down-to-earth humor and unabashed faith make an unforgettable impression.

Laugh out loud as the spirited Esmeralda learns how to love the unlovable.